Have Yourself a Deadly Little Christmas

Have Yourself a Deadly Little Christmas

A YEAR-ROUND CHRISTMAS MYSTERY

Vicki Delany

CROOKED LANE

NEW YORK

Published in the United States by Crooked Lane Books, an imprint of The Quick Brown Fox & Company LLC.

Crooked Lane Books and its logo are trademarks of The Quick Brown Fox & Company LLC.

Library of Congress Cataloging-in-Publication data available upon request.

ISBN (hardcover): 978-1-63910-463-5
ISBN (ebook): 978-1-63910-464-2

Cover illustration by Elsa Kerls

Printed in the United States.

www.crookedlanebooks.com

Crooked Lane Books
34 West 27th St., 10th Floor
New York, NY 10001

First Edition: September 2023

10 9 8 7 6 5 4 3 2 1

To my family, for giving me many
Christmases to remember

Chapter One

There are two types of people in the world: those who love picnics and those who hate them.

The picnic-loving camp can then be divided once again into two further types: those who love winter picnics and those who do not.

I am firmly in the former camp, in both instances.

My mother, however, is not, and she reminded me of such as she pulled her scarf tighter around her neck and shivered dramatically. "I am absolutely freezing, Merry. I do not know why this can't have been arranged for a pleasant, not to mention warm, indoor space. A restaurant preferably."

"It's a super nice day, Mom. Feel that sun on your face."

"Nice is a relative term. And the sun is not doing anything to compensate for the temperature." She rubbed her hands together. "These gloves are not going to be adequate. Dare I hope you have a spare pair on hand?"

"Sorry. No. Vicky brought mulled cider. A glass of that'll warm you up."

"I could use some help over here, Merry," Vicky Casey called.

"Have a good time, Mom," I said as I escaped for the bakery van where my friend Vicky Casey was beginning the all-important task of unloading the food and drink. "Sorry. Diva emergency."

Vicky laughed. "Always takes precedence."

"What do you want me to do?"

She indicated the folded red and green plastic tablecloths in her arms and nodded toward two bare picnic tables close by. "Those tables have been set aside for us. Let me lay these cloths, and then we can start arranging everything. Looks like the party's well underway."

The event Victoria's Bake Shoppe had been hired to cater was indeed well under way in our town park. Men lifted beer bottles glistening with moisture out of the ice-filled cooler close to the previously set-up drinks table, and women poured themselves glasses of wine. Jugs of lemonade and iced tea were on hand for the kids, the non-imbibers, and the designated drivers. My mom joined my dad at the makeshift bar and slipped her arm through his. He gave her a smile that lifted my heart, and asked if he could get her a glass of wine. She nodded graciously.

My mom might sometimes be "difficult" and my dad "eccentric," but the love they have for each other forms the bedrock of their lives. Dad was dressed in "civilian" clothes today. What passes as for normal for him, anyway—a plain brown winter jacket above dad-jeans bagging badly in the rear. Mom wore a knee-length camel coat with a fake fur collar and trimmed hood, a double row of ornate gold buttons running down the front, dark brown leather gloves, and a beige wool scarf shot with glistening golden threads. Brown leather boots with two-inch heels were on her feet.

It was a Sunday afternoon in December and we were at the annual picnic of the Rudolph Community Theater Players. I'm not part of the company, but my friend Vicky Casey had been hired to cater the food and Vicky roped me into helping. I'd left my store, Mrs. Claus's Treasures, in the capable hands of Chrystal Wong, one of my assistants. At three-thirty, Matterhorn, my Saint Bernard, and I had sprinted down Jingle Bell Lane to start loading Vicky's bakery van with all the wonderful things she'd prepared for the winter picnic. We sprinted as fast as Matterhorn ever moves, that is. He's a Saint Bernard, and laid back is the entire nature of his breed. Winter in Upstate New York is his favorite time of year, and at the moment he was resting on the brown grass beneath a giant old willow, being admired by numerous children. Any minute now, I knew, one brave kid would detach herself from the pack and ask if she could have a ride.

As if.

Vicky unfolded her tablecloths with a flourish. "Okay, the cider urn can go next to the desserts. I want to set up the sandwiches and the soup on that table, and the hot drinks and desserts on the other. Plates, soup mugs, cutlery, and napkins at the far end. The big plates are for the sandwiches; put the small ones for the desserts next to the cocktail napkins. I brought mugs for the mulled cider and hot chocolate."

"Are we bringing dessert out at the same time as the rest?" asked Alan Anderson, who'd also been roped into helping.

"Yes. Easier that way. Once the food's laid out, I'll tell Noel to invite people to serve themselves."

I took a large plastic tub containing rows of hefty sandwiches wrapped in butcher paper and tied with twine out of the van to the table as directed while Vicky arranged the urns containing the hot drinks

Alan grabbed the portable heater that would keep the soup warm. "I hope dinner's provided for the hardworking crew." He brushed a lock of overly long blond hair off his forehead and his clear blue eyes twinkled.

"You wish," Vicky said with a smile. "Of course it is. I made lots. That's turning out to be a good thing. Looks like everyone came."

"Weather couldn't be better." The warm winter sun shone in a brilliant blue sky. The temperature hovered at a few degrees below freezing, with no wind. Perfect conditions to gather outside, as long as everyone had bundled up. As a backup plan in case things turned nasty, the theater company had booked space in the community center, but such hadn't been needed. Not many people—Mom excepted—complained about taking the party outdoors.

I lifted the lid off a container and peered in to see rows upon rows of perfect cupcakes, the icing crafted to resemble miniature Christmas trees. "You went all out."

Vicky dropped her voice. "I was paid enough."

"In past years the picnic's been potluck in someone's back yard or basement. Don't tell me the company's that flush this year, and the play hasn't even opened yet?"

The Rudolph town park sits on the southern shores of Lake Ontario. Farther down the beach, a handful of families had set up portable barbecues and lawn chairs to also enjoy the day. The skating rink was open, and children and adults glided on skates with varying degrees of skill. A baby was being pushed in a specially designed stroller. On the other side of the rink, some of the students from Rudolph High were letting off steam in a rousing game of winter volleyball. There was no snow yet, but the waters of the lake were rimed with a touch of ice and no one dared venture in.

The theater company had taken over a large patch of ground near the bandstand. Before we arrived, an arrangement of colorful tablecloths had been laid out on picnic tables; lawn chairs set up for those who didn't want to sit on benches. Huddled in coats and scarves, people mingled and chatted and enjoyed their drinks. A few had gone down to the shoreline to watch the waves, keeping their toes a good distance from the icy water.

"I'm not being paid by the company, but by the new artistic director." Vicky nodded to a group of people gathered on the bandstand, watching the festivities, drinks in hand. Rudolph calls itself a Year-Round Christmas destination, and to that aim the tree at the center of the bandstand is refreshed with a live one once a month. This year's holiday season's tree was a twenty-foot-tall Fraser fir, adorned with countless gold and red orbs, some as big as soccer balls, some smaller than a golf ball. Colored lights draped over every branch lit up the gloaming. At four-thirty in the afternoon in early December, it would be dark soon.

"She's paying for this shindig out of her own pocket," Vicky added.

"Who's that?" Alan asked.

Vicky turned to him with an expression of shock. "You haven't heard? Everyone in town is talking about little else."

Alan shrugged as he opened the lid of the next container and peered in. "Oh, good. Vicky's famous gingerbread."

"Alan's never one for town gossip," I said. "Don't forget this is his busiest time of year. Gotta get all those toys ready for Santa to put under trees around the world. I'm surprised he agreed to help out tonight." Alan was a woodworker. He made many of the items stocked at Mrs. Claus's and at gift and toy stores all over this part of the state. In the lead-up to the Christmas season, he concentrated on toys and Christmas décor items such as candlesticks and ornaments; the rest of the year, he made furniture, gorgeous hand-crafted pieces that cost a heck of a lot and were worth every penny. As were his toys—made not only by his hands in his own workshop, often with wood he gathered on his own property, but with love. Alan also served as Santa's head toymaker at public events, standing by his side in a calf-length coat, waistcoat, breeches, and shoes with silver buckles, recording children's wishes on a long roll of paper with a feather-topped pen. Santa, by the way, is my own dad, Noel Wilkinson.

"I agreed at the mention of gingerbread," Alan said.

I laughed and gave him a hug. He kissed the top of my head. As well as furniture crafter, toymaker, and Santa's helper, Alan Anderson is also the love of my life.

"Catherine Renshaw," Vicky said. "That's her on the band-stand in the blue coat and matching hat and gloves, talking to the mayor. She's the new artistic director of the company."

"Don't know that name," he said.

The woman under discussion was in her early sixties, perhaps late sixties if she'd had some work done. She was of average height, wealthy New Yorker-thin, dressed in a cashmere-and-wool coat short enough to show off loose black slacks and ankle boots with three-inch heels. Brown hair with caramel highlights was tucked under a hat matching her coat. She held a wine glass in a gloved hand and waved the other hand in Sue-Anne Morrow's face. They were too far away for us to hear what was being said.

"Newcomers," Vicky explained as she made a last-minute adjustment to the napkins and I laid out mugs next to the urns of mulled cider and hot chocolate. "Tons of money, or so people say. They bought that big house on the lake where the old McNamara place had been, and they moved in over the summer."

"Oh," Alan said, "that house. Gigantic, ostentatious, totally out of place. A French chateau dropped into the center of Rudolph."

"Yup. That one. As a way of getting involved in her new community, Catherine volunteered with the theater group. Conveniently, Ron Fitzpatrick, who used to be in charge, although he never gave himself a fancy title like artistic director, declared his intention to quit over the summer, on the grounds of wanting to spend more time in California with the grandkids. Whereupon Catherine swooped in and took the job. Helped that no one else wanted it. Also helps that she's prepared to spend lavishly on this year's production. She's picking up the entire bill for this party, thus it's not a potluck in someone's basement."

"George Mann was told his homemade wine would not be needed this year," I said. "Mom told me he took that as a personal insult." As one, we turned to watch the not-happy-looking man standing on his own at the edge of the festivities, dressed in a tattered and faded jacket over a plaid shirt, jeans, and boots, all of which were weary with years of wear. George himself showed signs of years of wear, most of them spent outside winter and summer. He clutched a bottle of beer in a hand scarred from a lifetime spent on a farm. He looked as though he might not have bothered to have a shower and change before coming to the party after mucking out the barn.

"You seem to know a lot about the goings-on," Alan said to Vicky.

"Even from behind the scenes at my place, I hear plenty of the gossip."

"Anything I can do to help?" Rachel McIntosh asked. Rachel and her husband, Ian, owned Candy Cane Sweets, and the red-and white-striped shirt, red pants, and candy cane necklace she wore to work was visible under her open coat.

"Thanks, but we're good here," Vicky said.

"Is Ian in the play again this year?" I asked Rachel.

Her face tightened into an expression I couldn't read. "Starring role. Ebenezer Scrooge himself."

"That's good," Vicky said. "Everyone says a big part of the reason last year's play didn't do very well was because Ian had to drop out at the last minute."

Rachel shrugged.

"Everything okay?" I asked her.

She gave me a tight smile. "Perfectly fine. Thank you for asking, Merry. As you have everything under control, I see Irene over there. Haven't spoken to her in ages. Excuse me."

She slipped away and we finished setting up. Guests were already helping themselves to the cider, and the hot spicy scent of warm apples and cinnamon and nutmeg drifted on the air.

"I know just about everyone here," I said. "But who's that guy? The one on the bandstand, talking to Catherine and Sue-Anne?"

Vicky looked over. "Younger than most of this crowd. Nice hair." The man in question did have nice hair: thick, black locks curling slightly around his ears. He was around forty, slightly over six feet tall. As we watched, he laughed heartily at something Catherine said, displaying dazzling white teeth. He was, from this distance anyway, quite handsome and the cut of his winter coat hinted at a broad chest and shoulders underneath. "I haven't met him, but that must be Dave French."

"French? Is he related to the owners of the Carolers' Motel?"

"Yes. Lloyd French had a stroke over the summer, and his son's come to help run the motel. He's divorced, or so the female staff at my place say. Not bad looking."

"Is he?" I said with a sideways grin at Alan. "I hadn't noticed."

"I saw Lloyd talking to Noel when I drove up," Alan said. "I'd heard about his heart problems and I thought he didn't look at all well. I was surprised to see him here, as I wouldn't have thought the theater was an interest of his, but maybe he came at his son's suggestion."

"I can keep an eye on things now," Vicky said. "You two go and enjoy yourselves."

"I like the sound of that," Alan said. I did too.

People didn't need to be invited before they started drifting toward the food tables. Vicky had outdone herself, as she usually did, with hearty roast beef and homemade mustard on mini-baguettes, salmon and egg salad on thinly sliced white bread, and roasted red peppers and mushrooms on whole wheat rolls, along with a tureen of bright orange butternut squash soup made with the last of the season's fresh vegetables. And the desserts, of course—Vicky's justifiably famous gingerbread (a Rudolph Christmas tradition), coconut cupcakes, and glistening fruit tarts.

As previously arranged, my dad kept his eye on Vicky, and when she judged everything was to her satisfaction, she gave him a nod. He stood next to the food tables and announced, in the voice Santa Claus uses to guide the reindeer through a thunderstorm, that Mrs. Catherine Renshaw would like to say a few words.

Catherine descended the steps from the bandstand, smiling and waving, like Mrs. Claus on the back of the sled in the parade. Our mayor, Sue-Anne Morrow, isn't exactly a shy, retiring woman, but on this occasion she fell back to allow Catherine to be the center of attention. A man, whom I took to be Catherine's husband, walked slightly behind her. He was a reasonably attractive guy, about her age, just under six feet tall, with strong cheekbones, a sweep of thick silver hair, and light brown eyes.

Catherine graciously thanked Dad, and made a joke about finally meeting Santa Claus in her "old age," to which we all laughed politely. She then simply invited everyone to enjoy themselves, and they needed no further encouragement to dig in.

About fifty people were attending the picnic: the cast and crew of the Rudolph Community Theater Players and their families, along with donors and other supporters, and local celebrities such as the mayor and her husband. They were a fairly polite bunch, and they lined up at the food table, everyone telling everyone else to "Please, go ahead." I'd known most of these faces my whole life. Friends of my parents or of one of my siblings, town councilors from Dad's time as mayor, mothers and fathers of my mom's vocal students, former classmates of Vicky and me, members of Vicky's huge extended family, and volunteers with one committee or another, always dropping into our house to discuss strategy or budgets. Most of them were in their fifties or sixties, but a scattering of younger people had joined them, including parents of the kids diving headfirst into the food offerings.

Even my shop assistant, Jackie O'Reilly, was here. She'd told me, more than once, that she was an extra in the production although she was hoping that once the director saw how good she was, he'd give her a speaking part. Jackie's boyfriend, Kyle Lambert, had earlier been taking pictures for the local paper, as well as helping himself several times to the beer. He'd abandoned photography in favor of getting first in line for the food.

"Now there's a couple of folks I didn't expect to see," my dad said to me. I turned and looked in the direction he was facing. Two heavyset men were picking their way across the winter-brown lawn, both bundled up in heavy coats, gloves, and scarves. They had huge smiles on their plump round faces, jowls jiggling, hands extended. They greeted people loudly as they waded into the group.

"Politicians or real estate agents? Alan asked.

Dad chuckled. "One of each. The bigger one's Randy Baumgart-ner, mayor of Muddle Harbor, and the other fellow's John Bene-dict, owner of the biggest real estate office in these parts, outside of Rudolph, that is." Muddle Harbor was the neighboring town.

"Shall I set loose the hounds, Noel?" Vicky asked.

For a moment I was confused and glanced quickly to where Mattie, which is what I usually call Matterhorn, was comfort-ably stretched out on the grass, eyes closed, breathing deeply. My dad chuckled, and I realized it had been a rhetorical question.

"All are welcome to join us to celebrate the season of joy, isn't that what we say in Rudolph?" Dad said.

"I could make exceptions," Vicky said.

"Before you do that . . . he's spotted me. I'll go and make friendly. Randy!" dad bellowed, as he marched across the lawn. "What brings you here on such a fine day?"

Mayor Baumgartner's smile grew even wider, if that was pos-sible, and he thrust out a gloved hand. "Noel! Sorry we're late. Jack here had some last minute calls to make. Business never stops for the likes of him, does it?" He walloped my dad on the shoulder. "Looks like a great party. I hear good things about this year's play, and we wanted to see for ourselves. We might send some business your way."

"I'm afraid all this has nothing to do with me," dad said. "My wife has a role this year."

Vicky sniffed in disapproval. "As if Muddle Harbor has any business to send anyone's way. Never mind them, you two cute kids run along and play now. I can take care of anything that's needed." She made shooing gestures with her hands.

Alan and I decided to wait for the crowd to clear, and hope they'd leave something for us. The children had abandoned

Mattie at the call to dinner, and he was lying comfortably under the tree, his massive paws resting between his chin, alternatively snoozing and watching the festivities. I took a bottle of water to refill his bowl, slipped him a chunk of roast beef Vicky had thoughtfully provided for him, gave him a head scratch and told him he was a good boy, and then followed Alan to the drinks table.

Alan grabbed a bottle of beer out of the container of ice, and I poured myself a glass of wine. The drinks, like the food, had been paid for by Catherine Renshaw. The wine and soda glasses were real glass, too, not plastic or acrylic as would better suit a picnic in the park.

"Bring me another one of those," Lloyd French shouted to Alan.

Alan twisted the cap off the bottle he'd chosen for himself, and carried it over to the man. Lloyd was sitting in a folding chair, wrapped tightly in a blanket. His cheeks were red with cold, but otherwise his face was drawn and pale. Dark circles accented his watery eyes, and his breathing was ragged. He almost snatched the bottle out of Alan's hand.

"Thanks," he grumbled. "If you see that son of mine, tell him I'm still waiting for something to eat." He took a long glug of his beer and shook his head. "Too busy trying to impress all these fancy *theater* folks to see to his old man."

"I can—" I began.

"Not your job to look after me, young Merry." He looked around. "Where's that boy got to now?"

Alan and I exchanged glances and edged away. "Lloyd French has always been a man who likes to be in charge," he whispered to me. "Being incapacitated, even mildly, is hard on him."

"He's lucky his son agreed to move back and help out," I replied. "Not every grown child can, or will, do that. Hum . . . you seem to have lost your beer."

Desmond Kerslake, the long-time director of the Players, was taking a bottle out of the cooler. "Nice party, Desmond," Alan said. "Catherine's done a good job."

Desmond took a drink before answering. The look on his face was as though someone had slipped a slice of lemon into his Christmas eggnog.

"Catherine," he said, "doesn't stint. Not if it'll get her noticed." He stalked away.

"There's a story there," Alan said to me. "One I do not want to hear."

My mom and another woman hadn't gone for food. I took a step toward them, and then hesitated. The look on my mother's face didn't exactly speak of warm and friendly vibes. Alan, however, didn't recognize the signals as well as I did, and he walked up to them before I could warn him away. All I could do was follow.

"Aline, hi. Nice party," he said.

The tension at the corners of my mother's eyes and the anger around her mouth disappeared in an instant, to be replaced with a radiant smile.

"Alan! How lovely to see you, dear." She leaned forward to receive a peck on the cheek, which he provided. "It's been months since you've been around to the house for dinner. Merry, you must rectify that oversight shortly."

"I'll get on that right away, Mom. But be warned, only the promise of Vicky's baking was sufficient to tear Alan away from his workshop to come to this."

"A boy has to eat," Mom said fondly. "Paula, have you met my daughter, Merry? She owns Mrs. Claus's Treasures, on Jingle

Bell Lane. And this is Alan Anderson, who makes the most divine things out of wood you've ever seen. Merry and Alan, this is Paula Monahan. Paula's an important part of the theater family. Isn't that lovely?"

Probably only I, because I know my mother so well, heard the unsaid "not" at the end of that sentence.

"Are you in the cast, Paula?" Alan asked. "Or crew?"

I'd seen Paula around town, but I didn't remember having ever met her and I didn't think she shopped at my store. She was in her early forties, younger than most of the company, slightly taller than my five foot four, and slim beneath a padded black jacket. Heavy brown bangs peeked out from beneath her wool cap. "I play Mrs. Cratchit. My son, Eddie—he's around here somewhere—is Tiny Tim."

"Important roles. Tim, in particular," Alan said.

Paula didn't smile in acknowledgment. Instead she threw a not-friendly glare at my mother. "It is. As *some people* fail to understand. If you'll excuse me. I need to ensure Eddie finds something other than cake to eat."

"Sounds like an idea," Alan said once she'd gone. "I'm ready to hit the buffet. Merry?"

"Go ahead. I'll be with you in a minute."

He needed no further encouragement and barely managed to refrain from breaking into a run as he crossed the lawn.

"That was tense," I said to my mom. "What's with you and Paula?"

Mom sighed. "All these years I have refrained from engaging in amateur dramatics, no matter how hard Desmond and Ron worked to entice me. At last I succumbed. Much to my regret."

Mom wasn't exaggerating or bragging. The director and former artistic director of the Rudolph Community Theater Players

14

came on pilgrimage once a year to the house to beg her to join the group. In her glory days, my mom had been a professional opera singer. Not just a singer, but a true diva. She's sung solo parts with the Metropolitan Opera and at some of the best opera houses in Europe, including a sold-out performance of *Madama Butterfly* at La Scala, in which she sang Suzuki.

With her travel and performance schedule, it had largely been my dad—solid, sensible, small-town dad—who'd raised my three younger siblings and me. Mom was retired now, and she kept her hand in teaching vocal lessons to local children and a few adults who'd always wanted to sing but never had the chance to learn formally. She might be retired, but she was still every inch the diva. She'd never had anything but scorn for amateur theatrics. To everyone's surprise, probably hers most of all, she agreed to appear with the Rudolph Community Theater Players in this year's production of *A Christmas Carol*. Desmond Kerslake, the director, told her they'd be doing the musical version, and they desperately needed her help.

She not only would play the Ghost of Christmas Past, as well as Belle, Scrooge's former fiancée, but she served as the musical coach. When I'd asked how she could play both the ghost and Belle when the ghost shows Scrooge his youth, she said, "With a bit of deft maneuvering from stage left to center and a flick of a cape. Belle has the strongest female song in the entire production, no one else is remotely capable of doing it." She tried not to smile too widely as she said it.

"This," she now declared dramatically, "is going to be the death of me." All that was missing was the back of the hand held to the forehead and the drop into the fainting couch. "If not of me, likely someone else."

Chapter Two

"Don't take it so seriously, Mom," I said. "it's just an amateur production."

"Believe it or not, dear, I went into this intending to take it in the spirit in which it is intended. As you point out, an amateur production for the enjoyment of the participants and the entertainment of tourists anxious to get into the spirit of Christmas. It is not I who's being the diva here. Not that I ever acted the diva, of course."

I refrained from saying, *Are you really that unself-aware?* "You mean Paula? What's she done?"

Mom sipped her wine. Her cheeks had a pleasant rosy glow. Either she'd had more to drink this afternoon than she normally did or she was warming up and would never admit it. "I mean all of them. I've never seen such petty rivalries in all my days. Other than the time the Estonian baritone put bleach in the German soprano's tea because he wanted his lover, the Japanese soprano, to be promoted from understudy into the role of Tosca. Imagine! The man was a total fool, as though she, the German, wouldn't smell bleach in her tea before having a drink!"

Despite myself, I said, "What happened then?"

"The show was an abject failure. The German was dreadful. Simply dreadful. Far past her prime. They should have gone with the Japanese, but she, the German soprano, was sleeping with the company's primary donor."

"I meant what happened to the Estonian baritone? Was he arrested? Was that the end of his career?"

"Don't be silly, dear. You'd recognize his name from his recent triumph at Covent Garden if I told it to you."

That was unlikely, but I didn't say so. I get all my musical talent—and interest in grand opera—from my dad. Meaning I have none.

"As for this miserable company . . . Paula seems to think Mrs. Cratchit needs a more dramatic persona than is normally portrayed. And a far better wardrobe to go with it. But most of all she wants the role of Tiny Tim to be expanded."

"Tiny Tim's important."

"As he is. In small doses. He has only a couple of lines to say, including the one everyone knows."

"God bless us, everyone."

"See—even you know it. But it's not enough for Paula. She has all sorts of suggestions for increasing Tim's role. Including giving him a dance number when he throws off his crutch at the end. I dare not imagine it. The point being, dear, the kid can't act. He's awful. And far too big to be *Tiny* Tim." She pointed behind me. "That's him over there."

I turned. Eddie Monahan was ten years old but already topping five feet, and the word "pudgy" leapt instantly to mind. I'd earlier seen him piling his plate with sandwiches, and he was now demolishing his second round of dessert.

"Agreed that Tim Cratchit's supposed to be frail and on the point of death. That boy wouldn't be cast in a Broadway production, but this is amateur and community theater, Mom. You can't be picky."

"Perhaps I foolishly expected some degree of talent. Never mind that Catherine has ideas for the production, which rightfully fall in the realm of the director, and Desmond is not taking her suggestions well."

"Hey! Did you see that?"

"See what?"

"Eddie tripped that little girl. She's half his size, and he deliberately stuck his foot out. Her mother's coming over. No, more likely to be her grandmother. She's helping the girl up. She seems to be okay. Oops. Now the grandmother's saying something to Eddie. Here comes Paula, ready for battle."

My mom and I watched the scene play out: the weeping girl; the boy trying (and failing) to look innocent; the girl's indignant grandmother; the boy's protective mother.

"Irene Dowling," Mom said. "She's the wardrobe mistress, and I have to say that out of all the company, she's the one with the most genuine talent. What she can do with a scrap of leftover cloth is amazing. Her only flaw is she's not assertive enough. Every actor who's ever stepped foot on a stage or movie lot wants a better costume. Never mind dealing with the expectations of directors as to what can simply not be accomplished with the time and budget allocated."

People nearby stopped to watch the scene, now threatening to grow into a full-blown altercation. A man came running across the lawn, as Paula accused the girl of being clumsy. I decided I didn't care much for Eddie Monahan, no matter that he might be only ten years old. The smirk on his face as he watched the girl, tearfully huddled under her grandmother's protective arm, was not pleasant.

"Let it go," the man said to Paula. I assumed he was Paula's husband and father to the miscreant. He grabbed Eddie's arm. "You apologize to Lucy."

The boy stuck out his tongue instead.

"I said apologize. Or we're leaving now."

"You're overreacting, Kevin," Paula said. "Eddie didn't do anything. The girl fell. Children shouldn't be running if they can't bounce back from a fall."

"It was no accident," Irene said. "Eddie tripped her. I saw it happen."

"Are you sure about that, *dear*?" Paula said. "You have been here for quite a while and not been shy to make use of Catherine's excellent wine."

"Low blow," Mom said to me.

"Paula," Kevin said. "Let's have none of that. Eddie, are you going to say anything to Lucy, or are we leaving?"

"I'm sorry," the boy said in a ten-year-old voice.

"As am I," his father said.

"Apology accepted," Irene said. "From you, Kevin, if no one else." She led the little girl away.

Eddie sneered after them and then ran off in search of more desserts, which made me realize that if I wanted any food for myself, I'd better get moving. The boy's father leaned into his mother's face and spoke in a low voice. She snarled something in return and then marched away. Paula might have made a dig at Irene, but she headed directly for the bar in turn.

"Charming family," Mom said.

My shop assistant, Jackie O'Reilly, joined Mom and me. "Aline, hi. Isn't this great? So nice of Catherine to put this on, isn't it? Merry, are you thinking of getting involved in the production?"

"Absolutely and totally not. Alan and I came to give Vicky a hand."

This was Jackie's second year with the theater group. Last year she hadn't opened her mouth once, and this year she hadn't even stepped in front of an audience yet, but stars were dancing behind her eyes, and her dreams were of taking her award-winning performance to Broadway, maybe even Hollywood.

"Some non-Rudolph people have come to this," Jackie said. "That's great, isn't it? Word is spreading far and wide about what a fabulous production this is going to be."

Randy Baumgartner, bearing an overloaded plate in one hand and a bottle of beer in the other, had cornered Catherine Renshaw. He ate and drank and talked all at the same time with such speed I wondered if he had a third, invisible hand. Catherine's panicked eyes darted around, seeking escape, of which none seemed to be immediately forthcoming. His companion, the real estate guy, was engaged in what looked to be an intense, serious conversation with Dave French.

"I heard," Jackie continued, "Desmond's invited some of his Broadway friends to opening night. Isn't that exciting! I'm only in the chorus, but I hope they'll notice me. Anyway, while I have you, Aline, I'm wondering if you'd be nice enough to put a word in with Irene about my costume. I'm thinking something a bit more . . . flattering would be good."

"You're playing a Victorian washerwoman, Jackie, not Lady Mary Crawley. Or, perhaps more what you're thinking, a streetwalker. Which is irrelevant, as I am not involved in costuming decisions."

"You have a nice costume."

"I'm Aline Steiner," the diva said.

"Okay. Just a suggestion. Have a nice evening." Jackie ducked her head and scurried away.

"Amateurs!" Mom said. "Now that he's been fed, I might be able to tear your father away before anyone else asks me to improve their role." She stalked off, and I went in search of my own dinner.

Before I reached the food table, I glanced across the lawn to check on Mattie. A couple of small boys were edging nearer to him. He lay on the ground, watching them, eyes bright, tail slowly thumping. Eddie ran past me, heading toward them. I didn't care for that stick he was waving in the air, and I hurried after him, intending to intervene. Children should never approach dogs they don't know, but Mattie's sheer size keeps most of them away. He might be big, but he's as gentle as they come, but he's still a dog and he will react like a dog if he thinks he's being threatened.

Eddie charged the little group with a whoop and lifted his stick. Mattie let out a woof and lumbered to his feet. Before I could yell a word of command—to either dog or boy—someone intervened.

"Matterhorn, down," said a perfectly calm voice. "I will handle this." The dog dropped to the ground as though his legs had been kicked out from underneath him. "Put that stick down, young man, before I have to take it from you."

The stick dropped as fast as the dog had.

Diane Simmonds had formed an almost uncanny bond with Mattie. When I first met her, she told me her parents trained dogs for TV and movies, and she'd grown up around them. Sometimes I had a niggle of jealousy that my dog was better behaved for her than he was with me.

It would appear she had a similar effect on rowdy little boys. Diane Simmonds was the lead detective with the Rudolph Police

Department, so I suspect she had a good deal of experience with rowdy little boys. Not to mention rowdy big boys.

"You weren't going to hit that dog, were you?" she said to Eddie.

He mumbled something that might have been a no.

"Glad to hear it. Off you go, now."

Eddie bolted.

"If you want to pet the dog," Simmonds said to the two wide-eyed boys who'd remained, "You need to speak to the dog's owner first and ask permission. Here she is. Merry, hello."

"Thanks for . . . uh . . . this," I said.

Simmonds half-turned and beckoned to someone to join her. An older woman and a young girl stepped out from a row of bushes, brown and bare for winter. "Merry, I don't think you've met my mother, Judith. Or Charlotte, my daughter." The older woman had two sets of white skates thrown over her shoulder, and the girl carried her own. Their eyes were bright and cheeks glowed with the cold and the exercise. All three of them had the same small chin, huge green eyes, and curly red hair, although Judith's was heavily streaked with gray, Charlotte's was tied into a long braid, and Detective Simmonds's was cut smoothly at the back of her neck.

"Why don't you introduce those boys to Mattie while they're waiting," Simmonds said.

I smiled at the boys. "He's a good dog, but very big, so he can hurt you even though he doesn't intend to. You don't want to frighten him. If you hold out your hand to his face, like this, and move slowly, he'll get to know you and want to be your friend."

The first little boy did as instructed, and Mattie gave his hand a slobbering lick. The boy laughed and said, "That's wet." The second said, "Can I ride him?"

"He's not a pony," I said.

"Run along now," Diane Simmonds said, and they did so. "We've had a lovely day and we were heading for the car when I saw you and wanted to say hello." She pointed to the banner strung between two trees near the food tables. "Rudolph Community Theater Players. Are you part of the group?"

"Not me. My mom is, and Vicky's catering this picnic. I'm just helping her."

"What are they putting on this season?"

"*A Christmas Carol.* Opening night is Friday after next, and it's going to run until a matinee on the 24th. It's the musical version."

"I didn't know there was a musical version."

"Everyone's done some version of *A Christmas Carol.* Even the Muppets."

"I like that one," Charlotte said. "Can we go to the play, Mom?"

"Better get your tickets early," I said. "It's going to be a sold-out show."

"I'd like to see it," Judith said.

"Then we'll go. "We won't keep you," Simmonds said. "Have a nice evening. Take care of Merry, Matterhorn," she added. He woofed in confirmation.

Judith nodded to me, Charlotte gave me a shy wave, and Detective Simmonds walked away with her family.

Not a lot was left at the food table, but I was able to snag a roast beef sandwich and the scrapings from the bottom of the soup pot. While I ate, I stood to one side and watched the activity. My mom and dad had disappeared, and other people were gathering their things and preparing to leave. Irene was standing by the playground, a soft smile on her face, watching Lucy, her granddaughter, swing higher and ever higher. I didn't see either Kevin Monahan or his ill-behaved son, but Paula was refreshing her wineglass and offering the same to Jackie. Alan laughed heartily at something Ian McIntosh said. Dave French had moved on from the real estate agent, and was now chatting with Desmond Kerslake, the director, while Dave tried his best to ignore his father, Lloyd, frantically making gestures indicating he was ready to leave.

Catherine Renshaw played the room. Or the lawn, I should say. Her husband had freed her from the attentions of Mayor Baumgartner and once again she was all smiles and light chatter. More than just providing money to the theatrical company, she'd brought new life to what was becoming a rather stodgy old group resting on its laurels.

Rudolph, New York, wants to be known as America's Christmas Town. Here, we celebrate Christmas all year round. In July, the town goes all out to take advantage of its prime location on the shores of Lake Ontario and its Christmas Town theme, when Santa arrives for his summer vacation in a grand boat parade. He sets up his umbrella on the beach to meet visiting children, and high school students dressed as vacationing elves serve as his attendants, as does Alan in his toymaker getup.

We might play at Christmas all year, but it's the beginning of December when everything comes together. The hotels go all out with the decorations and seasonal activities, and the restaurants offer special menus featuring traditional holiday fare. Vicky's bakery goes heavy on the mince tarts and gingerbread and even old-fashioned fruitcake of the sort that people buy and almost no one ever eats. (Although Vicky's is fabulous!) The theater group always does a play with a holiday or Christmas theme, and it's an important part of the town's annual celebrations. Last year's production of *Miracle on 34th Street* had been an enormous flop, or so I'd heard. Mom told me the company was desperate this year to recover from that disaster. They'd never attempted a musical, but encouraged by the new artistic director to be bigger and bolder than ever before, they were taking a chance with *A Christmas Carol*.

By six-thirty most of the skaters had gone home, the lake resembled a cloth of smooth black velvet, and the trees surrounding the park were nothing but black shadows. The lights of the tree on the bandstand blazed with color. Houses surrounding the park had switched on their holiday lights and illuminated decorations. Alan came up behind me, put his arms around my shoulders, and pulled me close. "Nice night," he murmured in my ear.

I put my hands on his and settled into the embrace. "Nice enough. I think Mom's coming to regret getting involved in this thing."

"She'll forget her regrets the moment she steps on stage."

"Probably."

"She couldn't talk your dad into taking a part?"

"Ha. He's not about to take a role, to everyone's relief, I'm sure. He's busy enough with the Santa gig, but he agreed to help with the sets. I'm surprised they didn't ask you to be the stage carpenter."

"They did. As they do every year. And as I do every year, I told them I simply don't have time. Besides, they don't need a craftsman to make their sets. Hammer a few boards in place on the stage at the community center, and slap some paint on them.

It's done. Not like repertory theater where everything has to be carefully constructed in order to be able to be quickly broken down and then reassembled for the next show."

The party was starting to break up; people called good night as they headed for their cars. Alan and I went to help Vicky clean up.

Chapter Three

"Those earthenware dishes will be perfect," my mother said. "They have that cheap rustic look everyone knows costs an absolute fortune."

"Surely you're not buying a complete set of dishes for the play?"

"I'm not buying anything. I'm simply serving as a props scout. Isn't that the job you did when you were with *Jennifer's Lifestyle*?"

"Something similar. Before I was a design editor, I scoured secondhand shops and antique fairs searching for things to use in photo shoots, yes. But our magazine had a heck of a bigger budget than the Rudolph Community Theater Players."

"Catherine asked me to be on the lookout for items we can use on set," Mom said. "I get the feeling, dear, price is to be no object."

"That's no way to run a nonprofit endeavor."

My mother glanced around the shop. It was the Monday afternoon following the picnic, and she'd popped into Mrs. Claus's Treasures on her way home from a meeting at Catherine's house. Customers were browsing, and Jackie was ringing up pieces of handmade jewelry at the check-out counter. She'd made the sale by telling the customers the items had been made by a young woman who worked in this very store. One woman studied the toy selection while next to her two others were flicking through the limited selection of Christmas-themed children's books that were new additions to my stock this year. I'm not intending to compete with the Rudolph Bookstore, so I simply tucked the shelf into a back corner as an experiment to see if the books would sell. Over the summer I had the idea that a few titles would be a good match with the toys: one-stop shopping.

Mom jerked her head and slipped behind the curtain separating the storefront from the back rooms.

I could do nothing but follow. "Be right back, Jackie. Call me if you need anything."

"I won't," she said.

"What's up?" I said to my mother.

"This is not for public consumption, dear, but the Rudolph Community Theater Players is rapidly becoming more of one person's hobby than a nonprofit endeavor."

"Let's go into my office so I can check on Mattie. You can tell me what you're talking about in there."

Being a Saint Bernard, Mattie isn't welcome in my china shop, thus he normally spends most of the day in the office. His breed isn't known for having an excess of energy; the walk to and from work is usually enough for him, and he passes the time happily snoozing in the office. I pop in regularly throughout the day to fresh his water bowl and to take him for short outings in the alley. He opened one eye when Mom and I came in. Saw it was only me and closed it again. His water bowl had tipped over and a puddle was soaking into the carpet.

I picked up the bowl. "What do you mean someone's hobby? Surely the theater group's everyone's hobby. No one's being paid to take part in this, are they?"

"Catherine is taking it to excess, exerting more control than I think wise. She is, for example, making executive decisions about the set without consulting the set crew. George Mann attempted at one time to argue with her, and she simply walked away, leaving him in mid-sentence. He was fit to be tied, and you know how easygoing George usually is. I'm surprised he hasn't quit. Loyalty perhaps. He's been doing the sets for years. Decades probably. As for why I am here: Catherine suggested I keep an eye out for items to decorate the homes of the Cratchit family and Scrooge's nephew, Fred. Those dishes will make a nice addition to the background of the Cratchit's meager Christmas dinner when Ian, I, as Scrooge, and the ghost of Christmas Past pay them a visit."

I went to the washroom and filled the dog's bowl. When I came back, I said, "I'm not lending you any of my stock. I sell things, I don't rent them."

"Catherine told me to pay whatever necessary."

I put the bowl on the floor and gave Mattie a hearty scratch behind his ears. He grunted in contentment. "In that case, I'm happy to sell them to you. At full price."

"You fail to see my point, Merry. Catherine is taking over to a degree I consider unhealthy. Take this meeting we just had. I thought it was to be a gathering of senior cast and crew, but I was the only invitee."

"Why?"

"She warbled on about my years of professional experience. How I'm the only one she can count on to ensure the group has a true understanding of the meaning and importance of the stage."

"She's flattering you to get you on her side."

"Flattery," Mom said, patting her hair, "will not work with me."

I nodded sagely, as a way of preventing myself from rolling my eyes. My mother lives for flattery. The more lavish the better.

"I fear, dear, she is planning a coup. She's not happy with Desmond's direction, thinking him too restrained. She wants to get rid of Ian."

"Ian? You mean Ian McIntosh? Ian's been with the company forever."

"She doesn't think he has the gravitas to play Ebenezer Scrooge or the dramatic range to properly depict his change of heart."

"It's less than two weeks until opening night. If she fires Ian, who's going to step in to take the lead role?"

"She wants to ask Dave French. Dave is currently cast as the ghost of Jacob Marley and later as Old Joe."

"Not that it matters, but who's Old Joe?"

"The lowly fellow of the criminal element selling off Scrooge's possessions after his demise. As shown to Scrooge by Christmas Yet to Come."

"That would be the young and handsome Dave French?" I gave Mattie a final pat and pushed myself to my feet. I tried not to grunt too loudly in the presence of my mother. "I don't see him suiting either role."

"His looks might have something to do with it," she said dryly. "His youth, comparatively speaking, experience, and enthusiasm will bring something to the production if he's in the starring role. So says Catherine at any rate. He's been at all the rehearsals so he should be able to learn the lines quickly. Plus he's done some professional acting. But Ian's not to be trifled with, Merry. Ian is a founding member of the company and he's been in every production they've put on, usually taking the starring role. Other than last year, when he had a heart attack only a week before opening night, and had to drop out."

"Can Dave sing?"

"And there, my dear, is where Catherine has a problem. He does sing, and reasonably well too. Far, far better than Ian. Marley has the major male song in the entire production. Many of the other so-called singing parts are nothing but a lot of speak-singing." She let out a long theatrical sigh. "Although I am doing my best to keep them in tune. Ian cannot sing Marley, no matter how much rattling of chains he does. If Ian is replaced as Scrooge, and unable to play Marley, there's no other part suitable to his position in the company, and we'll have no one to take Marley."

"Did you tell Catherine this?"

"Of course I did. She assured me she has full confidence in my ability to instruct Ian. In little over a week, I'm expected to turn a candy store owner into a professional singer."

"As well as be a prop buyer."

"That too."

"Sorry, Mom, but I have to get back out there. Jackie's alone today, other than me, and we've been busy for a Monday. I have no advice to give you on this; you'll have to sort out your theatrical problems yourself." I told Mattie to guard the office, shooed my mother out, and followed her into the store.

Paula Monahan stood at the counter, chatting to Jackie. She turned to us with a bright, brittle smile. "Aline. Hello. Fancy running into you here."

"Considering my daughter owns this fine establishment, I can often be found here, yes."

Paula's smile didn't falter. "Jackie and I were just chatting about the costumes." Jackie nodded enthusiastically. "We both feel Irene needs to be given a freer hand. I'm sure she can come up with better designs, given the right direction."

"Do you want the plates, Mom?" I asked.

"Yes. Six sets, please."

"Jackie, can you wrap up set six sets of the blue earthenware design for my mom, please."

"In a minute," Jackie said. "I was saying to Paula that—"

"This isn't a place for theater company business. Aside from selling them six sets of blue earthenware dishes. Do you want a tablecloth and napkins too, Mom?"

"I'm not sure. Did nineteenth-century, working-class English families have tablecloths?"

"I doubt they had matching tableware. They certainly didn't know the word 'tablescape'".

"Sorry, but I couldn't help but overhear." A customer put down a box containing an Alan Anderson–made train set. "I have a degree in social history, and until well into the twentieth century, in both Europe and America, the working classes, and even quite a few members of the so-called middle class, wouldn't have even had enough cups to serve tea to guests. People brought their own when they visited."

"That's interesting," I said. "I've always thought we don't know enough about how the real people lived. Far too much *Bridgerton* and *Downton Abbey*."

"Can never have too much *Bridgerton*," another customer said.

"You're buying props for the play?" Paula asked Mom.

"Yes. I am."

"A play!" Customer Number One said, "I love live theater. What are you putting on?"

"*A Christmas Carol,*" Jackie said. "Opening night is Friday next week. December 15. At the Rudolph Community Center. I myself have an important role. It's going to be the musical production. Tickets are going fast."

"I might get some then," Customer Number One said.

"How much are the tickets?" Customer Number Two said.

"Uh . . ." Jackie said, "Aline, do you know?"

"Information is available online. Now, Jackie, I don't have all day. The dishes, please."

"Aline!" Customer Number One gasped. "Don't tell me you're Aline Steiner. I thought I recognized you from somewhere, and I'd heard you were living in Rudolph these days. I have to say, if you'll allow me, your interpretation of Carmen at the Met was the best I've ever seen."

Mom beamed. "How kind of you to say so. What did you say your name is, dear?"

I stifled a groan. Now I'd never get her out of here.

"I don't think the blue's suitable," Paula said. "Too modern. Do you have those dishes in another color?"

"We have brown." I indicated a shelf displaying more items.

"Much better for the way I intend to interpret Mrs. Cratchit. A hardworking, no-nonsense woman, who still finds time to do the best she can with limited resources for her husband and family. A dining room is a reflection of a woman's personality, wouldn't you agree? I'll take a full set. Six will be enough."

"You're buying these for the play?" I asked. "What about what Mom's going to get?"

"My small contribution to the production. Tell Aline it's my pleasure."

"Mom wasn't going to pay herself," I said, but Paula's attention had moved on. While Mom was entertaining an adoring

Customer Number One with details of her life post-retirement, including the important contribution she was making to the Rudolph Community Theater Players, Paula was pulling boxes of brown earthenware table settings off the shelf for the Cratchit family to dine on their roast goose (later turkey). "I don't think we want a tablecloth. If my legs are going to show, I'll need a fuller skirt, don't you agree, Jackie?"

"Yeah, I do. Do you think Irene would mind if I make some minor alterations to my costume myself?"

"What if she does? It's up to the artist to interpret their role, and costuming is so important as to how we see that role."

When Jackie played an elf on the Mrs. Claus's float at the Santa Claus parade a couple of years ago, she'd altered her costume to the point I was afraid we'd have an 'adults only' sticker slapped on us. I reminded myself that the goings on at the theater group had nothing to do with me.

"I have a small, although not insignificant, role in *A Christmas Carol*," Mom said modestly, "but I'm primarily acting as the musical director for the play. It's important to give young people a chance to shine, I'm sure you'll agree."

"What a treat." Customer Number One clapped her hands. "If you're going to be in it, I'll go online right now and get tickets. It was such an honor to meet you, Aline." She ran out the door at top speed, leaving the stack of children's books she'd been about to purchase unbought on the counter.

I glared at my mother.

"Perhaps," she said, "we should redesign the poster advertising the production. My name should be closer to the top. And in larger letters. I need to give Catherine a call."

* * *

A month ago, Jackie informed me that she'd be wrapped up in the play for much of December and would need time off, and this at our busiest time of the year. "I'm sure you'll understand, Merry, being the daughter and sister of performers as you are, that when the muse calls, one must follow."

I stifled a groan. I was the daughter and sister of performers all right, and I knew them for a bunch of overly dramatic, self-important attention-seekers. *Oops. Did I think that out loud?*

"How much rehearsal time do you need? I thought you were an extra."

"An extra for now. I'm hoping once the director sees the depth of my talent," she wiggled her body as though emphasizing where her talent lay, "he'll give me a speaking role." She then swept her arms to one side, in what I feared was an imitation of my mother. Jackie was an attractive woman, a couple of years older than me in her mid-thirties, of average height, with a soft round figure, clear skin, wide expressive eyes, thick black hair, and great bone structure. She'd been the class beauty in high school. Those had been her glory days, as Springsteen sang, and they remained the highlight of her life. It's one thing to be the prettiest girl in a small-town high school, and quite another to try to break into show business competing against all the other prettiest small-town girls. Not that Jackie had tried to compete—as far as I knew she'd never left Rudolph.

"The director's not new," I reminded her. "You've been involved before. You were an extra last year, right?"

"Work with me here, Merry. Catherine Renshaw is new and she has lot of influence on casting. As it is, I'm the understudy for Mrs. Cratchit. I need to be at every rehearsal, ready to step in at any moment." She lowered her voice. "Backstage rumor has it that Catherine and Paula Monahan, who's playing Mrs. C., are clashing constantly." Jackie wiggled her eyebrows. "Paula might not last much longer."

I'd agreed to give Jackie what time off she needed. As though I had any choice in the matter. She was flighty, self-obsessed (speaking of performers), and her attention had a tendency to wander. Despite all that, she was an excellent store clerk. That small-town prettiness attracted male shoppers, and her sheer, genuine friendliness appealed to women. She could convince people their heart's desire lay in that piece of jewelry, table setting, or holiday ornament they didn't know they needed. She was also ferociously loyal to me and to Mrs. Claus's Treasures. I didn't want to lose her. If I tried to argue about the time off, she might well walk out on me and worry about the consequences later.

Fortunately, Chrystal Wong, who'd worked at Mrs. Claus's part time throughout her high school years, was going to be home from college for the holidays, and she'd agreed to help out at the shop again. She was getting her degree at the School of Visual Arts in New York City, specializing in small jewelry design. Her pieces had been beautiful before, but as her education and experience grew they were becoming truly magnificent. Someday soon, I feared (hoped?) her work would be out of my price range. Chrystal would have been better suited to being in the play than Jackie, considering she'd taken vocal lessons from my mom for years. When I asked her about that, she'd laughed and said she had more than enough on her plate these days.

I heard nothing more about the progress (or lack thereof) of the play until Thursday evening. Jackie had left early, saying she had to get to rehearsal, and Chrystal and I were preparing for closing when my dad called me in a matter of the highest urgency.

"She needs a wrap. The heat's turned down too low in the auditorium at the community center, and no one can be found who knows how to raise it."

"Take Mom a wrap then, Dad."

"I'm on my way to a meeting of the children's party committee. I'm already running late, and we're gathering at Ralph's house. That's in the opposite direction to the community center. You close the shop at seven, Merry, and it's almost that now."

"Your house is also in the opposite direction to the community center from here. I walked to work today, as I always do, so that's far out of my way."

"Which is why I'm calling you. Take her one of those nice wraps from your shop."

"I don't rent my stock, Dad. I sell it."

"I'll call it an early Christmas present for your mother. The community center isn't far off your route home."

He had me there. The center was on my way, and I had no other plans for tonight. "Oh, all right. I'll take her something."

"I knew I could count on you, honeybunch. Didn't I tell you those capes would sell for women who don't always realize how cold it can get here when the wind blows off the lake?"

"That you did, Dad."

"Everything okay?" Chrystal asked me once I'd hung up.

"The usual. Mom's chilly so everyone has to drop everything, and Dad's not able to drop what he's doing so somehow it's up to me."

"You're lucky your parents care so much about each other, Merry. And about you too. Not everyone has that, you know."

"Everything okay at your place?" I asked.

She laughed. "I wasn't talking about me. Mom and Dad are fine. Except Mom's talking about having Grandma move in with them, and Dad's threatening to move out if that happens. He's not serious. I don't think she is either." Chrystal's face fell. "I hope she's not serious."

My phone rang before I could reply, and I checked the display. Vicky.

"Hey, Mer. I'm finishing up here, got a lot of prep done for tomorrow, so I'm in the mood to party! And by party I mean one drink in the bar at A Touch of Holly with a platter of calamari and home to bed by nine. Feel like living the wild life with me?"

"Sure. I'd like that. Mark working tonight?" Vicky's boyfriend, Mark Grosse, was head chef at the Yuletide Inn and naturally he worked most nights.

"Yup."

"I need to run an errand first. My dad's buying something for Mom, and I have to take it to her at the rehearsal, like right now. Can I meet you at the bar?"

"I'll come with you. I hoped you'd say yes, and I'm coming through your doors even as we speak."

The chimes over the door sounded and my friend walked in, phone to her ear.

"So you are," I said into my own phone. I hung up.

"Hey, Vicky," Chrystal said.

"Grab me one of those capes, will you, please," I said. "One of the shorter ones will do."

Chrystal took a cape off the rack and presented it to me with a flourish. It was gorgeous soft tweed in a teal and brown pattern, with a high wide collar and three big buttons, falling gracefully to the waist. When Dad suggested I stock them last spring, I'd thought him nuts. I own a Christmas-themed shop, not a women's clothing store. But, as usual, Dad had been right.

Spring had been unnaturally cool, and the capes had sold so well, I'd restocked for the holiday season for those who, like my mom, sometimes forgot to dress adequately for chilly nights.

"Your dad's buying your mom an expensive tweed cape, and you have to deliver it yourself, now?" Vicky said. "That seems weird."

I shrugged.

"Okay. Forgot who I was talking to for a moment. Weird is the definition of your parents."

"Good night, Merry," Chrystal said, "See you tomorrow."

I waved her out the door, went into the back to get Mattie and my bag, checked the door to the alley was locked, and then locked the front door behind Vicky and me and we set off.

Lights, laughter, and conversation flowed out of A Touch of Holly, the restaurant on the other side of the street. Traffic moved steadily on Jingle Bell Lane as Vicky, Mattie, I walked out of town. The other stores were closing, but tourists and locals enjoying a night out streamed into the brightly lit bars and restaurants.

"Did you do okay out of the theater picnic?" I asked my friend.

"More than okay. Catherine paid well, and most importantly on time, and we had almost no leftovers. Plus I had no wait staff wages to pay. Thanks again for helping out. You and Alan were lifesavers. Marjorie couldn't put in the overtime, something about a nephew's birthday party to go to, and Jamie wasn't feeling too well, so I sent her home early. How's business with you?"

"Good. Steady."

We strolled past the park and the bandstand, in no particular hurry. The air was sharp and fresh, the cold, clean air felt good on my face and in my lungs. I figured my mom wouldn't freeze to death before I delivered the emergency garment. Mattie followed his nose, sniffing under trees and around lampposts, also in no particular hurry. When we went back to town, I'd take him to the shop, where he'd wait for us while we were in the restaurant, but I knew he'd enjoy the walk first.

My house isn't far beyond the park, but before reaching it, we turned right, heading inland toward the Rudolph Community Center. I couldn't take Mattie inside, so I found a big tree on a patch of lawn under which to tie him up. "We'll only be a minute," I said.

He grunted in acknowledgement and settled himself down.

People, many of them carrying gym bags, yoga mats, or tote bags with their swimming things, were walking in and out of the building. Loud, thumping, rhythmic music came down the hallway from our left, which reminded me that I never had fulfilled my promise to get more active in the early fall during the store's downtime before the rush of the holiday season.

"We should go for a run one day," I said to Vicky.

She cocked one eyebrow at me and lifted a hand to tuck a lock of bubble-gum pink hair behind one multiple-pierced ear, showing the tattoo of a gingerbread cookie decorating her right wrist. Why?"

"For exercise."

"Why would I want to do that?"

Good point. Vicky was five foot eleven and, in proof that life wasn't fair, despite the fact that she baked for a living, she was as thin as a supermodel. Except for that one long pink lock, her black hair was less than half an inch long. Rows of piercings ran up both her ears, and her coat covered the dragon tattoos winding around her arms. She had a big, playful grin, and her blue eyes, heavily outlined in black liner and mascara, were always on the lookout for mischief. The first day of school, Vicky, already of ferocious height and determined temperament, for a five-year-old anyway, marched up to shy little me, cowering in a doorway, and declared, "You will be my best friend."

All these years later, I still was.

I, to my eternal regret, am not five foot eleven, and I definitely do not have the body of a supermodel. More like five four with a tendency to put on weight if I'm not careful. And it's hard to be careful, with Vicky as my best friend. She's always trying to get me to taste things she's thinking of putting on the menu at the bakery, or pressing the day's leftovers on me.

We stopped at the reception desk. "Hi, I've got a delivery for the Community Players." I indicated the cape tossed over my arm. "I think they're rehearsing here today?"

"Yup. They're in the auditorium. She pointed to the right. "Head down the hall and it's on your right."

We found the room indicated and opened one of the double doors to enter a small auditorium. Fifteen rows of raked seating faced the stage, with a single aisle down the center. Most of the lights were off, except for those illuminating the stage. A handful of people sat in seats in the first row. My mom was standing center stage, hitting a high note, facing Paula Monahan. A scattering of other cast members, including Jackie, were clustered in the wings watching. Everyone was in their street clothes.

Vicky and I tiptoed down the aisle, trying to be quiet. "I thought you said it was cold," Vicky whispered. "If anything, it's way too hot in here."

I whispered back, "Obviously, they found the person responsible for adjusting the temperature. He appears to have overcompensated."

Catherine Renshaw sat front row center, seated between Desmond Kerslake, the director, and Ian McIntosh, who was intended (so far) to play Scrooge. Eddie Monahan was two rows behind them, digging into an extra large bag of chips and kicking repeatedly at the back of the seat in front of him. Irene, in charge of costumes, stood alone at the bottom of the steps at stage left, a bolt of fabric cradled in her arms.

"Now you try that," Mom said to Paula Monahan.

"I can't sing that high," Paula said.

"Then why have you been cast in this play?"

"Because I can act!" Paula yelled. "Which is better than most of this bunch can say."

"Claws coming out," Ian said as we reached them. He didn't bother to keep his voice down.

"That," Mom said, "might be a matter of dispute. However, let me remind you that this is a musical production, and that means singing. And you, my dear, have one week to learn how to sing."

If looks could kill . . . Paula glared at my mother, and I thought it a good thing no knife-props were at hand.

"Can we go now, Mom?" Eddie called from the third row. "This is boooorrrring."

"You want boring, young man," she snapped, "you can wait in the dressing room."

Eddie muttered something rude. His mother ignored him.

"Aline, why don't you take Paula aside and do some private work on that song." Desmond stood up. "I'll admit it . . . uh . . . needs some work, but we're not at the Met here."

"We may not be at the Met," Catherine Renshaw said, "but as far as I'm concerned, that's no reason to let standards slip. It is precisely because I intend to achieve those standards I convinced

Aline Steiner to join our little company. Paula, I expect you to get that song perfect or I'll . . . I mean we'll find a replacement for you."

Paula put her hands on her hips and threw daggers at the other woman. "You wouldn't dare."

"Test me, please," Catherine said. "In the meantime, take your noxious child with you. That banging is seriously getting on my nerves."

Paula stalked off stage. Eddie continued kicking the seat. My mother turned to exchange a look with Desmond and caught sight of Vicky and me standing awkwardly in the aisle like eavesdroppers caught hearing things they shouldn't. "Merry, are you looking for me? This is not a good time. You can see I have work to do."

I held up the cape. "Dad asked me to bring you a wrap."

"Clearly, I don't need that now, do I?" She waved the sheet music in her hand in front of her face. "Desmond, you had better ensure they get the temperature in this place under control by opening night, or we'll have actors fainting in the wings. Not to mention members of the audience." She followed Paula off stage.

Vicky chuckled.

"Now that's done . . . Ian. Dave, places please," Desmond said. "Let's go over the scene when Marley arrives one more time. That one, at least, I'm confident we have down as it should be, but I'd like to see it again."

Dave bounded across the stage and stood in the center, feet apart, smiling broadly, conscious of every eye on him. Dressed in jeans and a close-fitting white T-shirt worn under an open blue checked shirt, he seemed to fill the space. He looked, I thought, like a man who worked out regularly. Ian sort of slipped up to stand next to him.

"If I can have a word, Desmond?" Irene took a tentative step forward.

"What is it now?" The director snapped.

She held up the bolt of fabric she was holding. It was a heavy black velvet, shot through with shimmering blue thread. "I don't think this will work for the Ghost of Christmas Future."

"Christmas Yet to Come," Catherine said. "Do use the correct terminology. I hope you're not planning to refer to Ebenezer Scrooge as Eb." She laughed lightly at her own witticism. Irene's look in return was not one of amusement.

"I need quiet here," Dave said. "I can't concentrate on my lines with all this irrelevant chatter going on."

"The matter of costuming," Irene said, "is hardly irrelevant to a production. As it happens, we'd do better with a suit hung over the back of a chair than your attempt at acting."

For a brief moment Dave looked confused. Then, realizing his skills had been insulted, he said, "That wasn't called for."

"Let's stick to the topic at hand, shall we?" Desmond said. "I trust you to make your own decisions about costuming, Irene, like you always have. With my final approval, of course."

"It's not you, Desmond, it's her." The wardrobe mistress threw a furious look at Catherine, sitting calmly in her seat. "She bought this extravagant thing, and insists I use it to make the cape for the aforementioned ghost. It is simply not appropriate. The spirit foretells Scrooge's doom. She's supposed to be terrifying, not dressed for a night at the opera."

"I happen to disagree," Catherine said. "That fabric was very expensive, and it will show beautifully under the lights."

"That's the point!" Irene yelled. "I don't want expensive, and I don't want beautiful. I want threatening. Use this for something else; I've already bought a plain black fabric for the spirit's cape."

"I told you to use the black for Mrs. Cratchit's dress, if you must. I want the velvet in the dramatic highlight in the graveyard."

"I heard that!" Paula ran on stage. "If you're talking about my costume, I'll take the velvet. It will make a nice dress to wear at Christmas dinner."

"Dinner at the manor house, perhaps," Catherine said. "Not the poverty-stricken Cratchit family's damp, crumbling tenement."

"The one with the complete set of earthenware dishes, as bought in a New York design shop," I whispered to Vicky. She gave me a confused look. "Catherine," I explained, "appears to be somewhat inconsistent in her approach to set and costume."

"If I may say—" Desmond tried to get a word in edgewise.

"You may not," Catherine said. "I have bought the velvet for the purpose I told Irene. We need not discuss it any further. Dave, dear, before you and Ian run through those lines, one more time, I'm wondering if perhaps you can exchange roles. Give Scrooge a try. You know his lines, don't you?"

"Yeah. I sure do."

"What!" Ian said, shocked at the very idea. "I'm not taking Marley."

"We have to be adaptable." Catherine smiled sweetly at him. As sweetly as a cat might smile at a mouse before pouncing. "Isn't that the byword of community theater? Adaptable. I thought it might be nice to see how it works that way. If I . . . I mean if we like it, Ian you can do some work with Aline on Marley's song."

Ian did not return the smile. Instead a vein pulsed in his neck and his eyes bulged. I remembered he'd suffered a heart attack last year, and hoped he wasn't heading for a recurrence. "Scrooge is the main character." He struggled mightily to keep his voice under some sort of control. "Let me remind you, *Catherine*, Marley's a bit part. He has one, count 'em, one scene. Besides, Marley's a tenor. I am not a tenor."

"Adaptability!" Catherine repeated.

Dave grinned. Ian fumed. Desmond sputtered. Everyone else watched, no one saying a word. Vicky wagged her eyebrows at me.

"I'm the director here." Desmond finally managed to get the words out. "I want them to act the scene as I have cast it."

"The way Mrs. Renshaw and I see it," Dave said, "is that Scrooge is always portrayed as an old guy. We're thinking someone younger, sorry Ian, would appeal to younger people in the audience. Tell them they need to change their ways because you never know when it'll be too late. Not wait until you're old. Like Ian here is."

"That's the way you and *Mrs. Renshaw* see it, is it?" Ian bit off the words.

Dave flashed a row of brilliant white teeth. "Yup."

"Anything else you two see which you think we need to be informed about?" Ian glared at Catherine. "Or is this a private matter?"

Dave smirked. Catherine touched her hair. Eddie continued kicking the seat in front of him.

"I will not be ambushed like this," Desmond said. "Catherine, you and I discussed giving the main part to Dave, and I told you straight out he isn't suitable."

"You did? When was this and why was I not told?" Ian's face was turning a highly unattractive shade of red.

"I don't discuss casting decisions with the actors," Catherine said.

"You obviously did with Dave."

"I needed to know if he was interested."

Vicky leaned over and whispered in my ear. "They could make a play out of this. I'd pay good money to see it."

My mom came on stage, wondering what was going on. Paula trailed after her.

"We're wasting time here," Desmond said. "Ian and Dave, carry on with the scene as I have instructed."

"I'd like to see how Dave handles Scrooge's lines," Catherine said. While Desmond was sputtering, Ian changing color, Dave preening, and everyone else looking confused, she'd remained comfortably in her seat, her hands folded neatly on her lap, her smile serene. The very picture of elegance, she wore a winter-white outfit of loose-fitting jacket, silk V-neck T-shirt, and wide white pants secured by a brown belt. A rope of pearls was around her neck and more pearls in her ears. A brown pump with two-inch heels dangled casually from the foot of a crossed leg. Despite the heat in this room, she hadn't broken a sweat or removed her jacket. Her makeup remained fresh yet subdued, her nails painted a soft pink matching her lipstick.

"I have been with this company since its inaugural season," Ian said. "I was a founding member, in fact."

"I respect that so much, truly I do," Catherine said. "Remind me of when that was? Was it during this century?"

Beside me, Vicky said, "Wow!" My mother's eyes opened wide at the sheer cattiness of the remark.

"Catherine, perhaps a word in private," Desmond said.

"Why don't we see how the scene plays out, as I suggest, and then we can chat?"

Mom stepped forward. "Irrelevant. Ian cannot play Marley. Marley's song is an important one, and Ian does not have the vocal range."

"He can fake it," Dave said.

"He cannot," Mom said. "Not if I am coaching him. Also, Dave's voice is too deep for Scrooge."

"I can raise my voice," Dave squeaked.

"Ironically, this time I have to disagree with you, Aline, dear," Catherine said. "I know I keep saying we want to put on a performance worthy of the Metropolitan Opera, of which you were so recently a shining light, but this is amateur theater. We can't get all we require. Much as we might want to. Particularly as regards a complicated musical production such as the one we're attempting."

For perhaps once in her life, my mother was struck speechless.

"If I have to take Marley, I quit," Ian said.

"That would be unfortunate," Catherine said. "But it is your decision."

I glanced between them. Ian was furious, Catherine calmly dismissive. Something else was going on here, I suspected, apart from a squabble over an unpaid role in a small-town musical production.

"I've an idea," said Paula, who had not been asked for her input. "If the part of Marley's ghost is up for grabs, I'll take it. Why does Marley have to be a man anyway and have a man's voice? There are too many male parts in this play. I can play both Marley and Mrs. C. They don't have any scenes together, right?"

My mother groaned.

Jackie leapt forward. "If both those parts are too much for you to handle, Paula, I'll step in as Mrs. Cratchit. I'm the understudy. I've learned all the lines, and I've been practicing at home. Kyle, that's my boyfriend, Kyle Lambert who takes pictures for the *Gazette*, he says I'd be great in the part."

"They would not be too much," Paula said. "I have no idea where you got that idea. As for Dave playing Scrooge, I have to say I'm with Desmond on this. Dave thinks he can get by on his fake aw-shucks charm." She rolled her eyes so dramatically that if it was an indication of her acting talent, she did need to be replaced. "He might be able to manage, barely, the part of the romantic lead in a Regency production, but as Scrooge, he is totally and complexly unsuitable."

Dave's entire body stiffened. He took a step toward her. "That's uncalled for. I am an actor. An actor acts."

Paula dismissed him with a wave. "If you're going to recast the parts, Desmond, then do it dramatically. Make a complete break from the past. Make a statement."

"I am not recasting the parts!" Desmond yelled.

"I've an idea. Even better than casting a woman as Marley," Paula said, "how about a female Scrooge?"

"I'm not going to remake those costumes," Irene said.

"You?" Dave said to Paula. "You think you can carry an entire play?" He let out a snort of dismissive laughter.

Paula bristled. "I don't see why not. Tell me again, Dave, why you left your oh-so-promising acting career behind. I had a look at your bio. Not many big parts, were there?"

"Enough of this!" Desmond roared. "Every one of you is out of line. Catherine, you started this mess. I will not continue to discuss this in front of everyone. Let's go outside. People, take a break."

Catherine rose from her seat in a smooth river of winter white. Desmond took a step backward. Even without the heels she would have towered over him. "I'm dreadfully sorry." She plucked her wool and cashmere coat off the chair next to her and slipped it on. "The time has totally gotten away from me.

Bruce and I have late dinner reservations tonight. I'll see everyone tomorrow. Six o'clock on the dot. Remember, we need everyone to be here to go through the entirety of the Fezziwig party. Don't be late." She gave the watching cast and crew a radiant smile.

"Merry, Vicky," she said as she passed us, me still clutching the unwanted cape. "How nice to see you both. If either of you is interested in joining our little group, please talk to me. Vicky, with that height you would have a marvelous stage presence."

No one said a word as she walked up the aisle pulling on her gloves, her heels silent on the thickly carpeted floor. The door closed behind her. Still, no one still said a word.

"Okay." Vicky broke the silence. "I'm thinking maybe two drinks at the Holly and a ten o'clock bedtime tonight."

Desmond broke out of his stunned silence. "We're finished here! Everyone go home! We'll do no more work today. I've had enough!"

"What did we decide about my role?" Dave said.

Desmond's expression indicated what he thought about that.

"Okay," Dave said. "We'll talk about it later."

"If you don't want to talk about my idea right now, that's up to you, but what about my private singing lesson?" Paula said.

"Didn't you hear the man?" Mom snapped. "We're done for the day. And not a moment too soon."

"Tomorrow then. Eddie, let's go. Where'd Eddie get to? Has anyone seen Eddie?"

"Probably raiding the snacks table," Ian said. "His usual hangout."

The cast and crew began to disperse. Some went backstage to get their things, some filed out of the auditorium. Every one of them was talking in low tones or listening to what was being said in low tones. No one, I thought, sounded happy. About anything.

"Disaster," a man said as he passed us.

"Doomed," his companion replied.

"Why don't we ask your mom if she wants to come for a drink with us?" Vicky said. "She looks like she could use one."

"Good idea." I waved. "Mom!"

She descended the steps from the stage. "Please remind me why I agreed to participate in this production." She ran her fingers across the cape in my arms. "That's a lovely garment, dear, beautiful soft tweed, but isn't it too warm for indoors?"

"I'm glad you like it," I said. "It's yours."

She blinked. "Mine? Nice as it is, I never wear brown, you know that. And I don't care for the length. It's too short. A cape must be longer, to allow for dramatic impact."

"Nevertheless, it's yours. As I told Dad, and I believe you on another occasion, I don't rent items, I sell them. It doesn't matter that you haven't tried it on. I carried it all this way, so I consider it used."

Mom looked at Vicky.

"Never mind," my friend said. "Just go along with it. Make her happy."

"That will mean there will be one happy person in this theater," Mom said. "I have no idea what's going to happen. Ian's not bluffing. Catherine and Ian seemed to be getting along fine when she first joined the group and rehearsals started, but all of a sudden, at the last minute, she wants to replace him. He'll quit if he loses the part of Scrooge, and Desmond might well follow. Dave will be a catastrophe in the main role; Paula's voice gets worse every time I work with her. Her son's a spoiled brat who won't take instruction; most of the extras have two left feet and keep crashing into each other in the dance numbers; Jackie's continually asking me . . ."

"Drink?" Vicky said. "Merry and I are going to the Holly. Would you like to join us?"

"Thank you, dear. It's nice of you to invite me, but I think not. I feel a headache coming on, and an early night will be welcome." She leaned over and brushed her lips across my cheek. I caught the familiar wave of Chanel No. 5. "I'll get my bag and be on my way." She headed backstage.

Vicky and I exchanged glances and then we broke into laughter. "Love how after overhearing all of that, Catherine thought we might want to get involved," Vicky said. "No thanks, I have more than enough drama at the bakery."

Desmond and Irene were huddled together in the hallway outside the doors to the auditorium when we came out.

"In the scheme of things, our little production is quite meaningless, Desmond," she said, "but I take my part as wardrobe mistress seriously. I don't know if I can continue. Nothing I do is ever good enough for Catherine."

"I hear you, Irene. I've been with this company for twelve years. In that time I've received more than a small amount of well-meant advice and not-so-well-meant criticism, but never before on this level. The blasted woman simply does not understand that this is not Broadway. I don't have professionals to work with. I have people who don't mind spending most of their evenings and weekends in a theater, some of whom have nothing better to do with their time. If Catherine insists on replacing Ian with Dave, I'm walking."

Vicky raised her eyebrows at me, and we scurried away before we could be caught eavesdropping.

Chapter Four

"**D**id you enjoy watching a bit of rehearsal last night, Merry?" Jackie asked me.

I stared at her. I realized I was staring and snapped my mouth shut. "Enjoy? Not quite the word I'd use. Didn't you notice some . . . shall we say tension in the group? Not to mention that rehearsal abruptly ended when the artistic director and the director almost came to blows."

She waved a hand in the air. "That's all perfectly normal. We theater people call it rehearsal jitters," she said as though she'd been center stage on Broadway most of her life. "Everyone's on edge because they care so much. Without that edge to provide the spark, the play would be boring."

"If you say so."

She fussed with a glass bowl containing an arrangement of colorful ornaments. "Do you happen to know what your mom's up to today?"

"No idea."

It was shortly after noon. Jackie had arrived for her shift, bubbling over with excitement as she stood on the verge of stardom (in her mind, if no one else's). Business had been quiet this morning, and I'd taken advantage of the time to rearrange the window display. Inspired by *A Christmas Carol*, I'd attempted to recreate a Victorian Christmas morning, with a small, but real, tree harvested from Alan's property, fully decorated with fake candles and colorful glass balls. Beneath the tree, I'd placed piles of empty boxes, wrapped in brown paper tied with string, overseen by a collection of porcelain Santa and Mrs. Claus dolls, complete with glasses perched on noses, caps on heads; her in a dress and apron and him in trousers with suspenders. They were accompanied by a couple of stuffed reindeer with bright bows tied around their necks.

Jackie picked up a red ball. She put it back. She picked up a gold one. She pointedly avoided eye contact with me.

"Is there something you want to ask me, Jackie?" I eventually said.

"Now that you mention it, Merry." She cleared her throat. "If you don't mind. I thought maybe you could tell your mom I'm free tomorrow morning. I don't start work until ten, so I have nothing on first thing."

"Why –? Oh, you'd like some vocal coaching?"

She grinned at me. "That's right. As part of the chorus, naturally I have songs to sing and I've been practicing like crazy, but I've also been working on Mrs. Cratchit's song. In case I'm called upon to step in. Kyle says I've got it down pat—"

As he would, if he knows what's good for him.

"A little extra coaching might help. Not that I have the part, I know that. But, I am the understudy, and looks like there might be some changes made in the cast, so I'd like to be ready."

"I'll mention it to her," I said.

"Thanks, Merry."

The chimes over the door tinkled and a group of women came in, wrapped warmly against the cold. No snow was in the forecast, but clouds were gathering and temperatures dropping steadily.

"Good afternoon," Jackie said. "Welcome to Mrs. Claus's Treasures. Let me know if you need any help."

"Thank you," they chorused.

"Susan! Look at that train. My Madison would simply love that for the new baby, don't you think?"

The women spread out around the shop, oohing and aahing over everything and calling to each other to come see what they'd found.

That's what I like to hear.

"Excuse me," one of them said, "Can I have a closer look at these earrings?" I ran to help her.

These women were decisive shoppers—I like that too. They piled an eclectic selection of items high on the sales counter and went back for more.

"Are you vacationing in town?" Jackie asked as she rang things up.

"We are. We're a bridge group, and we've come all the way from Iowa to visit America's Christmas Town."

That would make the town mothers and fathers happy. Rudolph had fought long and hard to be so recognized. It wasn't easy with competition from the likes of North Pole, Alaska and Snowflake, Arizona.

"We would have preferred to come over Christmas week, of course, but we can't leave the kids and grandchildren at that time of year, can we?"

"Much as we might want to," one added to gales of laughter from her friends.

"We're staying at the Carolers' Motel. Such a nice place. We'll be playing bridge and shopping and seeing the sights."

"Followed by more shopping and more bridge," another woman added. "One whole blissful week without those pesky husbands."

More laughter. I liked these women. They seemed to know how to have a good time.

"Will you still be here next Friday?" I asked. "*A Christmas Carol* opens for its seasonal run. It's going to be a great show."

"Oh, yes. I wouldn't miss that. We already have tickets for opening night! I'm so excited. When I heard that Aline Steiner, of all people, is in the production I insisted we add an extra day onto our holiday in order to see it."

"For years and years," another woman said, "Ruth tried to drag us to New York to go to the Met. Can't think of anything I'd like less than sitting through an opera." She shrugged theatrically, and Ruth gave her a good-natured poke in the ribs. "Imagine, six hours of *Gotterdammerung*. Spare me. I don't care for opera, but I enjoy musical theater. So—Ruth's idol's going to be in a play we can all enjoy. I call that a win-win!"

With that, they plunged into a renewed frenzy of shopping. Finally, Jackie finished ringing everything up. I helped her bag the items, and the women staggered out the door under the weight of their purchases, calling thank you as they left. One of them suggested a drink after all that hard work. The others heartily agreed.

"When I'm old, I hope I'm like them," Jackie said.

I looked at her in surprise. I think that's the first time I've ever heard my assistant engage in any sort of reflection. "Sixties isn't old, not according to Mom anyway, but I get your point."

The chimes trilled again, and Catherine Renshaw came in, trailed by her husband. This morning she was resplendent in a calf-length black wool coat worn with a black hat, bright blue woolen scarf, and low-heeled black ankle boots. Mr. Renshaw, whose first name escaped me, wore a casual gray jacket over slightly baggy jeans. A tear ran the length of the right thumb of his soiled leather gloves. He was freshly shaven, silver hair carefully arranged, after shave too liberally applied.

Catherine gave me an enormous smile and waved a sheaf of papers at me. "Merry. How nice to see you. And Jackie, looking lovely this morning as always."

What, didn't I look lovely?

"Why thank you, Catherine," my assistant giggled. "I *love love love* your scarf. Fabulous color."

"Do you know this is the first time I've been in your beautiful store?" Catherine said. "I can't believe the oversight, can you, Bruce?"

"Nice place," he said.

"You, darling, need to make a point of visiting regularly," she said. "That jewelry display in particular."

"Most or our jewelry, and much of our other stock, is made locally," I said. "Quite a bit of the jewelry's made by a young woman who works here part time."

"Isn't that special? I'm not here to shop today, but I will be back soon. In the meanwhile, while Merry and I are chatting, Bruce darling, I'm sure if you look hard enough, you can find a little prezzie for me."

He gave her a look I couldn't decipher, but she wiggled her fingers. "Off you go. Jackie, dear, do help Bruce select something nice."

"Happy to," Jackie said. "Anything in particular you'd like to see, sir? We specialize in Christmas decor and gifts, but we carry many other things for the home."

When the reluctant shopper had been led away, I said to Catherine. "You're here to talk to me? Why?"

She waved the papers at me. "I'm going up and down Jingle Bell Lane, such a charming street name, isn't it, asking everyone to put one of our flyers in the window. If you wouldn't mind?"

She held one up. It was a typical playbill. Name of the play in big letters, location, date and time of performances. My mother's name was prominently displayed as "musical director." That would make her happy. The other prominent name was Catherine Renshaw, "artistic director." That would not make Desmond Kerslake, the director, happy. His name was in such small print the nearsighted wouldn't be able to read it.

I held out my hand and she put one of the papers into it. "I'd be happy to display it. Word's getting around. A pack of women all the way from Iowa were in here a couple of minutes ago, and they've already bought their tickets. Too bad you missed them. They would have loved to meet you."

"Maybe you could have a word on my behalf with the woman who works at the shop next door? She was, shall I say, less than enthusiastic about taking a poster, and seemed rather suspicious about me. I can't imagine why. She eventually took one, but I fear it will end up in the trash."

"You mean Rudolph Gift Nook? That's Margie Thatcher you spoke to, and she's not exactly known for being civic minded." I'd never seen any sort of community promotion in her windows. Margie seemed to be convinced that keeping her doors open at the hours required by the town's business association was the most that could be expected of her.

She didn't even include being friendly or accommodating to shoppers as one of her duties.

"I'll mention it to her," I said. "But don't get your hopes up." More likely any word from me would have the opposite effect. The Nook and Mrs. Claus's were in no way competition for each other—Margie's store sold cheap stuff mass-produced in foreign countries—but for some reason Margie and her sister Betty, who'd owned the store before her, regarded me as such.

"That's the most you can do," Catherine said.

"Do you have anything a bit . . . less pricy?" Bruce asked Jackie, giving her back a necklace she'd removed from the display to show him.

"I hope you weren't too upset by our little imbroglio yesterday," Catherine said. "The theater family truly is like a family. We have our arguments and our disagreements, but it all gets sorted in the end. I'm terribly excited about this production, Merry, and with your mother's name at the forefront, it's bound to be a huge success."

"Do you have a background in theater?" I asked her.

"Sadly no. It was a passion of mine when I was younger, but I soon realized I have no talent. I'm better behind the stage. Organization is my forte. Bruce and I were not blessed with children, so we threw ourselves into our business endeavors."

"What did you do?" I asked, as I clearly was expected to.

"We own a group of furniture and appliance stores. Home Central Furnishings?"

"Oh. That's a big chain. There's a store in Rochester."

"We started the company from nothing when we were first married. One store in Albany, and we expanded from there. Such a lot of work, but so worth it to make a success of ourselves. These days, Bruce and I stay mainly on the sidelines, leaving the day-to-day running of the business to younger people with fresh ideas." The smile she gave me was tight, and I suspected she wasn't all that happy about that decision. They weren't much past sixty. Perhaps the idea to step away had been Bruce's alone. If so, that might explain why Catherine had thrown herself so fully into being the artistic director of a small-town amateur theater group. "It's long been Bruce's dream to move to a small town. I'm so glad we came here. Everyone's so nice. Exactly like the stereotype, isn't it? People in Manhattan have so little time for their neighbors." Another tight smile. Small-town living might be her husband's dream. It was not hers.

"I must be off. Plenty of businesses still to visit. Bruce, dear, you can catch up to me if you're still busy there."

"I'm done." He put a pair of earrings on the counter and dug in his wallet.

"I'll hang this in the window right now." I held up the poster.

"How kind you are." Catherine sailed out the door.

Her husband handed Jackie a twenty-dollar bill. She made change.

* * *

No more than five minutes later I was taping the poster to the front window, above the main display, when Paula Monahan came into the store. I could immediately tell by the Mrs. Claus's shopping bag she carried and the nervous expression on her face that I would not like what she was here to say.

"Hi, Paula. Look at this." I indicated the poster. "You just missed Catherine. She's delivering these to the shops on the street."

"Catherine," Paula declared. "I've had quite enough of Catherine, thank you. Which is why I'm here. I want to return these dishes." She plopped the bag on the counter. She was in a calf-length black coat, similar to Catherine's but of cheaper fabric, a blue scarf, and a black winter hat. Under the outerwear she wore jeans and running shoes.

"Why? Are they not suitable?" I asked.

"According to Catherine, no. You'd have thought she'd be pleased I bought them, out of my own pocket too, in an attempt to help the production out. You can be sure she'd have been more than happy to pay if her *darling* Aline got them." Paula sniffed in disapproval. She seemed to have momentarily forgotten Aline's my mother. "As for these," she shook the bag, "Catherine says they're not suitable. She wants something more colorful, to stand out on the stage." Another sniff. "I went around to her house earlier, hoping to talk some sense into her about the way the play's being cast, but she refused to hear it. Imagine, Dave in the lead part. He's such a hack. Doesn't bear thinking about. I have half a mind to quit outright, but I've been with the company longer than her, and I won't be driven out. I told her so. And then, to add insult to injury, when I showed her these plates, she said she doesn't want to use them. So I'm bringing them back."

"I can offer you a store credit."

"No, thank you. I'll take the money." She rummaged in her purse. "I have the receipt."

"We normally offer credit, not cash refunds."

"Surely you can make an exception in this case? I bought them for the play, not for myself. If you give me a credit, I don't know what else I'd buy here. Your store's nice enough and all, but I don't care for frivolities."

I gave in. As far as I was concerned, Paula's casting suggestions—to vault herself into the main role—had been way out of line, but nevertheless Catherine had done an injury to her pride. If refunding her the money would help a bit, I'd do it. "Very well. Can I have your credit card, please?"

While we'd been talking, Jackie had been busy in one of the store alcoves, helping customers select holiday-suitable serving dishes, and she'd missed most of the conversation. They made their selection, and Jackie carried the boxes up to the counter. While I prepared to ring through Paula's refund, Jackie put on a bright smile and said, "Paula, did you and Desmond sort out the casting? Are you taking Marley? Brilliant idea by the way, no reason Marley has to be a man, not in this day and age. Is Mrs. Cratchit free?"

Paula's face tightened. "I do not know why you keep nagging me about this, Jackie. I have no intention of not playing Mrs. Cratchit. Besides, my Eddie is Tiny Tim. I'm obviously going to be nearby for his scenes anyway, so I might as well be on stage. He's only ten years old. He has a delicate nature, and he needs my comforting presence in order to put on his best performance."

"You keep telling yourself that, Paula," Jackie said.

I blinked in surprise. Jackie was many things, but she was never deliberately nasty.

Paula snatched her credit card and the fresh receipt out of my hand and marched out of the store without another word. The door slammed behind her.

"I'm going for my afternoon break," Jackie snarled.

"You just got back from lunch."

"I can take my break whenever I want, can't I?"

"Yes, but . . . Never mind. If you're going to the coffee shop, can you bring me a latte, please?"

She also stormed out. The door slammed once again.

"What's got her knickers in such a knot?" The man she'd been helping said to me. "I hope it wasn't anything I said. You Yanks aren't usually so prickly."

"The dramatic temperament," I said. "She's involved in the community production of *A Christmas Carol* and there've been some disagreements among the actors, to put it mildly."

"They're putting on *A Christmas Carol*? Always a favorite. We might like to see that. Is it on now?"

"Opening night's next Friday. A week from today."

"That's too bad. We'll be long gone by then. We had a week in New York City, are spending a couple of days around here, and then driving up to Toronto to spend Christmas with my brother. Then it's back to Jolly Old England."

"And so to work," the woman with him sighed. "I hate work."

I smiled at her. "Sometimes, I do too."

*   *   *

The English couple left, and no one else came in. Grumbling all the while, I put the unwanted earthenware dishes back on the shelf. After about ten minutes of being alone in an empty shop, I stuck my head out the door and checked up and down the sidewalk. No one was heading my way, so I took the opportunity to slip into the back for a quick Mattie-check. I found him snoozing in his bed under the desk. He struggled to his feet when I came in. I gave him a rub on the top of the head and he rewarded me with a lick on my face. He then headed for the hallway.

"Sorry. No time for a walk," I said. "I'm only here for a quick check that you haven't upset your water bowl yet."

His giant brown eyes filled with so much sadness I feared he was about to cry. His ears drooped. He lowered his head. He sighed.

The chimes over the shop door tinkled, and I called, "Be right there."

"Drama queen," I said to the dog. "There's an idea. You should have a part in *A Christmas Carol*. You'd be no more of a prima donna than the rest of them. And how's this for a change—for once Mom's the calm one." I mentally cast Mattie in the production. He could play the Cratchit family dog. I gave Mattie another rub. He stepped backward—straight into his water bowl, tipping the whole lot onto the carpet.

"You did that on purpose." I considered leaving it and going out front to check on to my customer, but decided I'd better see to it while I was thinking of it. If we got busy, the day had a way of getting ahead of me. I grabbed the bowl and ran for the small staff washroom, calling, "I'll be right out. Please feel free to have a look around."

I heard a thump, and I stopped and listened. It didn't sound as though anything had broken, so I ran the tap and filled the bowl. I carefully carried the bowl of sloshing water back to the office and put it in a corner. "Try to get through to my dinner break on this," I said to the dog. He ignored it and pushed past me to stand at the door, wanting to go out. When Mattie stands in front of something, absolutely no one can get by.

"Move," I said.

He didn't.

I attempted to imitate Diane Simmonds's authoritative voice. "Matterhorn. You are in the way. Please move."

He edged ever so slowly to one side. I shoved him farther away and squeezed myself through the door. I shut the door firmly behind me and plastered my helpful shopkeeper smile on as I pushed aside the curtain and entered the store.

Have Yourself a Deadly Little Christmas

The first thing I noticed was that the door to the street was open. The second was that the store was empty. The third was that the Santa and Mrs. Claus stuffies next to the entrance had fallen on the floor. The customer must have left. I headed for the door, intending to shut it.

It was only then I saw a woman in a long black coat lying on the floor next to the center display table. She lay face down; her blue scarf was wrapped around her neck, and she did not move.

Chapter Five

"You left your store unlocked and unattended for several minutes. Did you think that was wise?"

"In retrospect, it obviously was not wise. But my assistant had gone on her break, no one was in the shop, and I wanted to check on Mattie. I was away longer than I expected because he tipped his water bowl and then he blocked the door, but I wasn't that long. I mean . . . this is Rudolph. It's midday on a Friday in December. No one's going to run into my store and snatch things off the shelves while I'm not looking, and run out again."

Detective Diane Simmonds raised one expressive eyebrow.

"Okay, that's pretty much what happened, right? Except for the stealing things part."

We were in my office. Outside, a uniformed officer guarded the door to the street while inside other cops picked through my things. A crowd had gathered on the sidewalk, asking what was going on. The forensic team was on its way.

I'd recovered from my shock almost instantly and dropped to the floor next to the unmoving woman. I rolled her over. The unseeing eyes of Paula Monahan stared up at me as I struggled to undo the scarf wrapped tightly around her neck with one hand while fumbling for my phone and calling 911 with the other.

The ambulance arrived first. I got to my feet and stood aside so they could do their work.

"Nonresponsive," one medic said.

"VSA," her partner said into his radio.

VSA, I know, means vital signs absent.

"Did you find her like this, ma'am?" the first medic asked me.

"Yes. Yes, I did. I stepped out for a few minutes and when I got back . . ." I breathed. "That scarf. It was around her neck. I removed it. I was trying to help."

"I call that interfering with a crime scene." Officer Candice Campbell came through the door.

Candice and I were not exactly friends. One drawback of living in a small town: your high school rivals can continue to haunt you into adulthood. Not that I'd ever been a rival of Candice over anything. In my mind anyway; she saw things differently. Which might be because Vicky had dated the hottest guy in our school for a number of months. The guy everyone knew Candice had the most enormous crush on. Or that Vicky had been the star of every sports team she was on, and Candice had never been more than an average player. All of which had nothing to do with me—I didn't even play school sports, and the popular boys only wanted to be friends with me to get close to Vicky—but Vicky was my best friend so Candice had seen it as rivalry by proxy.

"I had to check. She might not have been dead yet, Candy," I said. Okay, I can still be petty. Now she was a police officer, she hated the high school nickname, so I used it whenever I had the chance.

Her lips tightened, but she didn't reply.

"They're not dead," the second medic said, "until the doc says so. Let's make this a fast one."

I stood to one side as they quickly and efficiently loaded the unmoving body of Paula Monahan onto their stretcher and wheeled her out. A moment later, the ambulance siren tore down Jingle Bell Lane.

A crowd rapidly gathered in front of the shop. A second patrol car screeched to a halt in the loading zone, and another uniform got out.

My phone buzzed with an incoming text, and I checked it. Vicky: *What's up? Word says cops at MC. All okay?"*

MC meant Mrs. Claus's. I texted back: *That was quick*

Vicky: *Word travels fast*
Me: *Customer collapsed. Taken to the hospital*

"Detective's here, Merry," Candy said. "Tell Vicky Casey to mind her own business and put that phone away."

"How'd you know—? Never mind."

Detective Diane Simmonds had given me a sharp nod when she first arrived. All the winter-day-at-the-ice-rink-meet-my-mother-and-daughter friendliness was gone, leaving nothing but cop and witness.

Cop and suspect?

I assured myself that no one would believe I had any reason to want to do harm to Paula Monahan and put on my innocent face.

"Please wait for me in your office, Merry," Simmonds said. "I'll be in to talk to you in a moment. Officer Williams, can you escort Ms. Wilkinson? Ensure she doesn't make or receive any phone calls in the meantime. Officer Campbell, tell me what you found when you first arrived on the scene."

"I found Merry Wilkinson, proprietor of this establishment, here present, crouched next to the body with what is likely to have been the murder weapon in her hand."

"Hey!" I said. "That's making it sound like I had something to do with it."

"I'll get your statement in a minute," Simmonds said. "You're not in court, Campbell, and I didn't ask you to speculate. Tell me what you saw with no guesses or embellishments."

Candy had flushed an unattractive shade and glared at me. Somehow being reprimanded by Detective Simmonds would turn out to be my fault. In her mind at least.

"Are you working alone in the store today, Merry?" Simmonds asked me now.

"Jackie's here. I mean she was here earlier. She went on her break before . . . it happened. I suspect she's being kept outside, wondering what's going on."

"She was stopped from coming in the back door, yes. What time did she leave for this break?"

"I can't say for sure, but about ten minutes or so before I came in here to check on Mattie." I glanced down. The dog sat at Simmonds's feet, gazing up at her through liquid brown eyes overflowing with adoration. If she slapped the handcuffs on me and manhandled me out the door to face life imprisonment, he'd be cheering her all the way. *Traitor.*

"Do you know the dead woman?" the detective asked.

"I do. Her name's Paula Monahan. She was in the shop earlier and she left. Jackie headed out for her break almost immediately thereafter."

"Did Jackie going on this break have anything to do with the woman being here?"

I hesitated.

"Merry?"

"Paula has a part in *A Christmas Carol*. She's the mother of the boy you discouraged from throwing a stick at Mattie at the picnic on Sunday."

Simmonds nodded. "I thought so. I saw Jackie at the picnic as well. Is she in the play?"

"Yes, she is. She's an extra. There've been some minor disagreements between the cast and crew about the direction the play should take. Paula said something Jackie disagreed with, so she went out to cool down. That's all."

"I'll ask about these minor disagreements later. First, what time did Paula leave and Jackie go on her break?"

I thought. "I didn't check the time, but I'd say shortly after two. About five after, give or take. Paula came to return an item and didn't linger."

"Do you have any idea why she came back to your store so soon after leaving? Did she forget something?"

"I didn't notice anything she might have left behind. She didn't buy anything—rather the opposite. She came in the first time to return something she'd bought the other day. She happened to mention that I don't sell the sort of things she's interested in, so she didn't want a store credit. Maybe something did catch her eye and she decided she wanted to get it after all. I can't say."

Simmonds's phone rang. She checked the display and answered it. "Yes?"

I couldn't hear what the person on the other end was saying, and Simmonds's expression didn't change. "Got it." She hung up. "Mrs. Monahan was pronounced dead on arrival."

I dipped my head.

"How well would you say you know her, Merry?"

"Hardly at all. I'd never even met her before the picnic. She came into the shop earlier this week, I think it was Monday, and bought the items she returned today."

"I need to get out front and check out the scene for myself, but first, can you take me through what happened in the time leading up to your call to 911?"

I did so.

"No one other than you was in the store when you came in here to get Mattie his water?"

The dog leapt to his feet and let out a low bark.

"I'm not talking to you, Matterhorn," Simmonds said.

He sat back down.

"I do not know how you do that," I said.

"Please continue."

"No one had come in for about ten minutes. I looked out, checked the street, saw no one coming our way, so I figured I could slip out for a minute."

"No one coming your way. You mean no one on the sidewalk? It seems crowded out there now."

"People were on the sidewalk, yes. Lots of them. None who seemed to be purposefully heading in my direction. You sort of get to tell, if people intend to come in, I mean."

"But Mrs. Monahan came in. And someone came with or after her."

I swallowed.

"How long after hearing the door chimes did you go back out front?"

"A couple of minutes. More than five at a guess, but I can't be positive. I shouted to tell them I'd be right there, but I didn't see any need to hurry. This is the sort of shop where people usually browse extensively before buying. Few people need help right away. Other than men on Christmas Eve, that is. They run in half an hour before closing, desperately wanting someone to tell them what to get for their wives."

The edges of Simmonds's mouth might have turned up. Then again, it might have been a trick of the light from the too-strong lamp over my desk. "You heard no one else come in?"

"No."

"No signs of a struggle?"

"Those dolls on the floor by the door were on the table earlier, but other than that, no."

"You can go home, Merry. I'll need to talk to you again, but I know where you live and I have your number. Obviously the store will be closed until further notice."

I started to stand up. I sat back down. "You might want to know one thing."

"And that is?"

"I'm not directly involved, but from all I've seen and heard, the production of *A Christmas Carol* is not going well. The cast and crew are not getting on."

"You think someone killed Paula over a part in an amateur theater production?"

"I think nothing. I'm pointing it out."

"As I've taught you to do. Anyone in particular not getting on, as you put it, with Paula Monahan?"

I thought about my mom, but I said, "It's more of a general thing, I'd say. Everyone squabbling with everyone."

A knock on the door. Simmonds called, "Come in," and Candy Campbell did so. "Jackie O'Reilly's hanging around outside. She works here and wants to know what's going on. She says she was here not more than half an hour ago, so she might be able to help. I thought you might . . . uh . . . want to talk to her?"

"I'm finished with Ms. Wilkinson. Send Jackie in. It's possible she did come back in time to see something significant."

Jackie slipped around Candy and into my office. She held a takeout coffee cup in each hand. Her eyes were bright, and she was trying hard to suppress a self-satisfied grin. Jackie loved being the center of attention. I could imagine her making a big fuss outside, ensuring everyone saw her, insisting she could be of help to the police.

"Gosh, Merry, can't I leave you alone for half an hour without you getting yourself into trouble? Again. People are saying Paula Monahan was taken to the hospital. The cops have shut the store and most of this section of the street so you must think she was attacked or something, Detective. That's awful. You look okay, Merry. Were you here when it happened? Silly question: where else would you be?"

"Where were you when whatever happened, happened?" Simmonds asked.

"On my break. I'd been gone about twenty minutes and I was coming back when I saw the ambulance and the police pulling up, and then they wouldn't let me in. I'd only gone next door, grabbing a coffee from Cranberries. Here you go, Merry." She handed me one of the cups. "Sorry if it's getting cold, but I had to wait outside."

I took the drink from her and put it on my desk without tasting it. Simmonds didn't ask me to leave, and so I remained where I was.

"Tell me what happened after you went for your break," Simmonds asked.

"Like I said. I went to Cranberry Coffee Bar. I ordered our drinks and a cookie for me. I got to talking to Rachel McIntosh, from Candy Cane Sweets, who was on her own lunch break. She told me Ian, that's her husband, is considering quitting *A Christmas Carol*. He's been cast as Scrooge, that's the lead role, but there's talk of some changes to the casting, and he's unhappy about that. Then Irene Dowling came in. She's in charge of the wardrobe for the play. I asked her if any decisions had been made about my costume and she said no. Rachel mentioned Ian's thinking of quitting, and Irene said she might do the same."

Jackie's eyes opened wide and she sucked in a breath as a thought occurred to her. She spoke before I could stop her.

"Hey! I've just realized something. If Paula's in the hospital, she won't be able to come to rehearsals. So she might not be able to be in the play. That means I have the role of Mrs. Cratchit!"

Chapter Six

"You can't be serious."

"Perfectly serious."

"They arrested Jackie for murder?"

"Not arrested but took her down to the station for questioning. She walked right into it, Vicky. Opened her big mouth before I could stop her. Goodness knows what she's going to say next, so I figured she needs a good lawyer, and fast."

I was in the alley that runs behind the shops lining Jingle Bell Lane. A confused Jackie had been taken in for "questioning," and I'd been bundled out of my own store, along with Matterhorn. He, at least, was happy for the break.

"Aunt Marjorie!" Vicky yelled. "Can you call Dad, like now, and tell him we need someone to go to the police station as soon as possible? Okay, Merry. Marjorie's on it."

"Thanks."

The sound of the busy café faded away as Vicky moved into a quiet corner for some privacy. She dropped her voice. "You don't think—"

"That Jackie did it? Not for a minute. But, I have to admit, she has means, motive, and opportunity. Motive: she wants the part of Mrs. Cratchit, which is now unexpectedly available. Means: Paula's own scarf. Opportunity: Paula was alone in the shop, and at precisely the time Jackie would be expected to come in."

"I can't see Jackie, of all people, suddenly deciding to kill a rival and then having the gumption to actually go through with it. I mean, you have to be mighty cold blooded to strangle someone."

"I'm confident Diane Simmonds will soon realize that and let Jackie go."

"How confident?"

"Perhaps not as much as I'd like to be. Thus the need for your father. I have to go. I want to head over to Mom's and fill her in. Although she's guaranteed to have heard via the grapevine. Speak of the devil. A text is coming in now."

"Keep me posted," Vicky said as she hung up.

The text from Mom simply said: *???????????????!!!!!!!!!!*

Me: *Are you home?*
Mom: *Yes*
Me: *I'll fill you in. On my way.*

I led Mattie down the alley to the nearest side street and then up to Jingle Bell Lane. I peeked around the corner to see what was going on. A great deal was going on. The section of the street in front of Mrs. Claus's Treasures was full of police cars, blue and red lights flashing, and the sidewalk was packed with the nosy and the curious. Candy Campbell had been assigned to guard the door and she stood firm, feet apart, hands on her equipment belt, threatening scowl in place.

One person spotted me standing at the edge of the crowd and pushed his way through.

"Merry," said Russell Durham, editor-in-chief of the *Rudolph Gazette*. These days, being editor-in-chief of a small-town local paper meant he was also the lead (i.e. the only) reporter and the head (i.e. the only) staff photographer. And, on occasion, the copyeditor, the advertising salesperson, the janitor, and the person who went on coffee runs.

"I do not have a statement for the press," I said.

"Off the record then. What happened in there?"

"A customer collapsed and was taken to hospital."

"Obviously not from natural causes, not with that much police activity at the scene. Were you there?"

I made a face. "No. I was in the office. I didn't see anything. I didn't hear anything."

"People are saying it's a local woman by the name of Paula Monahan. Don't think I know her. Do you?"

"I don't have time to talk. I'm expected at my parents' house. Come on, Mattie."

Uninvited and unwanted, Russ fell into step beside me. "I'll walk with you."

"If you must."

"I must. No one's saying anything yet. Diane left a couple of minutes ago as chatty as usual. Meaning not saying a word. I shouldn't have bothered trying to get a statement out of her. Seems I was in the wrong place. Sources told me that a couple of minutes earlier, your own Jackie O'Reilly was rushed out the back door and stuffed into a cruiser. Care to comment on that?"

"Is Santa Claus using slave labor at the North Pole?"

He blinked rapidly. "Huh?"

"No, Santa Claus is not using slave labor at the North Pole, and no, I am not going to comment."

"Okay. What about the dead woman, then? Do you know why she was in your store?"

I stopped walking. Mattie didn't stop and I was jerked off my feet. Russ laughed. I glared at him, and he folded his handsome face into serious lines, pretending to be contrite. Russ was fairly new to Rudolph, having left his home state of Louisiana to work in New York City. His job in the Big Apple had not ended well, and he was looking for work when the position at the *Gazette* became available when the long-long-longtime owner and editor-in-chief finally decided to hang up his press badge and pack away the Underwood typewriter. Russ and I were friends, but I was well aware that Russell Durham was a newspaperman first and foremost.

"Can't you ask Candy what's happening?" Russ and Candy Campbell had been an unexpected "item" at last year's New Year's Eve celebrations at the Yuletide Inn. Come to think of it, it had been a long time since I'd seen them together.

He shifted uncomfortably. "First of all, it'd be more than her job's worth if she talked to a reporter on the QT, and I assume you know that, and secondly, we're not . . . we're taking a break from each other for a while."

"Meaning you broke up. Sorry to hear that."

"It was . . . complicated," he said.

"Always is." I wondered who'd instigated the breakup. Her probably. His reporter's instincts meant he wouldn't have been able to help himself from prying into police business. A woman can quickly get tired of a man if she suspects he's using her for his own reasons.

"To answer your question, I assume Mrs. Monahan came into my store to buy something, which is why people usually visit stores. I really do not know anything more."

"Why are you in such a hurry to get to your parents' house?"

I started walking again, not quite as fast as I had been earlier. "Because I'm a good daughter. Don't you visit your parents sometimes?"

"Sure. When I'm in New Orleans. I don't rush over immediately after I've been near-witness to a murder. I didn't arrive on the scene until the ambulance had left, but plenty of people were keen to tell me all about it. Rachel McIntosh said she knows this Paula Monahan from the community theater group. I overheard her saying something I found very interesting."

I stopped walking. This time Mattie did too, and he took the opportunity to have a good sniff at the base of a fire hydrant. "Okay. I'll bite. What?"

"She said she was surprised someone had attacked Paula Monahan. She'd have thought it more likely whoever was responsible would have it in for Catherine Renshaw. Now, I just happen to know, seeing as how I'm the arts and entertainment editor at the paper, that Catherine Renshaw is the new artistic director of the community players. I also know, because Kyle Lambert wants me to pay him to go to the opening night of *A Christmas Carol*, so he can take pictures for the paper, that Jackie has a part in the play. And, I now know because I asked Rachel, that Paula Monahan was also in the play. And, most of all I know, because everyone in town knows, that your mother is heavily involved in this year's production. You're hurrying directly from the scene of the crime, allegedly, to your parents' house. I put all those things I know together, and I'm beginning to suspect whatever happened to Paula has something to do with the theater group." He gave me a huge, thoroughly charming, boyish grin.

I was not charmed. I started walking again. "All those facts might be correct, Russ, but it doesn't mean Paula's death had anything to do with the group. She might have had plenty of enemies for other reasons. It might have been a random killing—a crime of opportunity."

"Do you think I should mention in the paper that a deranged serial killer is wandering the streets of our fair town seeking opportunities for murder?"

"Maybe not quite put it like that. My mom will want to know what happened, so I'm going to tell her. Seeing as how my store is closed and I have nothing better to do for the rest of the day."

He stopped walking. "Fair enough. Will you keep me posted if something comes up?"

"I will."

* * *

I expected Mom and Dad to be fully appraised about what had happened, but I had not expected so many of the surviving members of the Rudolph Community Theater Players to have assembled at their house already.

I knew something was up the moment Mattie and I turned the corner, and I spotted a driveway full of cars, and more lining the street in front of the three-story red brick Victorian house on a large lot in which I'd grown up. The garden had been put away for the winter, leaves raked, bushes wrapped in burlap, flowerbeds turned over. My dad would have loved to trim every bit of exposed foliage with blinking Christmas lights and erect a blow-up Santa riding in a sled pulled by nine reindeer on the front lawn, but the year they bought the house, my mom put her foot firmly down and it has stayed down ever since. Instead the roof line was trimmed with a single row of small, tasteful white bulbs and each entrance adorned with a huge live wreath of evergreen branches accented with a red velvet bow.

I let myself in through the kitchen door, to be greeted by a babble of voices coming from the front room. I settled Mattie with a bowl of water and a slice of cold ham I snatched out of the fridge and went to join them.

Apart from Mom and Dad, there must have been twenty people crammed into the living room. If I didn't know better I'd have thought they were having a party. Coffee and tea things were laid out on the dining room table, and more than a few people held bottles of beer or glasses of wine.

Things had happened so fast, I hadn't had time to give a great deal of thought as to who might have killed Paula Monahan. Russ's questions made me pause and have a close look at the assembled group. Did Paula's death have something to do with the play? Was one of these people a killer?

I shook my head. Far more likely, as I'd said myself, Paula had another enemy or enemies.

"Here she is now," Dad said.

As one the group turned to me. They all started talking at once.

"Let the poor girl speak," Dad said. He got up and came to stand next to me. "If you don't want to, that's okay, honeybunch."

"I'm fine Dad. I don't have much to say. You heard Paula collapsed in my store earlier and was taken to the hospital?"

People muttered and shook their heads in disbelief.

"I wasn't there at the time. I mean, I was there, but not there."

"What does that mean?" Catherine Renshaw cradled a glass of white wine in her perfectly manicured hands. "Bruce and I were in your store not more than an hour or two ago. You were there then."

"I wasn't in the store itself," I explained. "I was in the back. When I came out, I . . . found her. After it was over. The paramedics arrived and took her to the hospital."

"She died," Desmond said.

I nodded.

"Heart attack, do you think?" Dave French asked. "She was a young woman, comparatively speaking, but you never know, do you?"

"Rachel called me," Ian McIntosh said. "She was picking up a quick lunch at Cranberry Coffee Bar next door to Merry's shop, and she arrived moments after the ambulance did. The substantial police presence, including a detective showing up mighty darn quick, would indicate they don't think it's natural causes. Is that right, Merry?"

"They're investigating the possibility of foul play," I said.

"Preposterous," Irene said. "The poor dear had a heart attack. The police like to find any excuse to use their budget."

"Not always," my dad said. "We want them to take these things seriously, and time is important." He put his arm around me. "Can I get you a drink? Or coffee?"

"No, thanks, Dad. I'm fine. Paula came into Mrs. Claus's Treasures not long after you left, Catherine. Did you see her on the street?"

Catherine started. "Me? I did not."

"I was at Cranberries at the same time Rachel was," Irene said. "Jackie came in and we talked about the play for a couple of minutes." She couldn't help taking a surreptitious peek at Catherine from the corner of her eyes as she spoke. Catherine gave her an unfriendly glare in return, and the wardrobe mistress quickly looked away. "She left and a few minutes later we heard the commotion. Someone said Jackie's been arrested. Surely not. The idea's ridiculous."

"Not arrested," I said. "Taken for questioning. That's different."

"Maybe, maybe not," Ian said. "You, Merry, said you found Paula, but you weren't taken in for questioning. You're standing right here."

"Jackie did want the part of Mrs. Cratchit," Irene said.

"Enough," my mom declared in the voice that would easily reach the upper balcony at one of the great opera houses of Europe. "We will not go there. No one killed Paula to get a better part in the play."

"Maybe they mistook her for you, Catherine." Desmond smiled as he said the words, but I saw no hint of humor behind it.

Ian laughed and, under the focus of Catherine's glare, he flushed and quickly turned the laugh into a strangled cough.

"Most amusing," Catherine sniffed. "We look nothing alike. Perhaps they mistook her for you, Desmond."

"Stupid idea," Dave said.

Irene muttered something that might have been, "Not so stupid."

I also wasn't sure. That was an avenue Detective Simmonds might want to explore. Paula and Catherine didn't look at all alike, but their body shapes were similar. Same height, same approximate weight, same shoulder-length brown hair. Today, they'd both been in black coats with blue scarves. Catherine's clothes were finer and more expensive than Paula's, but the killer might not have stopped to notice those details. Did he see her from the back, think he recognized the woman in the long black winter coat and blue scarf going into the store, and follow? Perhaps merely intending to have words.

They, whoever they were, had only seconds to act—to see the store was empty, Paula was alone, decide to make their move, grab the scarf and twist it, kill the woman, and then flee. Had they acted in such a rush, and so impulsively, they got the wrong person?

A cold shiver ran down the back of my neck as I pictured the scene when I found Paula. Lying face down on the floor, scarf tight around her throat, twisted at the back of her neck. The police would be able to say for sure, but as far as I could tell she'd been attacked from behind. She likely didn't even see her attacker.

"Why don't you sit down, honeybunch?" Dad said. "You've a right to be upset."

Mom threw me a worried look, and I smiled at them both. "I'm fine. I came to fill you in, but I see word got ahead of me. As it does."

"Regarding our production, Paula wasn't at all important in the scheme of things," Desmond said. "Jackie's the understudy and a keen one at that. She can take the role. Irene, you should have time to adjust the dress to fit Jackie. She's taller than Paula, but it shouldn't much matter."

"I hardly think casting should be our biggest concern right now," Ian said.

"As I am not about to play amateur detective and solve the case for the police, it is my focus, yes. I'm sorry Paula died. She'd been a valuable member of our little group over the years, but what's done is done. We'll have to find another boy to play Tiny Tim. Unlikely Eddie's father will want him to continue in the play."

"One of Andrea Hopkins's boys might do," a woman said. "They're twins and the right age, and she's in the chorus."

Rather heartless, I thought, but then again these theater people could be single-minded. I snuck a peek at Mom. She was watching me, an expression of concern on her face, and I gave her a wry grin.

"You've decided to stay on as director, Desmond?" Irene said. "I'm glad to hear it. The production needs your steady hand. If you stay, I'll stay."

Desmond threw a not entirely friendly look at Catherine. She avoided his eyes. Dave said, "About that. As long as we're all here—I've been thinking about Scrooge. A younger person playing him will help to entice younger people to come. I—"

"Not that again. And not now!" Mom said. "Over the long, and I might say successful, years of my career, I was involved in many nontraditional presentations of classic opera. Not all of them entirely effective. I am reminded of the time I quit that ridiculous production of Wagner in Paris because the director decided the Valkyries, of whom I was one, would be dressed in schoolgirl uniforms. He wanted to make some sort of statement about the repressed power of young women today that—"

Dad cleared his throat. "A story for another time, dear. Your point is?"

"My point is, I can be as artistically adventurous and as *avant-garde* as the next person."

Dad and I exchanged glances. To our credit, neither of us laughed.

"*A Christmas Carol*, however, is not to be trifled with. It, more than most works, is firmly locked in time and place. That is what people expect. That is its appeal. The tradition of the Christmas season and the emotions it arouses."

"Thank you for your opinion, Aline," Catherine said. "I'll keep that in mind. You are, of course, highly valued as a soloist and our musical director, but you are not in charge of casting. I myself agree with Dave." She smiled at him. He smiled back.

Ian threw her a look that would curdle the mug of warm milk a child left out for Santa on Christmas Eve. "You two had better get that sorted, and fast. If I'm not playing Scrooge, I'm walking."

"That would be unfortunate, but it is your decision." Catherine stared at him. Ian's face tightened further but he turned away. A brief look of satisfaction crossed her own face, to be quickly wiped away.

Everyone began talking at once. The general consensus, it seemed to me, was that, other than Dave, the cast were on Ian's side and they didn't care for Catherine's proposed changes. I glanced at Catherine. The expression on her perfectly composed face told me she didn't much care what the rest of them thought.

I whispered to my dad, "This conversation seems to have moved far beyond its original intent. I'm leaving. I want to head back to the store and check on things. I honestly don't trust some of those heavy-handed cops not to knock over my china dishes or smash my porcelain dolls."

Before I could make my escape, Mattie let out a joyous yelp from the kitchen. Seconds later, the doorbell rang.

Dad left the living room and returned with Detective Diane Simmonds and Officer Williams.

Simmonds raised one eyebrow when she saw me. "I shouldn't be surprised to see you here, but I am. You travel fast, Merry."

"Not as fast as the news, it would appear."

"Can I get you a drink, Diane?" Dad asked. "Coffee? Tea?"

"Coffee'd be good, thanks, Noel. I had to leave the office in somewhat of a rush. Black, no sugar."

"Nothing for me, thanks," said Officer Williams.

"I'll get it," I said.

Mom stood up. This sudden infusion of company must have come as a surprise to her, but she was dressed for the occasion in a slim-fitting beige skirt with a blue silk shirt, a long silver chain, and earrings of blue sea glass. Her hair was folded behind her head in a chignon, and her makeup perfect but subtle. "Welcome, Detective. We're having an emergency meeting of the Rudolph Community Theater Players. One of our number has died, and we spontaneously gathered to remember her and to decide if and how to proceed with our production." She made the introductions in a volley of names and positions with the company. I had not the slightest doubt Diane Simmonds would remember them all.

I handed her a cup of coffee. She did not take a seat. She looked at everyone in turn. Some people returned the look with a vague smile, others fidgeted and glanced nervously away.

Catherine stood up. She crossed the room and extended her hand. "Catherine Renshaw, Artistic Director. So pleased to meet you, Detective. My husband and I are newly arrived in Rudolph. I'm sorry we had to meet under these circumstances." She talked as though most newcomers went to the trouble of introducing themselves to the local police. I wondered if Catherine or her husband had ambitions in our town beyond community theater. Such as the mayor's office.

Simmonds accepted the handshake. "I'm pleased to find you gathered here. It will save me some time. Speaking of time, let's get straight to the point."

"Paula. Please, what happened to Paula?" Irene asked. "Rumors are flying left and right. Is she . . .?"

"Paula Monahan died earlier today," Simmonds said.

"That's what we heard. I hoped that was wrong," Irene said.

People muttered; some bowed their heads. One woman crossed herself and another mouthed a silent prayer. No one spoke.

Simmonds sipped her coffee and studied the room. Finally, she broke the silence. "Before I begin, do any of you have contact information for Mrs. Monahan's husband? I paid a visit to their house but no one's at home."

Everyone glanced at everyone else and exchanged shrugs.

"The only number I have for her is her cell," Irene said. "Not many people have house phones these days."

"His number might be at the theater office. AKA my house," Desmond said. "We keep emergency contact information, insurance details, and the like for everyone involved. I don't have it with me."

"If we haven't had any success otherwise, I'll accompany you to get that when we're finished here," Simmonds said.

"Did you try calling the school?" Irene asked. "Paula teaches at Rudolph High. Classes are finished for the Christmas break, but the school office should be open today."

Simmonds nodded to the uniform, instructing him to make the call. He slipped out of the house. "Various witnesses have told me there's been some dissent in your group," she said. "Is that correct?"

Catherine and Desmond laughed. Irene choked. Ian said, "You might say that," in a voice not designed to carry.

"We're treating the death of Mrs. Monahan as a homicide." Simmonds paused, allowing everyone to express their shock, surprise, and dismay. Then she said, "The question I have for you all is, do any of you know of any reason someone might have wanted to cause her harm?"

Silence. More exchanging of looks.

Williams came back. "Answering machine says the office is closed for the weekend."

"Track down the principal or administrator and tell them what we need."

He slipped out again.

Detective Simmonds would have a heck of a lot on her plate in the hours immediately after a homicide. You wouldn't know that by her demeanor. She sipped her coffee. She said nothing, waiting everyone out. Someone would be bound to break the silence eventually.

Irene did. "I'd have been happy to bump her off just to get rid of that horrid son of hers. Sorry, bad joke."

"Was it a joke?" Simmonds asked.

"Yes! I mean, yes, of course."

"Go on."

"Paula's son, Eddie, was cast as Tiny Tim. He's a bully, and she indulges . . . indulged him rather than getting him under control. In my opinion, he was totally unsuitable for Tiny Tim, but casting decisions were made elsewhere."

"By which she means it was my decision," Desmond said. "As you well know, Irene. Eddie was the best option. Some of the girls in the children's chorus are excellent performers, but the boys are less than inspiring."

"I still can't understand why you always have to be so hide-bound and cast according to preconceived ideas," Dave said. "Things like Scrooge's age. What does it matter?"

"Not this again!" Desmond leapt to his feet and headed for the dining room table where the drinks had been laid out.

"Paula was an excellent Mrs. Cratchit," Catherine said, "She wanted her son on stage with her. I had no objections."

"Once again, might I remind you that casting is not supposed to be your responsibility," Ian said.

"What, pray tell, do you think is my responsibility if not oversight of the entire production?" Catherine snapped.

"It's supposed to be mine." Desmond poured red wine with a heavy hand. "You can handle the table settings."

"Staying on that subject," Irene said. "I hope someone has told Jackie O'Reilly she's now going to play Mrs. Cratchit. I saw her in town shorty before the fuss started but not since. She'll need to be informed. She's going to be very pleased."

Simmonds said nothing to that, and neither did I.

"It would appear casting changes are going to be made, whether you want them or not, Desmond." Dave drained his beer bottle and stood up. "If you have nothing else for me, Detective, I'll be off. Catherine, give me a call if you want to talk further about my expanded role."

"I quit." Ian didn't bother to finish his beer before also getting to his feet. His face was flushed, his eyes narrow.

"Don't be ridiculous," Desmond said. "You can't quit. I don't want you to quit. You are my Scrooge."

"Dave," my mother said in the calm, placating voice she used when she was trying to rehearse, and my siblings and I were running wild through the house with a pack of our friends. Come to think of it, it was Dad who had the calm, placating voice. Mom simply sang louder. "You are far better suited to Marley than Scrooge. Marley has one of the best solos in the entire production. Next only to mine as Belle, of course," she added modestly. Not.

Dave hesitated. He glanced at Catherine. Ian snorted. "What, you can't make up your own mind? You have to ask her for permission? Aline's right. You're Marley and I'm Scrooge. And that is that."

"We have one week until opening night," Desmond said. "Aside from anything else, that's not enough time for so much upheaval. An actor has to play the part they're suited for. Isn't that right, Aline? I'm sure there are parts you would have liked to have sung during your career, but you were wise enough to know they didn't suit your voice."

"Not that I noticed," Mom said. "But your point is valid, Desmond. Again, Catherine, please tell us what years of experience you bring to show business that you know what's better for this production than the rest of us."

Catherine glared at my mother. Next to me, Dad shifted uncomfortably. Simmonds had quietly melted into the woodwork, taking herself out of everyone's line of sight. The uniformed cop hovered in the doorway.

"And that," declared Desmond, "is final. I want this production to be the best it can be. I want to expand it beyond the limitations of amateur theater. I want audiences to reconsider spending hundreds of dollars on trips to New York City and Broadway tickets, when they can get almost as good quality here at home. With none other than Aline Steiner as the Ghost of Christmas Past, singing Belle, leading the chorus, and being our musical director, I . . . I mean we can achieve that. We will have a suitable tenor as Marley. Which is where you come in, Dave."

Irene clapped her hands.

My dad cleared his throat. "Must I remind you, Desmond, we don't exactly have Broadway production money going into our sets. George and his team and I are doing the best we can but—"

"But," my mother said. "That is not under discussion at the moment. Detective Simmonds, I fear we're taking up your valuable time with our petty little squabbles."

Simmonds stepped away from the wall. "Not at all. It's been most interesting. I repeat my question: is anyone aware of any reason someone might have wished to harm Paula Monahan, or of any enemies she might have had? Inside or out of your company?"

"You weren't happy with her singing, Aline, were you?" Dave said. "At the last rehearsal you had words with her and took her aside for private instruction, otherwise known as a lecture on her inadequacies. Let's be honest, Paula was pretty bad. Then again, she wasn't the only one. We can't all be up to the standards of a star of the Metropolitan Opera. I mean, isn't that what you're all saying? I get a minor part because I'm the one with professional experience and a half-decent voice. Would it have bothered you, Aline, if the musical parts of the production were a flop? Maybe some of your fancy opera friends are coming to see it and you don't want to be embarrassed?"

My dad stepped forward before I could. His beard bristled and his hair almost stood on end. "What do you think you're saying?"

Dave shrugged. "Just putting the idea out there."

"Well, you can stop putting it, or any other outlandish ideas you might have dreamt up, *out there*."

"If my mother killed everyone who offended her musical sensibilities, the world of grand opera would be a lot smaller." Dave's accusation was totally preposterous, and I attempted to lighten the mood. In that, I failed. Detective Simmonds was not laughing, and she had turned her intense stare onto my mother.

"You are not helping, Merry," Dad said.

"That was then," Dave said. "This is now. Sorry, Aline, but you're not a star anymore, are you? Does that bother you? Are you worried about what your former colleagues might think?"

"Now see here," Dad said.

Simmonds lifted one hand. "Shall we allow Mrs. Wilkinson to reply? Do you have anything to say to that?"

"Aline," Ian said, "is a highly valued member of our company, and we're lucky to have her."

My mother smoothed her skirt. "Thank you, Ian." She graced Dave with a radiant smile. "Considering I know nothing about Dave himself, other than he seems to think the ability to carry a tune without the necessity of a bucket excuses his considerable lack of acting talent, I assume he knows even less about me. So I will not grace his comment with a reply. Other than to thank him for his honesty."

Dave flushed and avoided everyone's eyes. He swallowed the last of his drink. I figured Dad would not be offering him a refill.

"You are here, Detective, to get at the truth," Mom said. "I fear the truth is sometimes not pleasant, therefore a police investigation is not either. Apple carts are upturned and long-concealed secrets revealed. Now, I believe you were asking if anyone knows of someone who might have had a reason to do away with Paula."

Catherine leapt in quickly. "I hadn't even met her before the first day I joined the group. And that was only a couple of months ago."

"I wouldn't say she and I were friends," Irene said. "We didn't socialize, or have much to do with each other outside of the group."

The others said much the same. Paula had been a member of the company for several years, but had never made any close friends among them.

"You'll have to look elsewhere for your killer, Detective," Desmond said.

"I'll do that," Simmonds said. "I'll be in touch if I have any further questions. Mrs. Dowling, you said you saw Jackie O'Reilly shortly before the police were called to Mrs. Claus's Treasures earlier this afternoon. Is that correct?"

"It is. We had a brief chat in Cranberry Coffee Bar. I was having lunch with a friend, and Jackie came in. She greeted me and said she was on her break from the store where she works."

"I'll need a statement from you about that, please."

Irene blinked. "Why?"

"Because I said so. Did anyone else see either Jackie O'Reilly or Paula Monahan in town today? Other than Merry, whose statement I already have."

"My wife did," Ian said. "Rachel. She called me with the news and told me she'd been talking to Irene and Jackie at the coffee shop minutes earlier."

"Why are you asking about Jackie?" Catherine asked.

Simmonds didn't honor that question with a reply. "You were in Mrs. Claus's yourself, earlier today, Mrs. Renshaw, were you not?"

"Yes, I was. I assume Merry told you about that. I visited the shops on Jingle Bell Lane today, hoping they'd put our playbills in their window. I didn't see Paula at any time, and I saw Jackie in the store, but not otherwise."

Officer Williams stepped forward. "I got hold of the principal at Rudolph High, Detective. She has access to staff records from her house, so she was able to give me Mrs. Monahan's husband's number."

"Good. I'll call him from the car. Mrs. Dowling, if you'll give me a minute."

Irene slowly stood up. "I don't know how I can help you. I didn't see anything."

"Perfectly routine," Dad said. "You were in the area at the time so you might have seen something you don't know the significance of."

"I'll help if I can," she said.

"Before you go, Detective," Ian said. "How did Paula die? You didn't tell us."

"I didn't, did I?" she replied.

* * *

"That is not a happy crew," Dad said once everyone had gone.

"I've seen worse," Mom said.

"I'm sure you have."

"But not often. As has been said about academe: sometimes the lower the stakes, the worse the infighting. As if a month from now anyone will remember who played Scrooge and who played Marley." She snorted and began gathering up glasses and mugs.

"Ian will remember," I said. "Dave will remember."

"Catherine and Desmond will never forget. Those two. Each of them could be marvelous in their own right. Desmond to direct to his heart's content, and Catherine to organize everyone and everything. Put the two of them together, and it simply isn't working."

"Catherine's new here, but Desmond's been around a long time," I said. "Has he clashed with people before?"

"I've not been involved with the company prior to this year, but I do hear things." My parents began carrying the dishes into the kitchen, and I followed. Mattie lumbered to his feet, his tail thumping.

"No one has openly challenged him before," Mom said. "Catherine challenges him, and that can often be a good thing.

Companies, professional as well as amateur, can get stuck in their ways. Clearly, in this case challenge is not inspiring Desmond to do better, instead he's digging his heels in."

"Does he have a theatrical background?"

"I believe so. He directed some off-Broadway productions, but his career didn't progress very far, and he moved to Rudolph a few years ago. He told us some of his old theatrical friends will be coming on opening night to see the play, and he's quite excited about it."

"What about Catherine? Why's she so keen?"

"She's new to town. Wanting to make an impression perhaps. To find a place in her new community."

"She and her husband ran a multibillion-dollar company," Dad said. "They started it from nothing and built it from the ground up. They recently retired and moved to a small town. They're still in their sixties; young to find yourself on the shelf." He hesitated. "As I well know."

"Nonsense," Mom said. "You're hardly on the shelf, darling. Sometimes I wish you'd slow down."

My dad had been mayor of Rudolph for many years. He was now not only the town's Santa Claus, and that's a far more vital role here than in any other community, but on the town council. He's actively involved in many groups to do with the welfare of Rudolph and Rudolphites.

"Back to Catherine," Dad said. "My guess is she's looking for something to do, some reason to feel important, and she doesn't understand that the management skills needed to run a corporation or a chain of big stores aren't the same as required when dealing with well-meaning volunteers."

"She's brought some much-needed funds to the company," Mom said. "As well as enthusiasm. Rumor had it they weren't likely to last much longer. Long-timers were leaving, either through advancing age or boredom. Not enough new people joining. Ticket sales for last year's production of *Miracle on 34th Street* were perfectly dreadful, putting the company in the red. Or so I've heard. Catherine's paying for a lot of things out of pocket. Never mind specially selected table settings, I, for one, don't come cheap."

"You mean you're being paid?" I said. "I thought this was an amateur show."

"I'm appearing as an unpaid performer, same as the rest of the cast. However, I'm charging my regular rates for extra vocal lessons. Many of the children, and some of the adults, in the chorus are in my classes, and I'm giving them additional tuition specifically to prepare them for the play. Catherine's paying for that. Not to mention Dave, who's new to me, and who's a perfectly acceptable tenor, although nowhere near the quality he would like to be."

"What about Paula and her son, Eddie, who plays Tiny Tim?"

"Paula's singing was hopeless, but she managed to get by in a sort of speak-singing style. That's what I was attempting to coach her through. Her acting skills were more or less on par with the rest of the cast. As for her son, Eddie isn't part of the chorus, and Tiny Tim doesn't sing. I don't know if he can or not."

"Never mind all that." My Dad wrapped me in a big hug. "It bothers me that my girl was so close to a killing. If you'd been in that room . . ." His voice trailed off.

I hugged him fiercely. Mattie rubbed his big body against my legs. "If I'd been in that room, it wouldn't have happened. I'm sure of it. I know it wasn't my fault. I'm allowed to take a break. But I still feel guilty."

"Richard and Lorraine came for dinner last night," Mom said. "Lorraine brought an enormous cake, and we scarcely touched it. Why don't you take the leftovers home?"

Mattie's warm soft fur, Dad's hugs, Mom's offer of (someone else's) baking.

What could be better?

Chapter Seven

I returned to Jingle Bell Lane, hoping the murder had been miraculously solved and I could open my store. Such was not the case. Most of the onlookers had dispersed, but Candy Campbell was still logging people coming and going through my doors. Cruisers and unmarked vans were still parked higgledy-piggledy on the sidewalk, ignoring the "no parking" instructions.

"Any developments?" I said to Candy.

"Not that I'm going to tell you."

Mattie sniffed at her pant leg. I believe you can tell a lot about a person by how they react to friendly dogs. Candy completely ignored him. Not easy to do considering he's a solid hundred and fifty pounds of fur and slobber and sheer personality. Which sort of proves my point.

She was dressed in her heavy winter uniform jacket with gloves on her hands, but a chill wind was whipping down Jingle Bell Lane. Candy's cheeks were ruddy with cold, and when I'd spotted her she'd been bouncing on her toes and rubbing her hands together in an attempt to get warm.

I peered past her shoulder. I could see people in white coveralls poking around my things. A section of the floor next to the center table had been marked off. "Did anyone say when they'll be finished here and I can have my business back?"

"Talk to the detective," Candy said.

"Okay. I will. Have a nice day. Come on, Mattie."

Candy cleared her throat. She shifted her feet. It must, I thought, get mighty boring standing here all day, doing nothing but watching other people doing the interesting things.

"Yes?" I said.

"The woman who died. They say she teaches at the high school. I didn't recognize the name. After our time, I guess."

"Must be."

"She was involved in the local dramatic society."

"She was. They're putting on the musical version of *A Christmas Carol* this year."

Mattie lost interest in Candy's boots, and began sniffing at the sidewalk in front of the doors, no doubt wondering why we weren't going in.

"I've been thinking of joining. You remember I was in the dramatic society at school."

Vaguely.

"I've always been interested in the stage. I considered acting as a career, but I decided on law enforcement instead. Much more important work, wouldn't you agree, Merry?"

"I suppose. I mean, yes. Important."

"I might like to join the local group." More shifting of feet. "I've been asked to join, but at first I didn't want to. Bunch of old fogies, putting on stale old plays. This year everyone's saying Catherine Renshaw's brought new life to the company. Shaken things up, provided fresh new ideas, bright new direction and focus. Not to mention lots of money. Too late for this year, but I might consider it for next. My singing is sort of out of practice. Do you think your mom would take me on as a student?"

I wondered what Candy was getting at. Mom would take anyone who'd pay her substantial fees, show up to lessons on time, and not expect miracles. "If she has space in her schedule. Why don't you ask her?"

"I'll do that. It would be nice to get my voice back in tune. Not that I'd consider singing professionally, of course. Law enforcement's my passion. And so important." She smiled at me. Her teeth chattered in the cold. "I suppose for some people selling Santa dolls and table settings is enough in life."

"It sure is cold, isn't it? Can't stand here chatting much longer. I'm glad I can take the afternoon off. I'm thinking of heading home, turning the heat up, slipping into my warmest jammies, putting my feet up, and relaxing with a steaming mug of hot chocolate topped with a mountain of fresh whipped cream." I rubbed my hands together in anticipation. "Come on, Mattie. Our work here is done."

I walked away, the dog trotting at my side.

Okay, I shouldn't have responded to a dig with a dig. But somehow, deep down inside, we're all still high school kids at heart.

Mattie and I didn't get far. Margie Thatcher came out of Rudolph's Gift Nook so quickly she must have been watching for me.

As one of the town's fathers, my dad's motto is everyone in Rudolph works for the benefit of everyone else. Meaning, when one business does well, all businesses do well. Margie, and her sister Betty who ran the store before her, didn't appear to have gotten the memo. At least not as it affected the relationship between the Nook and Mrs. Claus's Treasures.

She stepped in front of me. Five foot one of bristling hair, small angry eyes, and righteous indignation. "You again! More trouble at your ridiculous, overpriced store. Merry Wilkinson, you attract the worst sort of attention. I won't put up with it any longer. It's not enough that you're closed—again—for a police investigation." She stabbed a finger in the direction of Candy Campbell, who was no doubt watching the altercation with much interest. "But people are avoiding *my* store because of it. I'm taking my issues to the business bureau. This time, finally, I'll see you shut down."

I stepped to one side and said, "Good luck with that, Margie. I'll let my dad know about your concerns."

"And that," she declared, "is the problem with this entire town. Nepotism run amok."

"Have a nice day."

I tried to put both Margie Thatcher and Candy Campbell out of my mind as I walked. But that meant I was thinking about the death of Paula Monahan instead. Which reminded me that Jackie'd been taken in for questioning. When I got home, I'd give her a call. Hopefully Detective Simmonds had realized she'd made a mistake and sent Jackie on her way.

Mattie and I walked out of town in companionable silence. He sniffed at trees and fire hydrants. It was coming up to five o'clock, night was quickly falling, and the lights on the big tree in the bandstand had come on. Nearby houses glowed with holiday decorations. Despite the cold, the playground in the town park was busy with swinging, running, shouting children and watchful parents. Two elderly women, bundled up against the weather, sat on a blanket-covered park bench, watching the activity with gentle smiles on their faces. A banner had been strung across the front of the bandstand announcing the run of the play.

In its nineteenth- and early twentieth-century heyday Rudolph had been an important Great Lakes port. Ship owners and industrialists built grand Victorian mansions for their large and prosperous families. Then the shipping moved away, as did industry and young people, and like towns all along the lakes, Rudolph slowly began to die. Taking advantage of the town's name, largely under the influence of my father, Rudolph remade itself into a Christmas destination. The town's thriving once again, but not well enough for those grand old houses to return to their former glory. I lived in one half of the upper floor of one of them.

As we turned the corner, I could see my landlady, Mabel D'Angelo, sprinkling de-icer on the sidewalk. Ours is the best-kept property on the street. In the summer, the grass is perfectly cut at all times, the perennial beds lush and well weeded. Colorful annuals in terracotta pots or iron urns line the walkways and spill out of containers on the wide front porch. In the fall, the flowerbeds are turned over, every fallen leaf raked up, the bushes wrapped in burlap. Come winter, not a single flake of snow falls before Mrs. D'Angelo is out clearing the paths.

Mattie woofed in greeting, and Mrs. D'Angelo straightened from her labors. She wore a long, ragged scarf and a bulky winter coat that reached her ankles. Her ever-present iPhone, the latest model, was in her coat pocket and white wireless earbuds in her ears.

"Merry!" She waved the bag of de-icer at me. "What's this I hear? The whole town's abuzz. Naturally, my phone's been ringing off the hook, as everyone knows you live here." She smiled at me, her eyes alight with excitement and anticipation.

Naturally. Mrs. D'Angelo had one interest in life, and it wasn't care of her property. The reason our yard is the best-kept on the street is in the service of her keeping an eye on the goings-on of the neighborhood, so as to report to her vast network of contacts, who were presumably also watching their streets.

"I don't know much, Mrs. D'Angelo," I said. "I wasn't there when it happened."

Her face fell. Then it quickly rose again. "But it . . . the murder . . . happened at your store."

"I'm not sure if it's murder." I lied. "The police haven't said."

She waved that minor point away with a mittened hand. "Never mind what they say. Everyone knows. They say it's Paula Monahan, who teaches geography and history at Rudolph High. She's been there for five years, although she's lived in Rudolph longer than that. She was at Muddle Harbor previously. She must have been desperate to get out of there. I can't say I know her. I couldn't place the name offhand, but my sources tell me she and her family live on Oak Street. Nice part of town, although not quite as nice as this one." She took my arm. "I'm finished here, and the coffee pot's on. There's no snow in the forecast for tonight, but it never hurts to be prepared. The weather report's almost always wrong, isn't it? A cup of coffee would do me good, and you too, I'm sure. Come along now."

"I don't have time, sorry. I have to . . . do something."

"Nonsense." She dragged me to the porch and up the steps. Mattie trotted along behind. "We'll sit out here. It's warm enough out of the wind. I'll get the coffee and a bowl of water for Matterhorn. Such a nice dog."

She went inside. I grimaced at Mattie. "What can I do? She's a force of nature." My parents taught me to always be polite and accept hospitality when it's offered, but I did consider cowardly slipping silently away. Too late! She was back, with a tray bearing a coffee pot, two chipped mugs, a jug of cream, a plate piled high with freshly made chocolate chip cookies, and a bowl of water. She put the tray on the wrought iron table and the bowl on the floor for Mattie. He dove in.

My fate sealed, I took a seat in one of the white wicker chairs and settled back into the blue and yellow cushions.

"Now." My landlady dropped into her own chair and leaned toward me. "Paula Monahan. High school teacher. Husband named Kevin. He's an insurance broker. One child named Edward, who's said to be a hellion. She's active in the community theater group and is in rehearsals for the upcoming production of *A Christmas Carol*, in which she was supposed to play Mrs. Cratchit, as well as a member of the chorus."

"You know as much about her as I do."

Mrs. D'Angelo poured the coffee and shoved a mug toward me. "As I said, she teaches at Rudolph High. She's not popular there, not with the students or her fellow teachers. Norman King's granddaughter's also a teacher there. This is the young Miss King's first year teaching, and Norman says that she says that Paula, who should be mentoring her, is instead so unpleasant she's ruining Miss King's desire to continue in that career."

I wondered if I should put "young Miss King" on my suspect list. Not that I had a suspect list.

"Although," Mrs. D'Angelo went on, "Norman says his granddaughter doesn't have all that much to complain about. She's gone to California to spend Christmas with friends and is considering not coming back."

Scratch that name off my nonexistent list. I sipped my coffee. I refrained from spitting it out. You could stand a spoon up in there. The pot must have been on all day, waiting for a chance for Mrs. D'Angelo to drag some unsuspecting innocent bystander onto her porch. "Thanks for the coffee, but—"

"The police were around at their house earlier. No one answered the door. Norma Robinson, you know Norma, of course, dear."

Never heard of her in my life.

"Norma popped over when she saw them. To be of assistance, of course."

"Of course."

"She told them they wouldn't find Kevin at home. He's left. They're getting a divorce."

I choked on a mouthful of treacle-like coffee. When I could speak again, I said, "How do you know that?"

Mrs. D'Angelo smirked. As well she might. Usually her gossip was nothing but endless chatter reported by people I'd never heard of concerning people I didn't know doing things I didn't care about. But every once in a while, she could throw a good curveball.

"It's no secret on their street there's been trouble in the marriage for a long time. If people want to keep their private lives private, they shouldn't buy houses so close to their neighbors, now should they? Or keep their windows open. Never mind arguing in the driveway. According to Norma and some of my other friends, the severity of the Monahans' arguments has been increasing recently. Their latest dispute seem to be about the boy, Edward. The father thinks the mother is spoiling the boy. The boy, according to Norma, is a horror. Rude, ill-disciplined, slovenly, lazy. He is, despite all that, the apple of his mother's eye. Comes from having children late in life, I always say." Mrs. D'Angelo eyed thirty-something me carefully. She had no children, and Mr. D'Angelo had left the scene long ago. That didn't stop her opining on other people's drawbacks when it came to marriage and childrearing. "Not for me to criticize, of course."

"Of course not." I helped myself to a cookie. Mattie settled at the top of the porch steps and watched a small dog and its person walking down the street. The dog yipped and strained at the leash to get to Mattie. Mattie yawned.

"Things came to a head on Wednesday," Mrs. D'Angelo continued. "What day's today, Merry?"

"Friday." The cookie was surprisingly good, rich and buttery and full of chopped nuts. I took another.

"Two days ago, then. Kevin Monahan was seen dragging two suitcases and a computer bag out of the house at seven thirty in the evening and putting them into his car with a considerable amount of force."

"He might have been going on a trip."

"If so, he intends it to be an extended one. She, Paula, followed him out. They had words. According to Norma, she, Paula, was yelling to beat the band. And Kevin, as is normal for him, gave as good as he got. He told her he was leaving. She told him not to bother coming back. He said she could be sure of that. He said he was sick and tired of her nagging all the time, and she said she couldn't help it if she wanted to have a life."

"What does that mean?"

"Norma didn't know. Although she did know that Kevin thought she, Paula, was spending too much time with the theater company. His parents came to visit for a few days last week, and he was not happy when Paula said she wouldn't be able to spend time with them as she had rehearsals to attend. 'Fine, said Kevin, they don't like you anyway, but they're here to see Eddie'. And Paula said, 'Too bad, Eddie is also needed at rehearsals.' So then—"

"Your friend Norman overheard all of this?" I eyed the cookie plate, debating if it would be rude to have a third. I decided it would not.

"Norma. Not Norman. Do try to keep up, Merry. Norma has a beautiful deck attached to the side of her house, close to the Monahans' kitchen windows. She gets the full afternoon sun, so sits out there a good part of the time, even in winter if the day is nice The Monahans' windows are often open to let in fresh air."

"How convenient."

"As a parting shot, Kevin told Paula—"

"And most of the street," I muttered around the last bite of my third cookie.

"—he's going to try for full custody of Eddie. He then slammed the trunk of his car shut and drove away. At a speed that would have had the police pulling him over, had one been around."

"That is interesting." Maybe this case would get wrapped up quickly. Nothing like a battle over child custody to get people going to extremes.

If so, poor Eddie.

"Your friend told the police all this?"

"Of course, dear. Like a good citizen should." I didn't hear anything, but Mrs. D'Angelo jerked to attention like a dog catching a whiff of a squirrel invading his property. Although I only know how a dog reacts when he catches the scent of a squirrel from observing Alan's overly enthusiastic Jack Russell, Ranger. Mattie stretches and rolls over.

"Merry Wilkinson is here now," my landlady said.

"What?" I started to ask, then I realized she'd answered her phone and was listening on her earbuds.

"Yes, that's right. Paula was murdered in the middle of the day, in the middle of town. In Merry's store, of all places. Merry says she herself was lucky to escape with her life."

"Hey!"

"She's dreadfully upset. I've managed to calm her down with a freshly brewed cup of coffee and comforting conversation. Hold on a minute, I'll ask."

She spoke to me. "It's Cathy Dickens, dear. She wants to know if you noticed Paula behaving in an unusual way in the minutes before her untimely demise. Might she have had a premonition that death was imminent?"

"I told you, Mrs. D'Angelo. I wasn't there."

"Cathy has an intense interest in spiritualism. She's foretold events on more than one occasion."

I stood up. "I'd better be going. Thank you for the coffee." I called to Mattie, and we descended the steps.

"Now that you mention it," Mrs. D'Angelo said. "Merry says that's entirely possible."

*   *   *

Mrs. D'Angelo did seem to know a heck of a lot about the state of the Monahans' marriage, but as Mattie and I climbed the steps, I reminded myself that she wasn't above stretching the truth more than a little in the interest of making herself and her news seem important. Such as reporting to her friends that I not only saw Paula in the minutes before her death, but was somehow aware of her state of mind. It was possible, likely even, Mrs. D'Angelo's contacts did the same.

Still, if the Monahan marriage was breaking up and things threatened to turn ugly that would provide a powerful motive for murder.

I let us into our small apartment. Mattie ran into the kitchen and began pushing his empty food bowl around. A not too subtle hint that he'd like his dinner now.

I took care of that, poured myself a glass of wine, and dropped onto the couch. When I was comfortably settled, I called Alan and he answered almost immediately.

"Hey, Merry, what's up?"

"I wanted to hear your voice, that's all."

"That's nice. How's it sound to you?"

"Like normality itself."

"Is that a good thing?"

"Today it is."

"Things quiet at the store right now?"

"Quiet? Alan, what have you been doing all day?"

"Working. I'm in the shop. Getting a lot done. What's the time? Oh, almost dinner time. Are you on your break?"

I smiled to myself. Alan's woodworking shop was a place unto itself. When he was in there, crafting marvelous things out of wood with his own strong, gentle hands, he tuned out the entire world. The shop had a hotplate, on which he could make coffee or heat up a bowl of soup, and a fridge, well stocked with snacks and water so he didn't need to go into the house. While he worked, he listened to music from a streaming service, not the radio. He took breaks to let Ranger have a romp in the woods, but then went straight back inside. He didn't answer the phone unless it was me or his parents calling, or a customer or supplier he was waiting to hear from. And, often, not even then.

I didn't want to disturb his peace by telling him what had happened. But he'd hear about it eventually.

"I'm at home," I said. "I closed the shop early."

"Why?"

Briefly and as succinctly as possible I told him.

He said nothing until I was finished and then he simply said, "I'll come over right now, if you need me."

"It was upsetting, yes, but I'm okay. I'm going put on my pajamas and take my book to bed and take advantage of an early night. With a glass of wine. Or two. But first, I need to find out what's happening with Jackie."

"Okay. Call if you need to talk or want me to come over. Is the play going to go ahead, do you think?"

"I see no reason why not. Paula wasn't an important player. She had a small speaking role, and it can be recast. The auditorium's been booked, advertising paid for, guests invited, tickets sold, and the remaining cast and crew will want to go ahead with it."

We didn't talk for much longer. Alan told me what he was working on and a funny story about Ranger stalking a chipmunk around the woodpile. But Alan's not one for small talk, and even though it wasn't long after six, my day had been an exhausting one, and I had no idea what tomorrow might bring. We exchanged goodnights and hung up. I called Jackie, but got her voicemail. That might mean she was in jail, or it might mean she wasn't answering her phone. I left a message and asked her to return my call.

I then called Vicky, who also didn't answer. I finished my wine while leafing through a design magazine without taking in a word.

I was about to suggest to Mattie it was time for our nightly walk, when he lifted his head, let out a joyous bark, and bounded across the apartment with the sort of energy that could mean only one thing. Sure enough, seconds later, the doorbell rang.

"I wonder who that could be," I muttered. I knew full well who. Only one person ever got such an enthusiastic reception from my dog. That person was not me.

I left my apartment and ran down the stairs, Mattie hot on my heels.

As expected, Detective Diane Simmonds stood on the step, waiting for us. Mattie dropped into a sit and smiled up at her, expecting a pat.

She obliged. "You've done a good job training Matterhorn."

"Not so as I'd notice," I said.

"Pardon?"

"Never mind. Come on in. I assume you're here to see me, not the dog." I led the way up the stairs and into my apartment. I'd cleaned about a week ago, so it wasn't too terribly messy.

I nodded toward the empty glass of wine on the coffee table. "Can I get you something?"

"This isn't a social call, Merry."

"Oh. Okay. Have a seat."

She perched on the edge of a dining room chair. She didn't remove her jacket. Mattie settled himself at her feet. "Tell me again what you were doing between two o'clock this afternoon and when you called 911."

I did so. It didn't take long.

"You see, Merry, what I'm wondering is why you stayed in the back when you knew someone had come into your store."

"I told you. Mattie spilled his water and I refilled the bowl."

"I know you well enough to know you take your business seriously. Yes, Rudolph's a peaceful town. But no place is entirely crime or vandalism-free, and you stock a good many delicate items. As well as ones that are small and easily portable."

I didn't care for the look on her face. Even Mattie let out a low whine.

"What are you saying, Detective? I'm a small shop owner, and sometimes I'm working by myself in the store, or one of my employees is alone. One person can't be out front all the time. It happens."

"I'm wondering if you have reason to have not heard what was going on out front."

"What does that mean?"

"Not heard. Or not tell me what you did see or hear."

I opened my mouth. I closed it again. Mattie nuzzled the detective's leg. For once, she ignored him.

I might have mentioned that he doesn't care to be ignored. Head down, he crept across the floor to sit next to me. I put my hand on top of his head. I shifted in my seat. I wanted to get myself another glass of wine, but I was afraid that would look as though I was nervous.

Heck, I was nervous.

I picked up my glass and went into the kitchen. Mattie followed me. "I'm not sure what you're saying, Detective. I told you what happened, exactly how it happened. Do I wish I'd gone out front as soon as I heard the door chimes? Yes, I do. If I'd done so, Paula would likely still be alive."

"You think you could have stopped a killer?"

"I think this person saw she was alone and thus made his move on the spur of the moment. Her move. Their move. If I'd been there, things would have been different." I took my drink back to the living room. I sat down. "Maybe they would have been different." Then again, maybe I'd be dead too. I didn't say that out loud.

Simmonds stood up. "Thank you for your time."

"Wait. What's happening? What about Jackie?"

"Ms. O'Reilly's lawyer showed up very promptly. I assume that was your doing. You and Vicky Casey. Tom Casey himself will be representing Jackie."

"Does Jackie need continuing representation?"

"She left the station a short while ago, and she has been cautioned not to leave Rudolph."

"Meaning you still consider her to be a suspect. That's ridiculous."

"I consider not only her to be a suspect, Merry."

I shifted uncomfortably under the force of those penetrating green eyes. I took a sip of wine, taking care not to gulp it down too fast, or have too much.

"Thank you for your time. I'll be in touch. In the meantime, if you think of anything you might have forgotten to tell me, you can contact me at any time. I believe you have my number?"

"I do."

Simmonds headed for the door. Mattie stuck his nose out of the kitchen to see if it was safe to come out.

"Before you go," I said. "I learned some things about the state of Paula's marriage you might be interested in. If you don't know already, that is."

She turned. "What might that be?"

"Town rumor—"

"Meaning Mabel D'Angelo and her vast network."

"Uh. Yes. Anyway, the Monahan marriage was not on what you'd call solid ground. The neighbors report that Kevin and Paula could often be heard arguing. Kevin, supposedly, left her on Wednesday. Permanently. He was not only planning to seek a divorce but going to try to get custody of their son, Eddie." I smiled at the detective. I then killed the smile, realizing it must look exactly like Mattie when he thought he'd performed a particularly clever trick.

"Thank you for that information," Simmonds said. "In return, I'll tell you I spoke to Mr. Monahan on my way here. He admits he left the family home after a minor dispute, but he said nothing about a divorce."

"He wouldn't, would he? Not after hearing his wife died. Was murdered."

"He's in Rochester, staying with his brother. He and his brother were ice fishing most of the day, and he didn't get my call until they'd returned to the city."

Ice fishing. I can't think of anything I'd rather not do. "I hope you don't buy that. Who goes fishing in the middle of the afternoon? The fish are asleep. That's what my dad tells me, anyway. Besides, his brother is his alibi? Not a very good one."

"I'll make a detective of you yet, Merry. You may not be aware, but fishing, whether in ice or open water, is sometimes a euphemism for drinking beer while engaging in manly talk. Kevin Monahan and his brother arrived at the cabin belonging to a friend of the brother first thing Thursday morning. According to Kevin, not only his brother but the owner of the cabin and one other man were there the entire time he was. I've asked the local police to pay a visit to the friend, and I'll see what he has to say. But it's unlikely Kevin told me he was there, if he wasn't. It's not an isolated area, and other people were likely out fishing who might have seen him and his group. Kevin and his brother left the cabin shortly after five today because the brother has work tomorrow. He's an independent contractor."

That was it for that theory.

"Is someone looking after their son, Eddie?"

"The boy was spending time at the home of a school friend when his mother died. He stayed there overnight, and his father is on his way to collect him.

"Now, if you have no more suggestions as to how I should do my job, I'll be on my way." She put her hand on the doorknob and hesitated. Then she turned around and faced me. "I'm not entirely happy with your statement, Merry, but for now I'll accept it on face value."

"Thank you. I think."

"I don't want you getting involved in this case. You're too close to the people concerned."

"I don't see why you say that. I scarcely know the theater group. Other than Jackie, I mean. And my mom."

"Precisely."

Chapter Eight

My plans for an early night with a good book came to naught. My mind was too restless to allow me to concentrate on my reading or to sleep easily, and I tossed and turned all night. Detective Simmonds couldn't possibly think I was covering for Jackie? Or, even worse, for my mom? Simmonds hadn't suggested I myself had taken advantage of the empty store and killed the woman, but might she be thinking it?

Surely not. Simmonds knew me well. We were, I sometimes thought, almost friends. Then again, she was a cop first and foremost. I suppose being a detective means you have a suspicious mind. Must make life difficult, particularly in a small town where you know so many people from your child's school, amateur sports teams or social clubs, just being out and about and involved in the community.

Then again, I have a suspicious mind too, I thought, as I lay in bed running over the list of people who might have wanted Paula dead. The list was far too short. I didn't know anything about her life outside the theater company. I didn't even know much about her life inside the theater company, other than the few interactions I'd witnessed.

I must have eventually drifted off to sleep as I was awakened when it was still dark by the ringing of my phone. I fumbled on the night table for it, finally found it, glanced at the display, and was instantly awake. "Jackie, what's happening? Are you okay?"

"Yeah, Merry, I'm fine. Why wouldn't I be?"

"Because it's . . ." I checked the clock, ". . . quarter to six in the morning, and you were arrested yesterday for murder."

"I wasn't arrested, Merry. I was brought in for questioning as an interested party who might have been witness to events. I was assisting the police with their inquiries."

"Uh . . . okay."

"Tom Casey, Vicky's dad, came down to the police station. He said Vicky sent him because she thought I might need a lawyer. Wasn't that nice of her?"

"Very nice. What did Tom Casey tell you is going to happen now?"

"He said if I hear from the police again, I'm to call him right away and not speak to them until he arrives. Isn't that nice? Detective Simmonds told me I'm not to leave Rudolph without telling her where I'm going. I guess that's in case they need any more evidence from me. I'm staying at Kyle's until they catch the killer. He told Detective Simmonds I need round-the-clock protection in case the real killer thinks I can identify him. She said they don't have the budget for that. Mr. Casey said it wasn't necessary, but Kyle insisted if the police wouldn't protect me, he would. Kyle's such a darling, so thoughtful, don't you agree, Merry?"

Darling has never been a word I'd use for Kyle Lambert, but if it made Jackie happy to think so, so be it.

Jackie could be self-absorbed, a bit of a scatterbrain some-times (okay, a lot of a scatterbrain much of the time) but she wasn't an idiot. She must have realized by the direction of Simmonds's questions she was considered to be a heck of a lot more than a potential witness, and Tom Casey would have told her what was what. But if it suited her to ignore all that and believe otherwise, I wasn't going to correct her. I might have a word with Kyle, though. Kyle, on the other hand, was an idiot. But even he (especially he) was capable of manipulating a situation to his advantage. And what more of an advantage to him than to be seen by Jackie as her protector, saving her from the shortcomings of the police budget? "I'm glad you're okay. Why are you calling?"

"Do you need me to go into work? I'm scheduled for opening today. Detective Simmonds said the store will be closed until further notice, but I thought she might have told you something different."

"I haven't heard otherwise."

"Kyle says if I can't go to work because of an ongoing police investigation at your place of business, that's not my fault and I should still be paid for the full day."

I stifled a groan. Kyle—that idiot—made it sound as though the police were investigating my business practices or something. I hoped he wasn't going around town making it sound like that.

Then again, by now everyone knew what had happened anyway.

"You'll get paid," I said. Although I'd not have any income while the store was closed to customers.

"Great! Okay, Merry. Let me know when you need me back. I should warn you that my availability will be even less over the next couple of weeks now that I'm playing Mrs. Cratchit."

"Is that official? You have the part?"

"Yup." I could hear the pleasure in her voice. "Desmond called me last night. Isn't that great! I know I'm going to be fabulous in the role."

"Jackie, perhaps you shouldn't go around town being so excited about it. A woman died, don't forget."

She sighed. "Yeah, Merry. I haven't forgotten. You're right. I guess I just don't want to think of it that way. I can be happy to have the part without being happy at how it came about, can't I?"

"I suppose. I wouldn't let Detective Simmonds know you're happy, that's all."

"Mr. Casey told me to stop talking when she asked me about that."

"I'm glad to hear it."

"Anyway, as I'm not coming into work today, I need to see Irene about getting some changes made to the costume. I—"

"Can you sing, Jackie?"

"Sing? Yeah, kinda. I mean, how good a singer was Paula? Mrs. Cratchit is more of a talkie-singie role anyway. Do you think your mom will want to provide me with some private coaching? That'll be exciting. I bet I could learn to sing with a good teacher. I'll give her a call later. Oh, before I go, one other thing. You know Kyle's the photographer of record for the *Rudolph Gazette*, right?"

I knew Kyle took pictures the paper sometimes printed because they couldn't afford a staff photographer. Kyle got paid peanuts, but he was okay with that because he was, Russ had told me while putting air quotes around the words, *building his portfolio.* "Yes," I said.

"He'll be around the scene of the crime a lot today. In case the cops make a dramatic arrest or have a shoot-out with the suspect so he can be there as it happens."

"Jackie, the killer isn't going to come back to Mrs. Claus's. The police are taking forensic evidence, not setting a trap."

"You never know, Merry. You never know. Your mom and Paula didn't get on too well, did they?"

I hung up before I could tell her I'd dock her an hour's pay every time she so much as thought something like that.

As long as I was thoroughly awake, I stumbled out of bed and headed into the kitchen to put the coffee on. Yawning and stretching even more than I did, Mattie followed me. While the coffee was brewing, we went downstairs and I let him into the yard so he could have his morning sniff around the property to investigate overnight activity. A light snow had fallen, just a dusting, but it was a harbinger of things to come. It was bitterly cold, and I soon called to Mattie to come in. I gave him his breakfast and put bread in the toaster for mine. While I sipped my coffee and nibbled on thickly buttered toast, and Mattie checked the corners of the kitchen to see if he'd possibly overlooked a morsel, I opened my laptop to check for updates.

Nothing new either in the *Gazette's* online page or the police's official account. Nothing on Twitter but speculation and gossip. A lot of speculation and gossip. Some of it pretty far out there. I'd been told Paula was not a popular teacher, so I was pleased to see that the Twitter comments from her past and present students were polite and respectful. Some were perhaps over-the-top weepy and "grief-stricken," but that's normal enough these days when people freely express their emotions in public and, most importantly, want to be seen doing so.

I decided to get an early start on the day by doing what office work I could from home. I have access to most of my accounts from the laptop, so I was able to check on the status of items ordered but not yet delivered. Just over two weeks until

Christmas. I fervently hoped I'd have a store in which to display and sell the goods.

The winter sun was beginning to creep into the kitchen when Alan called. He's an early riser—the better to get into his workshop—but he knows I am not.

"Is everything okay?" I asked.

"Fine. Here anyway. I figured you'd be up early. You can't sleep when you have something on your mind, and what happened yesterday has to be on your mind. Am I right?"

"As you always are. I've been distracting myself by going over the orders I'm waiting for. I'm going to assume I can throw open the door of Mrs. Claus's to eager shoppers soon, and the Christmas season will progress as planned. I have you down for ten train sets, and I need them as soon as possible. They've been moving well. Also some of the angels and more of those necklaces, and several charcuterie boards in varying sizes. The boards can wait another week or so. They're popular with people who dash in at the last minute desperate for ideas for something to take to a dinner party with people they don't know well, or the family Christmas with relatives they only see once a year, if that."

"I'm on schedule. Ahead of schedule, in fact. As you're not going into work today, why don't you come around and pick up what I have? Save me a trip into town?"

"I can do that, but first I'd like to go to the store and see what's happening, if anything. I'll try and track down Diane Simmonds and beg her to let me know when I can reopen."

"Come for lunch. Bring Mattie. Dress warmly. You dress warmly. Not Mattie." He hung up.

I felt myself smiling. Alan was a man of few words. But what words he did use were always the right ones.

I returned my attention to my accounts.

* * *

At nine o'clock I was ready to head out. Mattie was also ready to head out, standing by the door, expression hopeful, tail and tongue wagging. But he was to be disappointed. I gave him a rub on the head and said, "I'll be back for you later."

I shoved him aside, which is never easy, and squeezed through the crack I'd made in the door. I didn't know what the day had in store for me, so I decided not to bring Mattie. Alan's place is about ten miles out of town; I'd have to come back for the car anyway, and I'd get the dog then.

Wendy, who lives in the other half of the second floor of Mrs. D'Angelo's house, was locking her own door when I came out, her daughter, Tina, in her arms. Tina was bundled up in so many clothes about all I could see was her pert nose. The little girl struggled to free herself and said, "Mattie?"

Wendy had told me Mattie was the first word Tina said. Even before Mama and Dadda. Wendy's husband, Steve, had pretended to be offended at that.

Or maybe he hadn't been pretending.

"I heard what happened," Wendy said. "I'm so sorry. You don't need trouble this close to Christmas."

"I don't need trouble anytime." We walked together to the stairs.

"Mattie!" Tina called as she passed my door.

"Is the play going to go ahead, do you know?" Wendy asked. "I hate to sound mercenary, but you can be sure Her Honor and the rest of the council are being precisely that." Wendy was a clerk at town hall. "The town's invested a lot in this play, and we know many people are coming here specifically to see it."

123

"What sort of investment? Money?"

Wendy laughed. "Are you kidding? No money, but they've been promoting it as an important part of the Christmas festivities. Now the Santa Claus parade is over, it's the centerpiece of the advertising campaign for the rest of the season. A lot of hopes are riding on this production, Merry. Last year's play was a huge flop. The hotels were still full Christmas week, but booking inquiries were down over the year before. Some people think that's because of the play. At least one hotel reported a cancellation specifically because the guests heard the play was no good so they decided to go elsewhere."

Wendy kept the stroller at the bottom of the stairs. She stuffed her squirming daughter into it and struggled to do up the straps. "You walking into town?"

"Yes. I need to check on the store, even if I'm not allowed inside yet."

"We'll come part of the way with you. We're going to my mom's for a late breakfast and holiday planning, then heading out to get started on our Christmas shopping." She saw the look on my face. "I'll save all the shopping I'd planned to do at Mrs. Claus's for next week."

"Thanks. Closed on a Saturday in December. It doesn't bear thinking about."

"Let's walk really, really fast. I'm late as it is. My mom's a stickler for punctuality. I cannot afford to be waylaid by Mrs. D."

I chuckled. We walked really, really fast, Wendy pushing the stroller ahead of her.

Cries of, "Merry! Wendy! If you have a moment . . . Wendy, is it true Sue-Anne's going to step into the role of Mrs. Cratchit?"

"I cannot imagine where she heard that one," Wendy said once we were out of danger.

"You don't think Sue-Anne has visions of stardom dancing in her head?"

"Not on the stage, no. I've heard a big time Broadway director is planning to attend opening night."

"That must be the person Desmond was talking about. Someone from his days in the city, he said."

"He's bringing people, and they've booked three rooms at the Yuletide. Sue-Anne will want to make a fuss over him. I think she's planning an after-party on opening night."

"The town can't afford to contribute to the play, but they can throw a party to impress some outsiders? How do my dad and Ralph feel about that?" Ralph Dickerson was the town's budget chief.

"It's unlikely they know yet. Unless they hear from unofficial sources." She gave me a wink and began to slow her pace. "This is our turn. You take care, Merry."

"You too." I waved my entire hand at Tina. "Bye! Bye!"

She gave me an enormous grin and enthusiastically waved five stubby fingers in return.

I carried on into town.

Margie Thatcher was standing at the window of the Nook when I passed. The look she gave me would have put Santa's reindeer off their food. For once I gave her some slack, because I was equally unhappy with the goings-on in the street. Yellow police tape was still strewn across the entrance to Mrs. Claus's. That would have a dampening effect on the mood of shoppers at this end of Jingle Bell Lane.

I went around to the alley to find the same situation there. With a sigh, I pulled out my phone and called Diane Simmonds.

"Merry," she said in greeting. In the background someone shouted at the printer.

"Detective. I'm at Mrs. Claus's and—"

"I trust you didn't go inside."

"I did not. I'm standing in the alley. It's cold out here. I'm calling to see if there are any developments. As in, when I can go inside my place of business, and more to the point, when can I open? It is the holiday season, you know, and I rely on making much of my yearly income—"

"Yes, yes. I'm well aware of your situation, Merry. I can assure you I've heard the same from other business owners at that side of town. Not to mention the mayor, who took pains to remind me of the importance of the holiday season to the health of the town's budget. A healthy town budget, she pointed out, means a healthy police budget." Detective Simmonds did not sound happy this morning. I took that to mean she had not made an arrest overnight. "I'm going over the preliminary forensic results right now. If I don't find anything that tells me otherwise, you can open tomorrow."

"Thank you."

"You might want to come in early."

"Why?"

"To clean up." She didn't bother to wish me a good day. She also hadn't given me the chance to ask if there were any further developments.

As I had several hours to kill before going to Alan's, I headed back to Jingle Bell Lane and made for Victoria's Bake Shoppe. I pushed open the door to be enveloped in the marvelous scents of fresh baking and good coffee. And the not so marvelous scent of wet wool drying. The place was full, every table taken, and a line waiting patiently at the takeout counter. The noise level was high as Marjorie, behind the cash, called out orders, diners chatted, cutlery clinked, and steam hissed from the industrial-sized espresso machines.

I took my place in line and while I waited, I carefully avoided looking at the high shelf where, once again, the best-in-parade trophy was prominently displayed. The two best-in-parade trophies, as we have a parade in July also, to celebrate Santa coming to Rudolph for his annual vacation by the lake. Vicky and Victoria's Bake Shoppe win the trophy almost every year. Mrs. Claus's Treasures never wins. Vicky insists it has nothing to do with the fact that she provides hot chocolate and fresh pastries for the judges to enjoy while they wait in the cold or the rain for the parade to pass.

This year I made the mistake of putting Alan's dog, Ranger, on my float to accompany Mattie. As we passed the judges' booth, on a flatbed pulled by George Mann's World War Two–era tractor, a squirrel chose that moment to break for cover and ran down a tree trunk and bolted across the street. Ranger's leash had been loosely looped around a cardboard pillar holding up the cardboard roof of the alpine rescue hut that was our theme this year. Mattie played the role of alpine rescue dog, complete with barrel tied around his neck. Let me just say that the chaos of Ranger jumping off the float, dragging the pillar behind him, the entire edifice collapsing, the children from my mom's singing classes alternately screaming or laughing (and thus not singing for the judges), me in my Mrs. Claus getup leaping off the flatbed in pursuit of the dog, and my mom trying to get the children under some sort of control, did not present the display in its best light. And thus, once again, Vicky's float emerged triumphant.

She tried not to gloat. Much.

Eventually it was my turn to be served. "One medium low-fat latte. One extra-large hot chocolate with as much whipped cream as allowed by law. One small blueberry muffin and one of the cinnamon and apple pastries, please. No, better make that two pastries."

"Having breakfast with your dad?" Marjorie, who's Vicky's aunt, asked.

"His reputation precedes him," I said.

I took the treats to Mom and Dad's house, hoping to find out if they knew of any further developments. Dad answered my knock on the kitchen door and gave me a welcoming grin. I held up the bag and the grin grew wider. "For me?"

"The muffin's mine." I knew not to bring baked goods for my mother. She never touched coffee either. I stepped into the house. Mom was at the kitchen table, scrolling through her iPad and sipping on a foul-smelling mug of her specially made herbal tea, supposedly good for the throat.

"You're up early," I said to her.

"Busy day. The adult chorus will be here shortly to work on the opening number. Which most definitely needs some work. The problem, Merry, with amateur theater—one of the many problems—is that people have jobs to go to. Today's Saturday, so this and tomorrow are the only days they can all get together outside of scheduled rehearsal times. The other problem with amateur theater is that a surprising number of them cannot sing. Not that that stops them from trying, bless their well-meaning little hearts." She sighed mightily. "I do my best."

I put the drinks on the table. "Someone implied yesterday that you might have . . . taken steps so Paula wouldn't spoil your reputation."

"If I cared about my musical reputation," Mom said, "I wouldn't have agreed to have anything to do with this thing in the first place. The very idea of *A Christmas Carol* as a musical is a travesty." She glanced up and gave Dad a warm smile. "In my opinion, anyway. Nevertheless, somehow, I got talked into it for the sake of Rudolph."

Dad smiled back at her. My parents were an odd match, perhaps proving the old adage that opposites attract.

His face turned serious when he looked at me. "Preposterous as the idea is, rumors such as that can focus police attention in directions they shouldn't go."

I gave him a nod.

Mom stood up. "Jackie O'Reilly, of all people, has asked to stay for a private lesson once the chorus practice has finished. Making silk purses out of sows' ears comes to mind." She left the kitchen, her iPad tucked under her arm.

When she was out of earshot, I asked, "Did Diane Simmonds come back? To question Mom about that accusation, I mean?"

Dad opened the bag and took out the pastries. He laid them on plates and we sat down. He took the lid off his hot chocolate and took a long drink. I sipped my latte and let him think. "She did not," he said at last. "I can only hope Diane knows the idea's as ridiculous as you and I do. If Jackie's coming here for singing lessons, does that mean she's no longer under suspicion?"

"Unfortunately she's still very much under suspicion. They don't have enough to charge or hold her, that's all. Tom Casey's representing her."

"Good man, Tom. Excellent lawyer."

I picked at my muffin. "I tried to tell Jackie she has to stop crowing about getting to play Mrs. Cratchit. Aside from the fact that it's in extremely bad taste, the chance to move up from understudy is the main reason she's under suspicion in the first place. I don't think she understands that she really is in trouble."

"You know I like Jackie a great deal, honeybunch, but she's not always as in tune to currents swirling around her as perhaps she should be. In fairness, people can sometimes be willfully blind to things they'd prefer not to think about. If I was your mother, I'd launch into a tale of some soprano, or maybe a tenor, who was about to be sacked and refused to accept it. But I am not, so is anything else happening with you?"

"On the good news front, I can open the store tomorrow. Should be able to open the store, that is, if nothing else comes up."

"Good to know. You don't need the loss of income, and any town trying to promote itself as a family-friendly holiday destination doesn't need crime scene tape strung across storefront doors and people scurrying past with eyes averted while muttering dark words."

"Sorta like the sidewalk in front of Scrooge and Marley must have been?"

"Precisely," Dad said. "Now, there's an idea for the set design for the opening scene. Minus the crime scene tape."

We ate and drank in silence for a few minutes.

"The thing is, Dad, someone killed Paula Monahan. Mom didn't do it. Jackie didn't do it. But someone did. I've been thinking it over."

"I didn't doubt you would, honeybunch."

"I don't know any of the other people involved well enough to know why one of them would want to kill her. It might not have had anything to do with the production. The woman had another life. She was a high school teacher. She had marriage problems. Her husband's left her, but Simmonds says he has an alibi."

"Alibis can be faked."

"True, but I think Detective Simmonds is a good enough cop to break a fake one."

"The end of a marriage is often a dangerous time for women," Dad said. "Is it possible the husband, Kevin is it, hired someone to do the deed? While he was establishing this alibi?"

"I didn't consider that, but it's possible, I suppose. Lots of things are possible. How much does a hit man cost, do you think? Something Kevin Monahan could afford?"

"I'm pleased to be able to tell you I have absolutely no idea what the going rate for a hit man is. I'd assume, as with most things, it varies by the quality and experience of the service provider. A professional with a good reputation, probably a lot. A drinking buddy who owes you a big favor—maybe not much at all."

"I'm wondering if it's possible Paula might not have been the intended victim."

Dad studied me over the top of his mug. A trace of whipped cream graced his upper lip. "Go ahead."

"I only interacted with the players a couple of times, but from what I could see, almost everyone was angry at Catherine. Except for Dave, for what I assume are reasons of his own."

Dad nodded. "Your mother told me it is not a happy set. As we saw yesterday when they gathered here. Back to Catherine, what are you thinking?"

"Paula and Catherine don't look at all similar, but they are about the same height and weight. Same shade of hair color. Seen from the back, both of them in black winter coats? Catherine was going up and down the street with her flyers, so it was possible she'd return to Mrs. Claus's at some time that afternoon. Did the killer get the wrong person?"

"That might be something to mention to Diane. The Renshaws are new to Rudolph, and I don't know much about them. Why don't I—?"

Dad broke off when his phone rang. He took it out of his pocket, glanced at the display, pulled a face, raised an eyebrow at me, mouthed "Ralph. Have to take it." He answered and said, "Good morning, Ralph, how are—"

A torrent of words poured down the line. I caught something about excessive expenditure, private ambition, out of line, and the looming threat of bankruptcy.

"It's Saturday, Ralph," Dad said. "I'm relaxing with my daughter and enjoying a delicious baked treat from Vicky Casey's place. Do we have to talk about this now?"

"Yes!" came through loud and clear. "I've called an emergency meeting of the budget committee. My house. Half an hour."

Dad blinked and put the phone away. "Looks like I have to go out, honeybunch. Sue-Anne has an idea for promoting the theatrical production, and Ralph is . . . shall we say not entirely sure it's a good one."

"Wendy told me about that this morning. Sue-Anne wants to put on a reception for the visiting bigwigs. Word got around fast."

"Did Wendy doubt it would? This is Rudolph after all." Dad popped the last of his pastry into his mouth. "Thanks for this. As for what we were talking about, don't get involved, Merry. Let Diane sort it out. It's what she does. I trust she told you the same?"

"She might have mentioned it in passing."

Chapter Nine

I detoured home via Jingle Bell Lane, to once again check out the situation at my store. Yellow tape still in place. Passersby still eyeing the storefront warily. Margie Thatcher still throwing daggers at me through the dusty main window of the Nook. Kyle Lambert lounging against a parking meter, camera around his neck, idly checking his phone.

I decided to take all that as good news. As long as the cops were not squealing to a halt on the sidewalk and pouring through my doors in search of fresh evidence, I should be able to open as planned.

"Hi, Kyle," I said. "Looks like not much is happening."

He shrugged. Kyle was a beanpole of a guy with a sunken chest, weak chin, and small eyes that regarded the world, and everyone in it, with suspicion. Upon prematurely leaving high school, he'd tried his hand as an artist. When that failed—totally and completely even in a town where his parents knew everyone, because he had not a speck of talent—he decided to take up photography with the help of a secondhand camera. In the meantime, he painted houses, filled in at the newspaper sometimes, and waited for his big break. Which, considering he was as lazy as he was untalented, wasn't likely to ever happen. Not in a field that competitive. "Yeah. Pretty quiet. I was hoping for some activity, like something that would make a great picture. But . . . nothin'. Not even any cops keeping people back."

"How long are you planning to stand here?"

"Huh?"

"I mean, the police have got all they need and left."

His eyes moved to his phone, bored with my conversation. "Not much longer, I guess."

"Where's Jackie?"

"She's gone for her singing lesson. 'Cause of her bein' in the play like, and now having a solo part. She's staying at my place. We think it's safer for her to be there, instead of alone at her place. Safer, in case the real killer comes after her next."

"But she was alone earlier?"

He tore his eyes away from his phone. "Huh?"

"Alone. Walking through the streets to go to her singing lesson. Earlier at your apartment. While you're here, waiting for the Pulitzer-winning shot."

"Oh. Yeah. Do you think the killer knows where I live?"

"I think maybe you should stop frightening Jackie, Kyle." I tried to choose my words carefully. "It's fine to be . . . concerned about her. But don't go too overboard. She'll be fine at her own place. The police will make an arrest soon."

A myriad of expressions crossed his face. Agreement with me, then uncertainty, followed by calculation as he tried to decide what was in his own best interests, and then a flash of concern as he finally thought about Jackie's best interests, circling back to agreement. He nodded. "Yeah, I guess. You are going to pay her for the missed day, right? I told her it'd be the right thing to do."

My phone buzzed with a text. "Gotta take this," I said to Kyle. "Have a nice day."

"Yeah, thanks." He lifted his camera and snapped a picture of me as I turned to walk away. The yellow police tape stretched across the doors to Mrs. Claus's Treasures would feature prominently in the photo, as would the store logo in the window. I did not want to ever see that picture in the pages of the *Rudolph Gazette* or, even worse, on Twitter.

I checked the text. Vicky: *Mark has a couple of sous-chefs off sick. Has to go in for dinner service tonight, so our date is off. Feel like pizza and bad movie at your place?*

Me: *Sounds like a plan*
Vicky: *I'll decide on the movie. You order the pizza*
Me: 👍

*   *   *

Mattie and I headed for Alan's shortly before noon. As we drove out of town, I told myself I was happy for the break. A whole day off, and in the runup to Christmas as well. Breakfast with Dad, lunch with Alan, dinner with Vicky. What a perfect day.

So I told myself anyway.

Alan lives about ten miles out of town, in a gorgeous nineteenth-century stone farmhouse situated at the end of a long lane, lined by ancient oaks and maples, now winter-bare. The house boasts three levels, a wide, welcoming wraparound porch, and miles of ornate gingerbread trim. The farm itself is long gone, the fields quickly reclaimed by woodland, and the lower level of the old red wooden barn converted to serve as Alan's workshop.

I parked next to the barn and opened the back door of the car. Mattie leapt out with as much enthusiasm as he ever shows.

He loves Alan's place, he loves Alan, and he loves all the marvelous scents in the woods surrounding the house. He doesn't love Ranger quite so much, but he tolerates the smaller, and far more rambunctious, dog.

Alan and Ranger came out of the house to meet us on the porch. At this time of year, the porch is stacked high with cords of good firewood in anticipation of the full strength of winter still to come. Ranger leapt up and down, yipping in an excess of excitement. He's a Jack Russell and excess excitement is his entire nature. He sniffed my boots, ran in circles around my legs, and then headed toward Mattie for more greetings. Mattie woofed in warning; Ranger decided discretion was the better part of valor and he hurried to sniff at the wheels of my car. I climbed the steps, and Alan gave me a kiss and wrapped me in a hug.

"Hard to believe," he said with a laugh, "those two are the same species."

"Good thing they're both males, or who knows what they might produce," I said.

"Ready to go?"

"Yup."

Alan's bulging backpack was waiting by the door. He put on his boots and coat and we called to the dogs and set off. It was bitterly cold, but the sun shone in a clear blue sky, and we were properly dressed for the weather. Alan had cleared some trails through the woods on his property, leading to a small stream tumbling north toward Lake Ontario. He and I walked slowly, holding mittened hands, enjoying the peace of the early winter woods. Almost all the leaves were gone now, the bare branches of the trees converted into sculptural silhouettes. Twigs, mulch, dying vegetation, and the residue of last night's light snowfall crunched under our feet. Ranger ran ahead, checking out everything, running back to encourage us to walk faster, and then dashing off again. Squirrels headed for shelter and dead twigs snapped as he passed. Mattie lumbered happily along behind us, occasionally stopping to smell something not far off the path. Mattie and Ranger were roughly the same age. Mattie topped the scales at around a hundred and fifty pounds. Ranger might be twenty pounds soaking wet, immediately after a big meal.

I always laugh to see them together.

After about a half an hour of walking, meandering up and down the trails, in no hurry to get anywhere, we reached the creek, gurgling happily as it flowed over rocks heading for the big lake. Alan had constructed a makeshift picnic table out of odds and ends of scarred or leftover wood and brought it here to create the perfect private picnic spot. In spring it was a riot of bright green vegetation and early wildflowers, in the summer thickly shaded in deep greens, in the fall a kaleidoscope of orange, scarlet, and rust. Even on the coldest winter days, the creek was so fast moving it rarely froze over.

Alan unpacked the picnic while Ranger explored the banks of the creek, Mattie rested from his endeavors, and I made myself comfortable and watched Alan work. He was a great picnic chef. Today he'd brought homemade onion soup, thick and fragrant, kept piping hot in Thermoses, hearty ham and cheese sandwiches, and crispy raw carrots accompanied by a spicy dip. Apples and chocolate chip cookies provided dessert and tea out of another Thermos our drinks. The dogs got water and a rawhide bone each. Even Ranger settled down to chew on his bone. Mattie made sure his was well protected.

"Want to talk about what happened?" Alan asked after we'd savored the first delicious sips of soup and bites of sandwiches.

"At the store yesterday? I feel like I've never stopped talking about it. First to Detective Simmonds, then to Mom and Dad, Vicky, and the half of Rudolph who didn't hear the story from someone else."

"I meant talk about how you're feeling. Your dad called me this morning, you know."

"I'm not surprised to hear that."

"Mabel D'Angelo phoned me last night."

"That I am surprised to hear. What did she want? How does she know your number anyway?"

"How does Mabel know anything? The secret network. Her and that bunch would put the CIA and the FBI to shame, if only they'd concentrate on facts rather than exaggeration and conjecture."

"And if the Russian mob and international terrorists operated out of Rudolph."

"That too."

"What did you tell her?"

"I played dumb. It wasn't hard." I swatted him with my napkin. "I told her I didn't know anything about it."

He lowered his spoon and studied my face. "Are you okay, Merry?"

"Yes, Alan. I am. If I wasn't, I know I have you with me."

"And your parents. And Vicky and Mark. Jackie too, although you don't know it. Half of Rudolph, come to that."

My heart might have swelled, just a little bit.

"I'm fine," I said when I could speak again. I scraped up the last of the soup. "I'm worried Jackie's going to talk herself straight into a charge of murder and someone else is going to talk my mom into one."

"What does all that mean?"

I told him my concerns.

"As for your mom," he said. "Let them try. As for Jackie, you're overthinking it, Merry. Simmonds knows how to read people like her, and she won't make a move without solid, concrete evidence. No one saw Jackie going into the store after Paula, right?"

"So far, no one's said so. As far as I know, anyway."

He tossed the last bite of his sandwich into his mouth. "Ready to get back? I'd like to stay longer, but I have work to do. I have an extremely demanding customer to make happy." He gave me a wink. "I'll help you load those items you ordered into your car."

Chapter Ten

"We've seen that one," I said to Vicky.

"We have? Are you sure?"

"I'm sure. About six months ago. We both hated it."

"Which," she said, "is why it's suitable for bad movie night."

"Too suitable. Find something else."

She pointed the control at the TV and flicked rapidly through the available offerings displayed on the screen. "How about this one?"

"No. It's supposed to be good."

"Is that a bad thing?"

"It is for bad movie night."

Vicky threw the control at me. "You choose something." She leaned back into the couch cushions, tucked her long legs under her, and picked up her glass of wine. Mattie snoozed in his bed on the floor, and Sandbanks, Vicky's ancient golden lab, rested his head on her lap.

I scrolled idly through the movie offerings on the various streaming services. "How's the old guy doing?"

"You mean Mark?"

"No, I mean Sandbanks and you know it."

She rubbed his ears. He grunted. "He keeps going. He's happy. He eats well, and sometimes he can summon enough energy to chase a bird out of the yard. If the bird's not too big and not too determined to keep his place."

I kept scrolling. The downstairs doorbell rang and I went to get it. As expected, it was the pizza delivery guy. He handed me the enormous cardboard box, warm from the food inside. I said, "Thank you," gave him a handsome tip, and skipped back upstairs. I got plates and paper towels from the kitchen and dropped the box onto the coffee table. Vicky and I dug in, pulling long strands of gooey hot cheese onto our plates.

"Yummy." Vicky said. "You don't want to watch a movie tonight, do you?"

"Not really."

"Things on your mind, I'd assume."

"Can't stop thinking about what happened."

When Vicky first arrived, she'd told me the latest gossip as related by her customers to her staff and from them to her.

In short, nothing new. No one knew of any reason why someone would want to do away with Paula Monahan. She wasn't a popular teacher, but there were worse, and no one had killed Mr. Saunderson, the math teacher. Not yet anyway. Paula and Kevin's marriage was on the skids, but people generally liked Kevin more than Paula so his innocence was predetermined. A customer had mentioned that it was too bad young Eddie Monahan hadn't been taken out instead of his mother and the abrupt silence falling over their table indicated the speaker had gone too far.

"Okay," Vicky said around a mouthful of pizza piled high with the things she liked: mushrooms, onions, red peppers, hot peppers, pepperoni, *and* sausage. "As you can't stop thinking about it, let's talk about it. Have you considered it might not have mattered who the victim was? Could it have been a random thing?"

"You mean we have a deranged killer running loose in Rudolph? They attacked a woman in broad daylight in a Christmas-themed store on the main street of your Year-Round Christmas Destination in the weeks leading up to Christmas? No, I have not considered that, and you can be sure if you mention it to anyone else, Sue-Anne, along with my dad and all the other town councilors, probably helped by the police chief, will ensure you never see the light of day again. I've heard rumors the dungeon beneath town hall is soundproof and the food is not catered by the best restaurants."

Vicky ignored my sarcasm. "That isn't what I meant. I meant random as in randomly chosen from a select group. Such as the cast and crew of the theater players."

"That makes no more sense than a random killer in general. Want another drink?"

She handed me her empty glass and helped herself to a third slice of pizza. "Hear me out," she said as I went into the kitchen. "Paula didn't have a particularly important role in the play. It's a small-town, amateur effort. Not as though this is Broadway or the West End, where people specifically buy tickets to see Hugh Jackman or Benedict Cumberbatch and might not come if their star can't put in the appearance. Meaning, no one had reason to kill Paula Monahan if they wanted to stop the play. But—" she paused dramatically, half-eaten slice of pizza in the air.

I put the refilled glass in her free hand and dropped onto the couch. "But?"

"Suppose someone did want to stop the play. Prevent it being put on. In order to do so, this nefarious person hoped to cause enough commotion and disruption the show would not go on."

"But the show is going on."

"That the plan failed to achieve its aim doesn't mean it wasn't attempted."

I leaned against the cushions and thought. "I suppose that's possible. But really, Vicky, who would go to that sort of trouble to sabotage an amateur theater production?"

"I can think of only one person—" She paused dramatically. "Or group of people."

"No."

"What do you mean, no? I haven't told you what I'm thinking."

"You have an obsession with the Muddites, Vicky. You see their hand behind every bad thing that ever happens in Rudolph. If we get freezing rain or an unexpected warm spell on Christmas Eve, you suspect they have a secret weather-changing installation hidden under town hall."

"You exaggerate. Please remember the saying, 'Just because you're paranoid, doesn't mean they aren't out to get you.' The Muddites hate us."

Vicky was referring to the people of the neighboring town, the awkwardly named Muddle Harbor. Like Rudolph, Muddle Harbor had once been a thriving industrial and shipping town. Unlike Rudolph, it had not been able to find something else to keep business going and the community prosperous once the major industry closed down. In my dad's opinion, the main reason Muddle Harbor couldn't move on is rather than try to come up with intelligent solutions to a difficult, but not unusual these days, problem, they preferred to blame all their misfortune on the townsfolk of Rudolph. They have been known to refer to us as "those blasted deer-people."

"Hate's a strong word, Vicky. Mayor Baumgartner and some of the townspeople came to the theater picnic. They smiled and made friendly. Surely they know any overflow from Rudolph's success will spill their way."

"Knowing and *knowing*, are two different things. Baumgartner doesn't want spillover. He wants Muddle Harbor to be the most important town in this part of the state. Remember the fiasco when they tried to fashion themselves as Easter Town?"

"Sadly yes. But—"

"No buts about it. It would be just like the Muddites to attempt to sabotage the centerpiece of Christmas week in Rudolph. Tomorrow's Sunday. You don't open the store until noon, and I can ask Marjorie to come in early. We ride for Muddle Harbor at dawn."

"I can't stop you from going, Vicky, but I won't come with you. The idea's ridiculous."

She helped herself to another piece of pizza and said nothing more about it.

* * *

Not quite dawn, but at quarter to nine I was standing in a patch of weak winter sunlight on the sidewalk waiting for Vicky to pick me up. Temperatures had dropped further overnight, and Mrs. D'Angelo had been spreading de-icer on her path and driveway when I emerged, still grumbling. She'd spread so much de-icer, I wondered if the stores had enough left for everyone else.

"Good morning, Merry," my landlady said cheerfully. She was thoroughly bundled up in a calf-length puffy pink coat, green woolen hat with a pom-pom on top, and purple mittens. "A cold but nice day. Always the best, I say."

"Morning."

"No snow in the forecast yet, but there's still time to get some before Christmas arrives. It's not Christmas without snow,

I always say. You're off bright and early, I see. Early for a Sunday, anyway. You normally like to have a nice relaxing morning on Sundays before going to the store. You must be pleased the police are allowing you to open again."

I didn't ask how she knew that. Mrs. D'Angelo had a "source" inside the police department, as well as at least one in town hall. Mrs. D'Angelo usually knows what's going on in the corridors of what passes for power in our little town before the mayor or chief of police do.

"Don't have Matterhorn with you, today? You mustn't be heading off for a walk or going into the store," she said, her eyes bright with interest.

"I'm meeting Vicky," I confessed.

"Oh, yes. Dear Vicky Casey. Such a lovely girl. I'm pleased she turned out so well, considering the history of the Casey family in this area. Her father excepted, of course. Any further developments between her and Chef Mark?" Mrs. D'Angelo eyed me carefully, no doubt waiting for a twitch of the eyebrow or something else she could use to report to her friends that a wedding was in the air. I hated to disappoint her. Correct that: I didn't hate to disappoint her in the least.

"Not that I know of," I said.

She hid her disappointment well. "I myself am going shopping later. I need a new dress for the official party." She waited for me to ask what party that might be.

"What party might that be?"

"Didn't you hear, dear? The mayor and town council are putting on an official invitation-only event following the opening night performance of *A Christmas Carol*. Everyone who's someone in town is going to be there. You haven't been invited?"

"My invitation must be lost in the mail."

"Donalda Schwartz got hers." Mrs. D'Angelo's face drooped ever so slightly at the confession, but then she perked up. "Naturally mine can't be far behind. I'm so busy these days, I can't wait for official notice before I search for something suitable to wear. Forewarned is forearmed."

"Here Vicky comes now," I said. "Have a nice day."

I leapt into the bakery van before it had time to come to a full stop. Vicky pulled away in a squeal of tires.

The first time we'd gone to Muddle Harbor on one of Vicky's "investigations," we'd been incognito. Our identity had been uncovered within minutes of our arrival, so we no longer bothered. Thus she picked me up in the white van clearly marked with the Victoria's Bake Shoppe name and logo.

I'd been adamant last night I was not going to stick my nose into the police investigation. So there. In particular I was not going to Muddle Harbor on some wild goose chase hoping to catch the mayor and town *burgermeisters* and *burgermeistrsses* plotting our demise.

Yet, here I was, tearing out of town on a freezing cold Sunday morning in a rickety (but pleasant smelling) old delivery van when I could have been asleep in my warm bed before rising to enjoy the luxury of a long leisurely breakfast.

Detective Simmonds had quite forcefully told me to stay out of it, and I'd been determined to do so. But such is easier said than done. The police investigation should be none of my business. Whatever happened in Paula Monahan's life that someone would kill her, was none of my business. I scarcely knew the woman. But she'd been killed in my store—and that meant, in Vicky's mind, anyway—the killer had made it my business.

I was forced to agree. As long as Jackie and my mother were under suspicion, however flimsy any case against them might be, it was my business.

Such was my reasoning to myself. Vicky never minds interfering in things that are none of her business.

"Okay," I said now. "What's the plan?"

"We'll go in open-minded and work from there."

"Meaning you don't have a plan. I thought you were going to come up with a plan."

"Spontaneous is always better."

"Not in my life. Acting under the assumption we're going to the Muddle Harbor Café, center of all activity in that town, I didn't have breakfast." Perhaps the only reason I agreed to come on this expedition was to have breakfast at the aforementioned café. They served a real American diner breakfast—fried foods, strong hot coffee, and plenty of both.

Vicky made a poor attempt to suppress a shudder. "I dare not think. I'll have some of your toast, to be friendly like as we work our wiles on them." Vicky, I knew, would have far more than my toast and would gobble up my bacon at the same time as she explained the relationship between heart disease and cholesterol and fat. A idea which, somehow, never seemed to occur to her when she was eating pizza.

The Muddle Harbor Café was gossip central in that town. If we were going to find out what was going on—not that I thought anything was—we'd start there.

Vicky began to slow as we approached Muddle Harbor. The sun was shining as it only can in winter, clearing the air and making the cold clean and invigorating. As we drove down Main Street, a bank of dark clouds passed overhead, turning the cold simply cold.

The shops were all closed, many of them permanently. "For rent" signs hung in papered-over windows, next to doors needing a good coat of paint. Limp wreaths and burnt-out bulbs hung from the scraggy trees, and many of the Christmas decorations in the store windows looked, to my experienced eye, cheap, tawdry, and too much used.

"I honestly don't know why they bother," Vicky said as she pulled into a parking spot. "Hey! I've got a fabulous idea. You could offer to help them spruce up the downtown. Hire yourself out as a design consultant."

"Because they'll be so favorably inclined toward me after I demand to know if they killed an innocent woman to make Rudolph look bad. Sometimes, Vicky, you don't always think things through."

"Sure I do. I also plan for contingencies. Judging by all these cars, my plan's working. The café's busy."

She was right about that. In an otherwise empty street, the block in front of the restaurant was full of cars and pickup trucks. Vicky and I got out of the van and approached our destination. The windows of the Muddle Harbor Café were decorated for Christmas, and although the decor might not be to my taste, they'd gone to some trouble. The decorations weren't covered in dust, and the blinking lights all worked.

We pushed open the door and were immediately enveloped in the scent of strong, hot coffee and frying bacon and pancakes. Winter coats were slung over the backs of chairs or hung on hooks by the door. The restaurant was almost full.

I'd like to say all conversation died and everyone turned narrow, suspicious eyes onto us. Instead they ignored us, except for the waitress who called, "If it isn't the pride of Rudolph, Vicky Casey. And her friend. Sorry hon, I forgot your name."

"Merry."

"Merry, right. Noel Wilkinson's daughter. Look Randy, John, Vicky, and Merry are here. The usual for you girls? Or would you prefer pancakes today? The Sunday special. A sky-high stack of buttermilk pancakes served with an extra side of bacon or sausage, plenty of butter, and enough real maple syrup to drown a duck."

"My arteries are closing as we speak," Vicky muttered.

"No thank you," I said. "I'll have two poached eggs, please."

"Two poached eggs, soft, with bacon *and* sausage. Side of mushrooms and onions. Hash browns done to the point of being burned. Wheat toast and coffee. Comin' up."

My mouth watered, and I might have rubbed my hands together in anticipation. Janice, owner and head waitress of the Muddle Harbor Café, had a prodigious memory. That was exactly the way I liked my all-American diner breakfast.

"Muddy water and dry cereal, for you, hon?" she said to Vicky.

"I'll share Merry's toast," my friend replied.

Formalities over, we looked around the room. Longtime married couples read their newspapers or phones and paid no attention to each other. A group of young mothers bounced toddlers on their knee or rocked strollers as they enjoyed their weekly breakfast outing. A family dressed in their Sunday best, ranging in age from mid-90s to infant, had taken a large table. Three men in ball caps, heavy sweaters, and thick pants shoveled pancakes into their mouths. Ice fishermen, I guessed.

The group seated around the center table were the only ones paying us any attention, while they tried to pretend they weren't. Dirty plates had been pushed to one side, crumpled paper serviettes tossed on the table, coffee mugs refilled. Five men, including Mayor Baumgartner and Janice's brother, John Benedict, the real estate agent. They'd been joined by someone I hadn't expected to see: Dave French, Jacob Marley himself. He had a cup of coffee and an open laptop computer on the table in front of him. Jack and the man next to him were reading the screens of their iPads. Randy Baumgartner , still old school, had a pad of yellow legal paper and a pen.

Janice began clearing the used dishes. "I, for one, think it's a good idea," she said. "What with the renewed interest in tourism in this part of the state we'd be wise to be ready."

Pointedly she didn't mention that all the renewed tourism came via Rudolph as she carried her loaded tray into the kitchen.

"Hi," Vicky said, approaching the men's table, huge smile slapped into place. "Nice to see you all. Having a nice meeting?" She craned her neck to read the mayor's notes.

"Yes," Dave said.

"Mighty productive." Baumgartner pointedly put his hand on top of the paper. "I'm sure you'll agree, Ted."

Ted was an older guy, and I'd never seen him before. Well into his eighties, hair thin and a greasy gray, eyes dull, face dark and lined with a lifetime of work he hadn't got much pleasure out of. His clothes, faded, with ground-in dirt, also showed a lifetime of work. "Like I said, my daddy built that place."

"And it'll soon be in the grave, like your daddy." Dave slammed shut the cover of his laptop. He drained his coffee. "You have my offer, and you know how to reach me."

"We'll work something out," John Benedict said.

"You better!" Janice yelled as she came out of the kitchen. "Are you two girls going to take seats or do you want to eat your breakfast standing up?" She didn't wait for an answer before pouring coffee into a mug at a place at the counter.

"It's the best deal you're going to get, Ted," Randy said. "A good deal for Muddle Harbor, too."

"Don't much care if it's good for Muddle Harbor." Ted lumbered slowly to his feet and grabbed his coat—fabric torn, hem frayed, buttons missing, mud-streaked—off the back of his chair. "I'll talk it over with the wife." He walked out.

"As good as done then." Mayor Baumgartner rubbed his hands together.

"What does that mean?" Dave asked.

"Ted's wife makes the decisions in that family. Always has. She keeps sayin' how it's time for them to move to Florida. She wants to buy a trailer in the park where her sister lives, but they don't have the money. Not yet. The property's as good as sold. You can count on that." The mayor stood up and held out his hand.

Dave shook it. "I hope so. I don't have an unlimited amount of time, plenty of other deals out there." He reached for his own coat.

"Poached eggs up!" Janice yelled, coming out of the kitchen carrying a laden plate, delicious aromas rising from it.

Oh, my gosh, that all looked so good.

"I forgot an important appointment!" Vicky yelled back. "Merry, pay the lady. We have to go."

"What? I haven't had my breakfast."

"You can have something at my place."

"But you don't do bacon and poached eggs."

"Can't be helped. You can thank me later. Dave, hold on a sec." She ran after him. "I've a question about the production of *A Christmas Carol*."

I put a twenty-dollar bill on the counter and gave Janice an awkward smile. "Sorry."

"Your friend's mighty weird. I'd worry about her except all you folks over in Rudolph can be mighty weird." She scooped the money up and didn't bother to offer me change.

"Shall I see you at the reception, Merry?" Mayor Baumgartner asked me. "I trust your parents are planning to attend."

"Reception?"

"The opening night reception for *A Christmas Carol*, which Sue-Anne is organizing. Naturally she's invited all the dignitaries from the surrounding communities. I hear a state senator will be coming."

"In that case, I'll come with you," Jack said. "I need to talk to the senator about getting that highway to come closer to the east end of town. Plenty of people ready to build houses on land out there if it does. Don't know why no one in Albany answers my calls about it."

I found Vicky and Dave French on the sidewalk outside the café, zipping up coats and pulling on gloves. A man approached us, walking a black Lab. Man and dog gave us suspicious looks and quickly crossed the street. If Muddle Harbor hoped to be a tourist destination, they had to get over that innate distrust of strangers.

"Paula's death hasn't set things back too much," Vicky was saying to Dave when I joined them. "Regarding the production, I mean?"

Dave tightened the wool scarf around his neck. The wind whistling down Main Street was sharp and bitterly cold. "The show must go on, as they say. Have a nice day." He set off down the street.

Vicky and I followed. I let Vicky do the talking—it's what she does best sometimes.

"Merry and I often come to Muddle Harbor for Sunday breakfast. It's nice living in a town where everyone knows you and your family, isn't it, but we need a break sometimes."

"Seems to me you're well enough known here. As for breakfast, you didn't have any." He looked both ways before crossing the street, as we had been taught in kindergarten. No cars were coming so he stepped off the sidewalk. Vicky did not look both ways before following. I scurried after them. After looking both ways.

"It's more about the outing than the eating. A girl has to watch her weight, you know," said Vicky, who did not know any such thing.

Dave shoved his hand in his pocket and his car, a ten-year-old Toyota Corolla, flashed its lights in greeting. "I guess I'll see you two back in town." He didn't sound as though that was something he was particularly looking forward to.

"As I said, we come here most Sundays," Vicky replied cheerfully. "I've never seen you here before, though. First time to Muddle Harbor, Dave?"

His eyes narrowed and he turned to look at her. I wasn't sure if he was getting suspicious at the direction her chatter was taking, or if he was simply not interested in standing in the cold engaging in said chatter. "Not had the time before. Or the interest." He glanced up and down the street—at the boarded-up shop fronts, the empty parking bays, the erratically flashing festive lights. He put his hand on the car door.

"If you don't mind my asking," Vicky said.

His look indicated that he did mind, but he was too polite to say so.

"I'm wondering what brought you here today. Looked like business, rather than a social gathering. John Benedict is in real estate, and I heard something about selling property." She gave him the full strength of her totally innocent smile.

He didn't smile back.

"My family's very connected, you know," she continued, undeterred. "The Caseys have been in Rudolph since its founding, and there are a heck of a lot of us. Merry's father is just about "Mr. Rudolph" himself as far as everyone's concerned. We're always on the lookout for business opportunities, aren't we Merry?"

"We are? I mean, absolutely. Always on the lookout. As scouts, she means. For our families' interests."

"You're in hotels, right?" Vicky persisted. "Must be super interesting."

"Not so as you'd notice. Yeah, hotels. Hotel. One motel, if you insist. My folks own the Carolers' Motel in Rudolph."

"Nice place," I said.

"Not so as you'd notice," he repeated. He shook his head. "My dad had a stroke last year, and Mom's not up to managing the place herself. I came back to help them out. It was supposed to be a temporary thing, until Dad recovered. But . . . it's dragging on. And on. Frankly, I want them to sell it, but they won't hear of it. Dad insists he'll be back on his feet any day now." He let out a puff of air. "Not gonna happen. He's fooling himself, and he won't hear a word I say about selling it. Meanwhile, I'm stuck being the dutiful son and managing the dump. So I thought, long as I'm here, I might as well make the best of a bad situation and look into expanding."

"Expanding into Muddle Harbor," Vicky said. "Great idea."

"If I can get the price down on that firetrap of a place on the highway, I can put some money into fixing it up. Not going to turn it into a luxury resort and spa, but at least I can make it a slight bit better than the local version of a Bates Motel it is now. Old guy thinks he's driving a hard bargain." Dave smiled for the first time all day. "He's gonna fold like a paper napkin. Who knows, maybe it'll be the start of the French hotel empire. Something to rival the Hiltons."

"They started out with one small budget hotel," Vicky said.

"Is that true?" I asked.

"How would I know? That's not the point. So maybe it'll all work out okay for you, Dave?"

"Okay? Not what I wanted out of life but if this deal works out, it'll do temporarily. Give my parents some extra income, so Dad will get off my case. Finally. I was at loose ends anyway. Ugly divorce, career not going anywhere. I was ready for a new start, looking for opportunities to get my career back on track, when Dad got sick." His face twisted. "My father and I never have gotten on. He doesn't approve of my choices in life and has never hesitated to tell me so. I might not have come back to help him out, but Mom asked me to, and . . . What else could I do?"

"Divorced, are you?" Vicky asked.

The look on his face softened, and something twinkled in the depths of his eyes. "Interested?"

"Me?" She giggled in a very un-Vicky-like way. "I'm taken. Merry is too, sorry. I have girlfriends and cousins, lots of cousins, if you get my meaning." She winked.

He cracked a grin. "I might be. I wasn't brought up here. My folks moved to Rudolph when I was in college, when they bought the motel. It's not always easy, moving to a small town at my age. Getting to know people, I mean. People have their own circles of interests and friends already. I'm trying to be active in the community. Because I can sing and I have some acting experience, I figured the players would be a good start." His face fell and his voice dropped. "To be honest, I hoped to meet women. Not a lot of single women in a small town like this. I thought they might gravitate to something like amateur theater."

I was absolutely freezing, just standing here in the wind. I considered suggesting we go back to the café to continue our chat, or at least seek the shelter of a storefront, but I figured that might ruin the mood. Dave was chatting comfortably now, Vicky leading him on.

"Instead, they're all old or married. Most of them old *and* married. Either that or high school kids."

"Terrible about Paula. Do you have any thoughts about what might have happened?"

I heard voices calling goodbye and looked across the street. Mayor Baumgartner and his party were leaving the café. They shook hands on the sidewalk, headed for their own cars, and drove away.

"Nope. I didn't know Paula at all. Outside the group, that is." Dave laughed without humor. "Believe me, I had no interest in getting to know her better. The way she dragged that talentless kid around after her, always nagging Catherine or Desmond to give him a bigger part. She saw herself as a stage mother, managing his career as he went on to TV or movies. No secret to anyone she and her husband were on the outs. Not a scene I want to get involved in. Not again."

"Catherine seems highly competent," Vicky said. "As artistic director, I mean."

"She is. And that's the whole problem with amateurs, right there. Everyone thinks they're entitled to an equal opinion. Whether they know what they're talking about, or not. Usually not."

I was losing contact with my extremities. I wiggled my gloved fingers and shifted my booted feet in a failed attempt to get some warmth into them as I glanced at Vicky out of the corner of my eyes. Other than asking Dave if he killed Paula, I couldn't think of any other reason to keep standing out here in the cold. "Mustn't keep you," I said. "I'm sure you have places to go and things to do."

But Vicky wasn't finished yet. "Why are you staying in the production then?"

"I'll finish what I started," Dave said. "And appear in their stupid play. I'll be Marley as per Desmond's stuck-in-the-past vision. But I won't be back next year, I'll tell you that. If I'm unlikely enough to still be stuck in your town. No insult intended. I'm sure it's a nice place. For some people."

"We like it," I said.

"Catch you later." He moved to get in the car, then he hesitated. "I might have said more than I should. I'd appreciate it if you keep this between us, for a while anyway."

I couldn't think of what he'd said that was confidential, but I nodded agreeably as Vicky made a "my lips are sealed" gesture.

"I wouldn't want to get into a bidding war on that rundown motel," Dave said. "I can only afford it if I get it at a rock bottom price."

Chapter Eleven

"Are you satisfied?" I said to Vicky as we pulled out of Muddle Harbor.

"Reasonably. Accommodation is tight in Rudolph at the height of Christmas season, as well as Christmas in July. A nice, reasonably priced motel not too far away, with plenty of modern upgrades, is sorely needed. I'm thinking I might approach Dave if his deal goes through. He can add freshly baked and delivered breakfast pastries as an extra enticement to guests."

"I meant about the murder."

"Oh, that. I don't know we learned anything we didn't know, did we? I will begrudgingly admit I might have made a mistake in leaving with Dave rather than staying in the café to continue our inquiries. We never did get the chance to ask the movers and shakers of Muddle Harbor what they might have done to sabotage the production. A return visit might be required."

I groaned.

"As for Dave himself . . . Nothing other than he's looking for a girlfriend and not having much luck. If he wants luck, he needs to drop the poor-me line mighty fast."

"I disagree. I think we can move Dave higher on the suspect list. Not that we have a suspect list. But we should. I'll start one."

She glanced at me. "Why? He clearly didn't have any time for Paula, but she was no threat to him."

"Can we be sure he didn't, as you put it, have any time for Paula? He said he didn't. Murder suspects don't always say what they mean."

"True enough, and he was quick—too quick?—to mention her brat of a son and her shaky marriage."

"I believed him about that. Not that my impressions are all that meaningful. I've been wrong about people before."

"Once or twice," Vicky mumbled. "Max Folger comes to mind."

I ignored that. Vicky never had approved of my no-good, cheating ex-fiancé. But she was wise enough not to say so when he and I were together. "It has crossed my mind," I said, "that Paula might have been mistaken for someone else."

"Like who?"

"Catherine. Think about it, Vicky. Our killer found the shop empty, but for one woman. They acted quickly, probably on impulse. No time to think. Just do it and worry about the consequences later. I believe it's possible Catherine might have been the intended victim and the killer made a mistake. If that's the case, did Dave intend to kill Catherine?"

It was a Sunday morning and traffic on the highway to Rudolph was minimal. Bare trees and brown grass lined the roadway. The sun had come out the minute we crossed over the Muddle Harbor town line. Not the first time that happened, and not the first time I'd wondered if it was nothing but a coincidence.

"Why would Dave want to kill Catherine?" Vicky asked.

"Maybe they were having an affair? He openly told us he was hoping to meet women, and openly complained that all the women in the production are old and married." I realized Jackie is neither old nor married, and I made a mental note to ask her what she thought about Dave.

"Doesn't that exclude Catherine then? She's both. Married and old, in comparison to Dave, I mean. She's what, nearly sixty, and he's not much more than forty, at a guess."

"Don't be ageist, Vicky. Catherine might be a lot older than him, but she's still attractive. Well groomed, well dressed. She's also, judging by appearances, well off if not out-and-out rich. And powerful, in the tiny world of Rudolph amateur theater anyway." I thought about how Catherine argued for Dave to be promoted to the main role, not caring about upsetting long-time members of the company such as Desmond and Ian. Did she think Dave would be better in the Scrooge part, and thus make for a better play? Or did she want to make her young lover happy with the expanded part, regardless of its effect on the production?

"Say I buy that," Vicky said. "I don't, but never mind that now. They were having an affair. So what? She's married, but he isn't. He's got nothing to lose by ending it. No need to go to extremes."

"True, but there's a lot of emotion wrapped up in illicit relationships. Passion, pride, self-esteem. Guilt. He said he's divorced, but is he? Maybe the divorce hasn't gone through yet and he can't afford to be caught out, but Catherine was getting more serious than he intended."

"All that's speculation, Merry. You got nothin.'"

"You're right about that."

"I wonder if the Muddle Harbor Sunday supper crowd gathers at the café at five thirty for the early bird special. I saw it advertised. I bet they serve hot turkey and gravy on white Wonder Bread with canned peas on the side."

"I'll never know," I said.

*   *   *

As long as I was thinking about Catherine . . .

Vicky dropped me at home and headed to the bakery to get back to her ovens. I saw no sign of Mrs. D'Angelo, for which I was grateful. My landlady had a way of getting me to confess to things I'd prefer not to. I suppose that's why, in my dad's and Alan's opinion, she'd be a good recruit for the CIA or FBI.

The shop opened at noon today. It was ten o'clock now, so I had a while to do some investigating before going to work. Not that I was investigating. Just being curious. I let Mattie have a short romp in the yard and then put on a fresh pot of coffee and sat at the kitchen table with my iPad.

Catherine and Bruce Renshaw were the founders of Home Central Furnishings, a big-box store with branches all over the Northeast. In my previous life, I'd been a prop stylist and then a design editor at *Jennifer's Lifestyle*, one of the country's top monthly magazines. We'd never worked with Home Central— their line was too mass-produced and budget for us—but I knew of them.

I started with the business news and learned that Catherine and Bruce retired two years ago. Retirement had not been voluntary. They'd been kicked out by the majority of the board after several years of steadily declining revenue. I read back in time to learn there'd been dissent in the business for a long time. Bruce and Catherine openly clashed over the direction they wanted the company to take. Bruce was a traditionalist: big spaces with four walls stuffed full of display rooms and stock. Catherine was an early proponent of online shopping and rapid delivery. By the time Bruce and his faction realized online was the future of retail, it was too late for Home Central—other companies had captured most of the market share. Several of their stores closed over the past ten years and others downsized. Revenue continued to steadily decrease, along with the value of the company's stock.

Catherine, I thought, would not have been pleased. She'd had a vision and wanted to expand, but Bruce resisted. From what I could find, they were still shareholders in the company, but their shares would be worth a fraction of what they'd been at the company's height.

I then turned to the more gossipy sections of the internet. Seven years ago, Catherine had thrown open her Westchester home for the benefit of a charity Christmas tour. The pictures reporting on the event showed expansive grounds, huge old trees and well-trimmed bushes, a large pool (closed for the winter) complete with pool house. Inside, a roaring fire in a massive fire-place, walls of windows, shelves of books, good art, a gleaming kitchen of chrome, marble, and glass. The article mentioned that the Renshaws enjoyed summer vacations at their beach house in Sag Harbor.

Estates in Westchester and beach houses in Sag Harbor weren't cheap. They were, in fact, a considerable leap up from a substantial, yet comparatively modest, house in Rudolph, New York, no matter that it was lakeside.

More pictures of the couple, her resplendent in gown and jewels, him in a tuxedo, attending galas for the New York Phil-harmonic or the opening of a special show at the Metropolitan Museum of Art. In one photo, the beaming couple posed with the cast of the biggest show to hit Broadway in ages. I found nothing along those lines more recent than three years ago.

The Renshaws had clearly come down in the world. Did they mind? They were still comfortably off. Catherine dressed impeccably; she donated lavishly to the theater company. On the other hand, the Rudolph Community Theater Players was a far cry from opening night at the Philharmonic or backstage at a talk-of-the-town Broadway play.

As for her spending on the production, I wondered if that was a point of contention between the couple. Possibly, if she was spending more than they could afford. I thought back to the picnic. Bruce Renshaw had seemed happy enough in his wife's world, moving in her shadow. Would he have been able to pretend to be enjoying himself if he was resenting what the picnic was costing him?

Possibly. If he didn't want people gossiping about him.

On the other hand, maybe he *was* okay with it. I'm computer literate, but no more than most people my age who run their own business. Meaning I have no hacking skills. I'd love to have a peek at the Renshaw's finances, but that wasn't going to happen. They'd started Home Central with one store and built it into an empire by themselves. I could find no evidence that they'd inherited family money or had help opening the first store. They still had shares in Home Central along with some probable investment income, but I assumed that wasn't adequate to maintain their Westchester and Sag Harbor lifestyle.

If Bruce Renshaw was watching his wife spending more than they could afford on her hobby?

Yes, that might be a motive for murder.

I reminded myself Paula had died, not Catherine, and I was only speculating that Paula had been mistaken for the other woman. If Bruce Renshaw had wanted to murder his wife, surely he'd have had a better opportunity to do it.

But had he?

The first person the police look at in a murder is the partner of the deceased. Had Bruce been biding his time, waiting for the opportunity to get rid of Catherine? He'd been with her when she came into Mrs. Claus's Treasures, but they might have separated when they left. Had he later thought he'd seen her returning to my shop, and flown into a rage, thinking she was about to spend more money that he could ill afford? Had he followed her, and realizing the shop was empty, struck without taking care to be sure he had the right woman?

How likely was it he'd mistake someone else for his wife? Catherine and Paula were wearing similar but not identical coats the day in question. Even if they looked moderately the same from behind, wouldn't Bruce recognize his wife's coat? Maybe not. Some men could be blind to that sort of thing. My dad came to mind. He'd once lavishly praised Mom on the new dress she was wearing to a summer dinner party. It was, she icily informed him, the same thing she'd worn to a different gathering only the previous week.

I shook my head and pulled myself out of that line of thought. I am not a police officer, which means I don't have police resources. Bruce might have been in full view of a hundred people when Paula died. He might have been having lunch with the chief of police and the mayor.

As for my theory of Catherine being the intended victim . . . I was running down a rabbit hole in pursuit of that idea.

It then occurred to me Catherine might have been spending on the theater production as a way of recording a loss for tax purposes. Such was entirely possible: wealthy business owners know how to game the system. I couldn't see it as a motive for mur- der, though. Then again, might she have been using the theater company as more than just a hobby or a tax loss? Might she be spending on the production as a way of covering up something more nefarious? Such as stealing from it? Did Paula know something about Catherine that Catherine didn't want everyone else to know? Had Catherine decided she needed to eliminate Paula?

Possible. Then again, just about anything was possible. I next looked up what I could find on Dave French. That's not an uncommon name, so initially I had trouble locating him. I searched for the Carolers' Motel and found a thoroughly up-to-date web presence, almost certainly Dave's handiwork. The "about" section told me the motel was a proud family business, owned and operated by Rudolph residents, the French family. I recognized Dave's parents from their pictures, having seen them around town, but I didn't know them well. A short bio was provided for Dave. The only interesting tidbit was that he had a degree in theater from Barnard College at Columbia. Interesting, I thought. He said he had some acting experience. "Some acting" is a far cry from an actual degree.

Armed with that information, I went to IMDb. Sure enough, David French had had a couple of minor—very minor—roles in Hollywood musicals and comedies. His parts were listed as "Boyfriend 1" or "Singing Waiter 2." No mention of anything he'd been in in the past three years. He was, the bio informed me, divorced from actress Veronica Halston French, and the couple had no children. Veronica Halston French, I learned, had an acting career no more distinguished than that of her ex-husband. Although she, now under the name Veronica Halston, was still getting minor roles, whereas he'd not been in anything lately.

I leaned back in my chair. That information opened up several cans of worms. Dave wasn't happy at abandoning his dreams of stardom to run a budget motel in Upstate New York under the eye of a disapproving parent. Was he trying to get his foot back on the bottom rung of the show business ladder by joining the Rudolph production? Someone mentioned a Broadway director was coming to the opening night performance. Did Dave see this as his big chance to get back in the game?

Had Paula, somehow, stood in his way?

I couldn't think how. Marley's solo's the best male song in the play, but that character only appears in one scene. The starring role, of course, is Ebenezer Scrooge. It was Desmond, as well as Ian, not Paula, who stood in the way of Dave getting the more important part.

No way could anyone have mistaken Paula for Desmond, no matter how much of a rush they might have been in.

My ringing phone snapped me back to the real world. I recognized Jackie's number and answered.

"Are you not coming in today, Merry? I told you I'm leaving at two for rehearsal, and Chrystal and I are swamped here."

With a shock I realized it was already half past one. I should have been at the store at noon. "I'll be right there. I got . . . involved in balancing the store accounts and lost track of time."

"Okay. I have to say, Merry, we had to do some mighty fast cleaning before we opened. The police are not very tidy. They left gray dust on everything and didn't bother to put things back in the correct places on the shelves. Cleaning stock should count as performing extra duties, don't you think?"

"No, I do not think. But thanks for doing that. Wait for me, will you? It shouldn't matter if you're a few minutes late to rehearsal."

"That wouldn't be very professional of me, Merry."

"Whatever," I said.

I grabbed my bag, shrugged on my coat, called to Mattie, and we headed off.

Mattie never likes to hurry, but he does enjoy the cold, so today he was happy to walk alongside me at a brisk trot, and we arrived at the store in good time. I came in the back way, settled Mattie in the office, hung up my coat and scarf, put my purse into the desk drawer, changed boots into shoes, slapped on a smile, and went to work.

The smile turned into a real one when I saw how satisfyingly busy the store was, with buyers as well as browsers. Chrystal was behind the counter, ringing up one of Alan's handmade toy train sets. Jackie was helping a woman choose table linens. Jackie pointedly checked her watch when I came in. I ignored her. I was the boss here, after all.

"This selection will do nicely," the customer said. She carried a box of place mats—Santa and the reindeer crossing a star-studded night sky—and matching napkins to the counter.

I slipped up to Jackie. "Come into the office before you leave?"

"Why? I'm leaving now. It's two o'clock, Merry. We're expected at rehearsal at two thirty, and I need something to eat first. This is important, you know. As the understudy, of course, I thoroughly memorized Mrs. Cratchit's lines, but I need to work with my fellow actors on movement and—"

"I'll pay for your lunch. How's that?"

"Okay."

"Be right back," I called to Chrystal. She gave me a wave, as Jackie and I slipped behind the curtain.

I didn't take a seat in my office, but Jackie dropped into the visitor's chair and swung one leg over the armrest. She was dressed today in a slim-fitting black and red checked dress over black leggings. "What's up? If this is about me closing the store a few minutes early the other day, I can explain. I was—"

"You left early? When was that?"

"Oh. You don't know about that? Never mind." She gave me that totally "what, me?" Jackie smile. "You don't want to leave Chrystal alone out there too long. She's young and needs supervision."

Last year Chrystal threatened to quit when I promoted Jackie to assistant manager, mainly to stop her nagging but also because I'd been spending a great deal of time away from the store. Chrystal complained that Jackie was overly enthusiastic in her new role of "managing" the store's only other employee. I had to give Chrystal a substantial raise to convince her to come back this holiday season.

All of which had nothing to do with why I wanted to speak to Jackie. "Have you heard anything more from Detective Simmonds?" I asked. "About the murder. And . . . your involvement?"

She waved a hand in the air. "I told you not to worry about that, Merry. I'm obviously in the clear. She hasn't been around to see me or called me since Friday."

Which might simply mean she was building her case, slowly and steadily. I didn't point that out to Jackie. "That's good. I ran into Dave French this morning. We got to chatting about the play."

"And?"

"And, I like him. He seems like a nice guy. He's not entirely comfortable in Rudolph, though. Feels out of things. Trying to find a way to fit in."

"I guess."

"Did he . . . suggest you and he get to know each other better?"

"That's clever, Merry. You know it's a line from the play, right? The Ghost of Christmas Present says—"

"Yeah. I know."

Jackie fluffed her hair and gave me a knowing grin. "I'll admit Dave's not a bad looking guy. He suggested we go out for a drink after rehearsal one night. I said I was meeting Kyle and invited him to join us. He suddenly remembered another appointment." She winked at me. "I've been thinking about suggesting we have that drink some other time, but I'm not quite decided on that. Between you and me, Merry, I'm not sure if Kyle's truly the one for me."

I didn't say, "At long last." But I thought it.

"I'm not getting any younger, you know, as my mom never fails to remind me. I mean, I'll be thirty-five soon. Dave's like what, over forty? I suppose that's old, but not too old. He's divorced and he says he and his ex get on really well, so that's good." The smile disappeared. "Still, he runs his parents' motel. Kyle's preparing for a career as a professional photographer. He's hoping to get a job soon with one of the big newspapers, on the crime beat. Either that or the celebrity circuit. He's not sure which yet."

"Kyle can keep hoping."

"What's that mean?"

"Nothing. Did Dave tell you if he has any acting experience? As a professional, I mean?"

"He said he'd been in movies." Jackie shrugged. "Nothing I've ever seen, and he's not in movies now, is he?"

"Did you ever notice anything . . . shall we say particularly friendly between Dave and any of the other women?" Jackie was not what I'd call a student of the human condition. If it didn't concern her, she didn't much care. But I asked the question anyway.

"Not really. I mean they're all a lot older than him, except for me and Paula, but she was married. He and Catherine get on pretty well, but that's only because she wants him to have a bigger part, right? Desmond and Ian don't agree. Ian threatened to quit altogether. I'm on Catherine's side, although I didn't say so. I don't want to make enemies, you know. I mean, Scrooge is like always played by an old guy. *Booorrrring*. Why not shake things up a bit? That's what Catherine and Dave wanted." She checked her watch again and stood up. "I have to go. Being on time is important to Desmond. He's a real stickler and he expects us to do our best. That's good right? Kyle says I shouldn't let him boss us around the way he does. It's not like we're being paid to be in this thing, Kyle says, but I still think it's important to act professionally."

I studied Jackie's face, thoughts racing. Obviously, her part in the play was very important to her. How important? Could it be possible Jackie killed Paula to get Mrs. Cratchit's role? As I'd told Vicky, Jackie, of all people, had means, motive, and opportunity.

Jackie cocked her head to one side and watched me in return. Her long hair fell around her shoulders, her eyes were wide, and her expression held nothing but a question. Certainly not guilt, or even fear at being found out. I gave myself a mental shake. Jackie had worked for me ever since I opened the store. I knew her well. As well as we can know someone, that is. I was confident that not only did she not have that amount of anger or ambition in her, but if I was wrong, and she had killed for a part, Jackie didn't have the wits or the guile to keep quiet about it.

She held out her hand. I looked at it.

"Lunch money?"

"Oh, right."

* * *

We close at five on Sundays, and it was almost fully dark by the time I locked the doors. Chrystal groaned and bent backward to give herself a nice stretch. "I'd say that was a good day."

"It was. I'm particularly pleased at how well your jewelry sold."

"And Alan's toys. Keep this up and you'll be out of stock by Christmas Eve."

"Fortunately I know my suppliers. Speaking of which—?"

"I'm off tomorrow and Tuesday, so I'll be hard at it in my workshop. I'll have some more pieces to you on Wednesday."

"You're a doll."

After Chrystal left, I did some rearranging of the shelves. Aside from the latte and muffin Chrystal got for me when she went for a coffee run, I hadn't had anything to eat all day. I thought sadly of my calorie-laden breakfast, abandoned in Muddle Harbor. I had no plans to see Alan tonight, and I didn't dare call Vicky in case she was serious about going back to the café in time for the early bird special. I wondered what Diane Simmonds was up to tonight. She led a busy life. She was a single mom and a police detective. She might not appreciate a call at this time on a Sunday evening.

Then again, she was a police detective and she did have a murder case on her plate. I gave her a call.

She answered right away. "Merry. I was wondering when I'd get your daily call."

"I don't call every day. Do I?"

"As good as. What's up?"

"You asked me not to interfere in the investigation—"

"Ask isn't the correct word. I believe I ordered you not to interfere."

"Okay. I'm not interfering." I crossed my fingers behind my back. "But I have been thinking about it. I'm allowed to think, aren't I?"

"I'd stop that if I could, but it doesn't seem feasible. Go ahead. I assume your thinking led you to having questions."

"If you're not busy? My questions can wait until tomorrow." In the background I heard someone call, "Good night, Detective."

"You're still at the office?" I asked.

"I am. Going through bank records, witness statements, prior police reports, and forensic results. All the tedious details involved in a modern investigation. Sometimes I think I'd like to be Inspector Lestrade, hailing hansom cabs and rushing off to consult with Sherlock Holmes. Lestrade never had to wait for a DNA analysis."

"I'll be your Sherlock Holmes," I said.

"Don't push your luck, Merry."

"You mentioned bank records. Shall I assume you know that the Renshaws have seen a substantial decrease in their financial status lately?"

"I won't ask how you know, as it's more or less public knowledge for those interested enough to poke into their affairs. That's irrelevant to this case. If you want to know about the Monahan family's finances, I'm not going to tell you."

"I have a theory." I quickly told her my thoughts about the killer mistaking Paula for Catherine. "You've been told Catherine isn't loved by everyone in the theater group?"

She didn't reply immediately, which I took as a sign she was seriously considering my theory. "It's a stretch, Merry," she said at last, "but I will admit the time and location of the murder has led me to conclude it was very much a spur-of-the-moment thing."

"As the timing is so exact, you must be able to pin down people's alibis."

"It helps."

"And?"

"Sometimes it doesn't help. One thing about exact timing, Merry, is it can be difficult to establish that an individual was somewhere at a precise time. Let's say, for the sake of argument, a person of possible interest claims to have been shopping at Jayne's Ladies Wear at two fifteen on Friday. The shop clerk might be able to tell us this person was in their shop sometime in the midafternoon, but at the exact time Paula Monahan was being murdered? Much less certain. They might not even remember this person being in the store. Places get busy, one customer blends into another. Or so I've been told. Another person might claim to have been jogging on the lakeside trail between one thirty and two thirty. Did anyone see this person on the trail? Maybe, but they didn't check their watch and make a note of the time. I told you Kevin Monahan, Paula's husband, has a solid alibi and that alibi remains solid. Of one thing I am sure—Jackie O'Reilly and several other members of the theatrical company were at your end of Jingle Bell Lane between two o'clock and your 911 call, but no one can say exactly where each of them were at any given time."

"What about Paula herself? Do you know where she went after leaving my store the first time?"

"I have a fair idea. She left your store, according to you yourself, shortly after two and almost immediately following that

Jackie went on her break. Paula returned around two fifteen, again according to you, a couple of minutes before your call to 911 was logged. In that time, it would appear Paula went to the library. She asked the woman behind the counter if they had an illustrated edition of *A Christmas Carol*. She was told all copies were out, and she left immediately. The librarian's sure of the time, as a few minutes later she saw the emergency vehicles go past and checked her watch."

"That must be why Paula returned here so soon after leaving," I said. "To buy the book. It's prominently displayed on the book rack; she might have seen it when she was in, and decided to check if the library had it first. Her son Eddie was supposed to play Tiny Tim in the production. Perhaps she wanted him to have some exposure to the source material." Seemed a bit late to be doing that, but she might have finally realized the rest of the cast was not happy with Eddie in the role and figured he needed some inspiration.

"That might be, but I'm not going to speculate as to her thought process. The important thing is the librarian says Paula was alone when she left. Now, if I'm to get home in time to have supper with my daughter, which I'd very much like to, I'll say good-night."

"One more quick question, if you don't mind. Hello? Are you there, Detective?" I'd been hung up upon. I shouldn't be too disappointed. Simmonds had told me one piece of information: other than Kevin Monahan, no one had an alibi that could be positively verified.

And Jackie was still very much in the frame.

* * *

In for a penny, in for a pound. Isn't that the saying? Meaning, go big or go home.

I was heading home, but on the way, I'd go big.

The cast of *A Christmas Carol* were rehearsing tonight. Opening night was less than a week away, so rehearsal would be intense. Almost certainly Catherine Renshaw would be there, keeping an eye on everything.

Thus, this would be a good time to pay a social call on Bruce Renshaw. I switched off the lights and locked up the store. Mattie and I headed down Jingle Bell Lane. The other stores were closed or closing, but light and laughter spilled out of the bars and restaurants. It was still very cold, but temperatures were supposed to rise to slightly below freezing tomorrow, and a good amount of snow was expected later in the week. Snow was always welcome in Rudolph in mid-December. It made everything look Christmas-y and put the tourists in a holiday mood. Also known as a shopping mood.

Mattie gave me a questioning look as we passed our house. "Just a quick errand," I said. "Then home for dinner."

The Renshaw house was only a few blocks farther along. It was located on the lake side of the street, on a good-sized piece of property with mature trees and extensive flowerbeds, now turned over for winter. The thirty-foot pine in the center of the lawn was decorated for the season with thousands of tiny white bulbs, as were the evergreens in tubs on either side of the front door. The house itself was a modern construction that looked as though, as Alan said, it was trying to imitate a French chateau: all fake turrets, miniature balconies, several chimneys, grand sweeping staircase leading to an impressive front door.

No cars were parked in the circular driveway and the doors to the three-car garage were closed, so I had no way of knowing if my quarry was at home. I climbed the steps. A huge wreath accented by more white lights and a giant red-and-green checked velvet bow graced the front door. I pressed the bell and could hear the sound faintly echoing inside the house. Mattie sniffed at the door and then dropped to a sit next to me. His big tail thumped.

I rang once more and was about to give up when the door opened and Bruce Renshaw glared at me. "Yes?" He was dressed for an evening at home in khaki pants and a wool cardigan, brown slippers on his feet. The slippers looked to be well worn and much loved.

"Hi. I'm Merry Wilkinson. We met at the theater group picnic?" I hadn't actually met Bruce there, but I'd seen him. That's the same thing, isn't it?

"I remember. You're the woman who owns that store in town. Catherine's not at home." He grimaced. "She's at yet another rehearsal."

"You might have heard that Paula Monahan died in my store. I was the one who found her."

"I heard."

"It's, as you can imagine, been preying on my mind. A lot. I keep going over and over what might have happened to her and wondering if I could have done anything to prevent it."

He said nothing. I would have expected some expressions of sympathy at the least. "I know you're not as closely involved with the theater group as your wife is—"

"That's an understatement. I have no idea why she's so wrapped up in that thing. Bunch of small-town amateurs." If we hadn't been standing on his front step, he might have spat.

"Uh . . . okay. It's natural for people who are new to town to throw themselves into community activities, don't you think? Particularly in a small town such as this one, where people go back generations and connections between people are tight. That sort of community can be hard to break into, sometimes."

"I suppose."

"Unlike in New York City. You lived in New York, right? I did too, for a while. Always something going on. One party after another. One good cause to support after another."

"What do you want, Merry?"

I was cold and getting colder. Bruce had to be too, but he made no move to invite me in. I could smell a touch of fragrant smoke drifting down the hallway. They must have a real wood-burning fireplace.

"I mean," I floundered, "it's nice of Catherine to throw herself into the play the way she has. Do you know if she has any other plans to continue her involvement in the community? I heard the Santa Claus parade fund is needing organizers as well as donors."

"You'll have to speak to her about that. Good-night."

The door shut firmly in my face.

Okay.

I looked at Mattie, still smiling up at me. "That went well."

We trudged back home. I don't know what I'd been expecting. That Bruce Renshaw would invite me in, offer me a seat by the fireplace (I'd been sensing applewood logs), hand me a twenty-year-old whiskey served in a cut-glass tumbler with just a splash of water, and tell me the intimate details of his and his wife's financial situation while Mattie snoozed on what was very likely an expensive rug?

In the past, I believed I could sometimes uncover things Detective Simmonds, with all her official resources, could not. People didn't see me as an authority figure or a threat—or didn't care if they were wasting my time—so they talked more freely to me. Simmonds herself had never quite come out and said I was a help. But she'd hinted at it. I thought she'd hinted at it.

Can't win 'em all, I guess.

We'd barely taken two steps up our driveway before Mrs. D'Angelo was on the front porch calling, "Yoo hoo! Merry," and waving. Mattie barked and headed toward her. I couldn't pretend I hadn't seen her, so I followed him.

"Good evening, Merry," my landlady said. "Snow's on the way. Most welcome, I say. It's not Christmas without snow."

"That's true."

"A bit cold for a walk tonight, don't you think? I happened to be watering the plants in the front window when you went by earlier."

"Mattie never minds the cold," I said. "Speaking of cold, we won't keep you." She'd come outside so quickly, she hadn't paused to put on her coat or gloves, and was dressed in only a tatty sweater over her housedress. I gave the leash a gentle tug and began to turn. Then I reconsidered. "Actually, we weren't just walking. I paid a call on Bruce Renshaw. Do you know him?"

Her eyes gleamed with the opportunity for fresh gossip. "Not personally, but I've heard a thing or two. As you can imagine, dear, some of the townspeople were curious when the Renshaws first arrived. Naturally."

"Naturally. They were quite the power couple at one time, I've heard. Retired now, although they seem young, as far as wealthy business owners go. Have you heard why?"

Something crossed her face. A look of—shock? Disappointment? The realization of failure? Her mouth flapped open. It closed again. "I . . . I don't know," she admitted at last. "I . . . never thought to wonder. I mean, that's none of my business of course. Although, come to think of it, I did hear that some of the local tradespeople are disappointed Bruce Renshaw isn't as . . . generous as they'd hoped." She pulled her phone out of her pocket. "Why don't I see what I can find out for you, dear." She ran into the house without another word.

Chapter Twelve

When we got home, I fed Mattie first, and then began fixing my own dinner. I chopped whatever vegetables were on hand and put on a pot of rice to make a simple stir fry. I dished it up, but before sitting down to eat I went in search of a pad of paper and a pen. I found what I needed, and while I ate I considered what I'd learned about "the case" and prepared to make notes.

I divided the paper into columns: Suspect. Motivation. Likelihood. I alternately munched on my dinner and chewed on the end of the pen. I studied the paper for a long time and then I swept it up, crumpled it into a ball, and threw it across the room.

Who was I kidding? I was spinning my wheels, going in circles, getting nowhere with this. It wasn't up to me to do anything anyway.

Paula had been killed in my shop, and I'd been the one to find her. But that was no reason for me to get involved in trying to find the killer.

My mother had been accused, but not entirely seriously. Even Jackie couldn't really be considered a major suspect.

I didn't know the theater people well, if at all. I certainly knew nothing about their lives, their fears, their hopes. As Bruce Renshaw had reminded me—it was all none of my business.

I was going down rabbit holes chasing after my favored theory: first assuming Paula's death had something to do with the theater group, and then trying to prove Paula had been killed being mistaken for Catherine. I needed to remember Paula had a life outside amateur theater. A life I knew absolutely nothing about.

Paula's husband, Kevin, was the most likely suspect: he'd argued with her only days before, a divorce had been threatened, child custody cases could be horrific. He had an alibi, but alibis can be broken. If he'd hired a killer to do the deed, then the police would find the evidence they needed.

Not me.

I had to trust in Diane Simmonds to do her job to the best of her abilities.

It was Christmastime in Rudolph, and I had a store to run.

* * *

I went to bed early and slept well, free of thoughts of the death of Paula. I'd gone to bed so early, I was up even before the winter sun. Which was just as well as when I was putting the coffee on Mrs. D'Angelo called.

"Good morning, Merry. I have a partial report for you. More information will be coming in throughout the morning, but I knew you'd be anxious to hear my preliminary findings."

"Report? Report on what?"

"The Renshaws, of course. What you asked me to find out last night."

"Oh, that. I've decided not to—"

"The general consensus is that they are, in the words of one of my contacts, flat broke. Broke, of course, is a relative term. They bought that big house on the lake, but in comparison to what they were used to it's a substantial comedown. Tradespeople say she's not so bad, but him! Ha. He bargains down to the lowest possible price and is so late paying some firms have had to threaten legal action."

I remembered the one occasion the couple had been in my store together. Catherine suggested Bruce get her a gift, and he begrudgingly bought one of the cheapest things in stock.

"They rarely eat out at restaurants, and never just the two of them. Although Catherine Renshaw has cultivated friends, largely though her participation in the theater company, they do not entertain at their home with anything more extensive than a coffee morning, or something similar."

"Thanks, I—"

"You're probably wondering about the state of the marriage itself. I can find not a whiff of scandal. Doesn't mean there isn't any, of course. The subjects might have been discreet." She sniffed in disapproval at the very idea. "One of my friends said it's obvious Bruce adores her, Catherine. She's more circumspect, and on occasion she's seemed almost cold toward him, but she might simply be one not to display her feelings in public." Another sniff of disapproval. "I have to go. A call's coming in. It's Donalda. She's sure to have something important."

I blinked. I almost felt sorry for Bruce and Catherine. I'd decided their affairs had nothing to do with me, but I forgot to call off my crack investigation team.

* * *

As I was ready for work early and temperatures had risen over-night, I decided to take Mattie for a proper walk this morning. We headed away from town and the nicely groomed lakeside paths to a small patch of woodland left largely untouched where I could let Mattie off the leash for a romp.

Not that Mattie ever truly romped—but you get the idea.

This close to town the woods were never entirely quiet, and the path joined up with the ones in the park so it was a popular place for morning walkers. I stuffed my hands into my pockets and strolled along, enjoying the fresh scent of the winter woods and the soft crunch of forest debris under my feet. Mattie fol-lowed his nose.

He stopped abruptly, lifted his head, let out a woof of greet-ing, and ran around a bend. I hurried after him to see what had caught his interest.

A woman dressed in winter running gear sat on a park bench, holding her hand out to the big dog. He sat in front of her, tongue lolling, tail thumping. "Rachel," I said. "Good morning. It's a nice day for a run."

Rachel McIntosh turned her head toward me. I bit my tongue. "I'm so sorry. We didn't mean to disturb you."

"It's okay, Merry. I'm always happy to see this big lug." She gave Mattie an enthusiastic scratch behind his years. His entire body wiggled in delight. "He cheers me up, no end." Her voice broke.

Rachel had obviously been crying. Her nose and eyes were red, her cheeks streaked with tears, and she clutched a bundle of tissues in her gloved hands.

"Are you . . . okay?" I asked.

"Not really." She wiped at her face. "But I will be. I have to be, don't I? It's going to be a busy day in town."

"If you're sure. We'll leave you alone. Come on Mattie, let's go." The dog made no move to stand up. He whined softly and rested his head in Rachel's lap. She ran her fingers through his thick fur.

"Why don't you sit for a bit, Merry." She wiggled over slightly, making room for me on the bench. "Unless you're in a hurry to get to work, that is."

"No. No hurry. We're enjoying the morning quiet." I tucked my coat beneath me and took a seat next to her, and we sat together in silence. She blew her nose and wiped her eyes. Mattie stayed near her, but his ears and nose twitched as something small moved through the undergrowth close to us.

"The rest of the season's looking promising, don't you think?" Rachel said at last.

"I do. The play's always a good draw. Last year's was a disaster, but this year's production seems to be attracting people. I've heard advance ticket sales are good."

Rachel burst into a fresh round of tears.

I didn't know what I'd said, but I hurried to apologize. "Gosh, I'm sorry. I forgot Ian's an important part of the group, but wasn't he ill last year? I seem to remember he had to drop out and the person who took his place wasn't very good. That's what people said, anyway."

"Ian." She sobbed. "Ian. We've been married for almost thirty years. We have two children. I'm hoping for grandchildren someday in the not-too-distant future. I thought it was a good marriage. It was a good marriage."

"Oh, dear. I'm so sorry." I patted her shoulder awkwardly. Mattie nestled his head deeper into her lap.

"I don't know what to do, Merry. I don't know if I can forget and forgive."

I felt absolutely awful. Awful for poor Rachel, weeping for her marriage. Awful for me—totally unsure of what to do. Finally, I asked, "Has Ian talked about . . . moving on?"

"No. He's said nothing. He doesn't know I know. But the wife always finds out eventually, doesn't she? Perhaps I should have been more involved in the theater group. But I have the store and the kids, even though they're grown up now, and my own friends and interests. I never thought . . ."

"You shouldn't have to pretend to enjoy the same things he does," I said. As I spoke, my mind raced. Was Rachel telling me Ian was involved with a woman in the Rudolph Community Players? She must be. Ian and Rachel had been married a long time. They owned a house together as well as Candy Cane Sweets, although Rachel was the one who managed the store and worked there. As well as the house, they must have savings and investments. When a longtime marriage breaks up, the financial details can get complicated. In any divorce, children take sides, and they were almost certain to side with the innocent party—with Rachel.

"How long have you known?" I asked.

"A couple of weeks," she sniffed. "I've been waiting it out. Hoping it was just a brief, temporary thing. That he'd return to his senses. It is over. Now, finally. But he's not the Ian I know. I knew. He's bad tempered, irritable, refuses to talk to me." She wept some more. "I don't know if I can forgive him, not just for the affair, but for shutting me out so completely."

Ian must have been having an affair with Paula. It was over because she died. Understandable Ian would be upset about that. Be not himself; not able to talk about it.

But could it be more than that? Was it possible Paula been pestering Ian to leave Rachel? Paula's own marriage was on the rocks. Had she told Kevin, shortly before he was observed by members of Mrs. D'Angelo's network stuffing his belongings into the trunk of his car, she was leaving him for Ian?

Had Ian not wanted that to happen? Had he intended to stay married to Rachel, and the thing with Paula to be nothing but a "harmless" fling? When he realized Paula was serious, that Paula had ended her own marriage, had he acted to put a stop to her intentions?

Had Ian killed Paula?

Poor Rachel.

"I'm sorry, Merry," she said. "You don't need to hear my troubles."

"I don't mind. Everyone needs a shoulder to cry on sometimes."

"You're kind."

I patted her back and dared to ask the question uppermost on my mind. "Has Ian said anything to you about Paula's death?" I asked.

"Paula? Goodness, I've been so wrapped up in my own misery, I almost forgot about poor Paula. He's shocked, of course. We all are. That such a thing could happen in Rudolph in the middle of the day. People are saying it must have been her husband. What's his name again?"

"Kevin."

"Right. Kevin. But the police haven't arrested him, have they? I heard he's gone to Rochester to stay with his brother and his family for a while. He took his son with him. Surely they'd remove the child if the father was under suspicion for murder? People are always too quick to jump to conclusions, don't you think?" She blew her nose. "Thank you for listening to me Merry, but it's time we were going. I want to finish my run, and then I have a store to open and so do you." She gave Mattie a final thump on his side and started to stand.

"Hold on a sec," I said. "You almost forgot about Paula. Ian's no more upset than anyone else about her death? Isn't Paula. . . . I mean, weren't you telling me Ian was having an affair with Paula?"

"Paula? Heavens no. Ian was fooling around with that Catherine Renshaw."

Chapter Thirteen

What do you do when you know things you'd rather not know?

Rachel gave me a weak smile and a spontaneous hug, Mattie another hearty slap, and ran down the path toward town, her bright red jacket and pants a welcome splash of color in the gray and brown woods.

All the reasons that flashed through my mind as to why Ian might have killed Paula now switched to Catherine. Had Ian killed Paula, mistaking her for Catherine?

Last night I'd told myself I was finished with this case. I took my dog for a nice relaxing walk in the winter woods before starting another busy day in the store I loved (most of the time). And now here I was, thinking about the whole blasted situation once again.

Should I tell Diane Simmonds what Rachel had told me?

I decided not to. Not immediately, anyway. Rachel hadn't asked me to keep her confidence, but surely she had a right not to expect a tearful park bench confession to be spread all around town.

Not that telling the police was spreading it all around town. But close enough.

"Another fine mess you got me into," I said to Mattie.

He paid me no attention.

Now I was thinking about it, I couldn't stop thinking about it. I hadn't seen any signs of undue affection between Ian and Catherine. If anything, the opposite. They barely managed to be polite to each other, and sometimes got perfectly snippy. I'd assumed they were clashing over the direction in which to take the play. Instead they were showing all the signs of a relationship gone bad and two people who couldn't avoid still having contact with each other. As much as they might not want to.

Catherine wanted Ian out of the main role and the younger and handsomer Dave in it.

Had Ian ended the affair, and favoring Dave was Catherine's way of showing her disapproval? It was possible, likely even, she wanted Ian to quit. Regardless of who ended it, no one wants continuing evidence of a failed relationship hanging around. It was for that very reason I'd left Manhattan, which I loved, and my job at *Jennifer's Lifestyle*, which I adored, and came home to Rudolph: to get far away from Max Folger and the woman who'd taken control of the magazine, the one he left me for.

Ian, obviously, had no intention of being pushed out by Catherine. For one thing, he'd been with the company far longer than she had. For another, Desmond, the director, as well as the majority of the cast and crew supported him.

Had Ian McIntosh seen Paula going into Mrs. Claus's in her black coat and blue scarf, and in his anger mistaken her for Catherine? Had Ian decided to end his relationship with the artistic director once and for all?

*　*　*

"How was rehearsal yesterday?" I asked Jackie when she came into work.

"Do theater people bicker all the time?" she said in reply.

"If you go by what my mother says, yes. Egos are on the line, I suppose. More than in many situations."

"I have my part down pat. Desmond said I've slipped into the role as though it had been mine all along." She preened. If Desmond had said that, I considered it to be rather tactless, considering the initial actor had died. "Speaking of your mother . . . She wants me to move to the back of the row during the big numbers. I don't think that's a good idea, and I said so. The audience wants to see someone young and energetic on stage."

Speaking of egos—Jackie had essentially told the rest of the chorus they were old and decrepit.

"Desmond said I could stay in the front, if I didn't sing quite so loudly. Your mom said it wasn't a matter of volume." Jackie's face twisted as she thought. "Do you know what she meant by that?"

"Not a clue."

"I asked Irene to make some adjustments to my costume." Jackie stuck out her chest and wiggled her top half. I choked. "She didn't want to but Desmond said that would work. Why not make Mrs. Cratchit young and pretty, eh? Although with Rick Reid playing Mr. Cratchit it's a stretch to think we'd be married. Still, that's show business, right, Merry? Our job is to make the audience believe."

"I suppose it is." My sister Eve is an actress, trying with limited success to make it in Hollywood. She has a lot to say about young and pretty versus having talent and being a suitable age for the part. My other sister Carole is an opera singer, like our mother. Even in that world, where you'd think the voice and physical presence were everything, such wasn't always the case.

"What's happening about the role of Scrooge?" I asked. "Is Ian keeping the part or is it going to Dave?"

"Catherine and Desmond seem to have stopped arguing about it. Your mom's with Desmond. She says because Dave's the better singer, and Marley has the best song, then Dave has to be Marley. So there. People don't argue with your mom much, do they Merry?"

"My dad doesn't even argue with Mom."

"Opening night's Friday, so Catherine finally admitted, although not in so many words, it's too late to be recasting."

"How did Ian react to that?"

She shrugged. "He didn't say anything, but he looked pleased."

The chimes over the door tinkled, and we both turned to greet the first customers of the day, two couples in their late middle age. Well groomed, well dressed, expensive coats and boots.

"Welcome to Mrs. Claus's," Jackie said. "Please let me know if you need any help."

"Thank you," the younger of the women said in a deep Southern accent. She smiled broadly as she looked around, taking it all in. "Everything in your town is so absolutely charming. The stores, the restaurants, the decorations. The lobby of our hotel looks like a French alpine village, and the gardens at night . . . The perfect Christmas wonderland."

"That's nice to hear," I said. "Is this your first visit to Rudolph?"

"Yup," said the man with her, his accent equally broad. "When my wife suggested we come to New York State for

Christmas, I couldn't think of anything I'd rather not do. Not all that fond of the cold myself." He suppressed a shudder.

"We're hoping for snow," the woman said. "And lots of it. Right, Will?"

Will shuddered once again. "Not me. I intend to spend most of my time sitting by that lobby fireplace with a cup of mulled wine."

"And going to the play of course. That's the only way I could get him here," she said to me with a laugh. "Will's been a fan of Aline Steiner for years; it just about broke his itty-bitty heart when she retired. When he heard she's appearing in a musical play in a little town in the middle of nowhere, Will couldn't get tickets fast enough for us and our friends, who are also opera buffs. We're going to opening night."

"Aline's—" Jackie began.

"Also directing the chorus," I interrupted before she could mention that Aline's my mother. It's hardly a secret around town, but I didn't want opera lovers pitching tents in the alley hoping to get a glimpse of their idol dropping by.

Will smiled at me. "I don't suppose you happen to know her favorite restaurant or coffee shop?"

"Sorry, no. Let us know if you need any help."

*　*　*

The diva herself came into the store shortly before closing, looking every inch the diva in a double-breasted, floor-sweeping navy-blue coat with gold buttons, a matching blue hat, and blue leather gloves. She held a takeout cup in one hand and a large shopping bag in the other.

"Hi, Aline," Jackie said from behind the counter. "We had people in this morning who are big fans of yours."

Mom tried not to look too pleased. "How nice."

"What brings you here?" I asked as Jackie returned to ringing up purchases.

She indicated the bag she carried. "Some shopping. I needed a new dress to wear for the opening night after-party. It's going to be a very dressy affair, dear, so I hope you have something suitable."

"Me? I haven't been invited."

"You haven't been invited?"

"Nope."

"A shocking oversight on Sue-Anne's part. She's so gushy over having a senator and professional theatrical people she's forgotten who's important in Rudolph. Consider yourself invited. Plus Alan, of course. You can't show up by yourself. Bring Vicky and her date too."

"Kyle will be taking pictures for the paper," Jackie said.

"I hope he's learned how to use the focus by then." Mom sipped from her cup. "I went into Cranberries to get a drink before my next appointment."

"Where are you off to now?"

"I'm meeting with Irene for one last fitting of my Belle dress."

"Can you remind her it would be great if she can make my dress fit a bit better?" Jackie asked.

"No," Mom said.

"Before you go," I said. "Do you have a minute, Mom?"

"I don't suppose it matters if I'm a few minutes late. Why?"

"I have something I want to talk over with you. A . . . family matter. Come into my office. You okay here, Jackie?"

Jackie glanced around the empty shop. "I figure I can manage, thanks."

"What family matter? Has something happened I should know about?" Mom asked when were in my office with the door closed.

"A little white lie. I don't want Jackie trying to eavesdrop, that's all." I took a deep breath. Seeing Mom with her Cranberry Coffee Bar cup and her mentioning Irene reminded me of a few things. Irene had been in the vicinity shortly before Paula died. She'd told Jackie she was thinking of quitting the production because of interference from Catherine. I myself overheard her complaining to Desmond that Catherine was trying to override her costuming decisions. If it was possible Paula had been killed in mistake for Catherine, then Irene could be considered a suspect.

Even if Paula had been the intended victim, Irene might still be in the frame. She'd been furious at Paula at the picnic in the park when Eddie bullied her granddaughter. If Eddie was a bully on that occasion, it was entirely possible he continued bullying the other children in the play. Had Irene had enough and decided the best way to get rid of Eddie's participation in the community players was to eliminate his mother? Which is precisely what happened: according to Rachel, Kevin had taken his son to Rochester. Eddie Monahan would not appear as Tiny Tim.

"Irene," I said. "What do you know about her, Mom?"

My mother raised one perfectly sculpted eyebrow. "That question is so out of left field, as your father might say, I have to ask why you are asking. You are not, I hope, involving yourself in any more police matters. Didn't you learn your lesson the last time?"

"I'm not involving myself in anything. I'm curious, that's all. Don't you remember you and Dad encouraging all us children to be curious about the world around us?"

"And wasn't that a mistake," she said. "As for Irene, I'd never met her before joining the players. She doesn't sing; she has no involvement, far as I know, in town affairs. She's married and has grandchildren, but I don't know what her husband does, nor have I met him. I've never been to her home. She's done the costumes for the plays for many years. She mentioned once that she enjoys sewing for her granddaughters. I cannot bear to think of what that means. Plaid pinafore dresses and blouses with bows at the neck, no doubt."

"What about her costumes?"

"I'll freely admit she does an excellent job, from what I've seen so far. Someone mentioned how pleased Irene is because this year they're putting on something with a historical setting so she can go all out with the ladies' dresses and the ghosts' costumes in particular."

"Have you ever seen her display any signs of temper? Or of repressed anger?"

"She has her own ideas about the wardrobe selections, and strong ones. She insists she takes direction from Desmond, but I'd say it's more she tells him what she intends to do and he doesn't argue. She has little patience for interference, and because of that she doesn't get on well with Catherine, who also has strong ideas and little patience. Such, Merry, is life in a theatrical company. But we don't go around killing each other over it."

Except someone had.

"I do not know why you are asking this, dear. Irene, I'm sure, is exactly what she appears to be. A grandmother with an all-encompassing hobby."

"How important that hobby is to her, I'm wondering."

My mom brushed my cheek in a kiss and a wave of Chanel No. 5. "Stop wondering."

195

Chapter Fourteen

I heard little more about the case for the next two days. Jackie told me she'd been interviewed again, this time by a "dreadfully handsome" officer from the state police who'd been sent to help with the investigation. Jackie seemed to think his attentions were a good thing. I didn't agree, but I didn't tell her so. Mom reported that Detective Simmonds had been talking to the members of the theater group, but no one had anything new to tell her. I decided not to tell Simmonds what I'd learned, and observed, and speculated, about Ian and Catherine. If the evidence was there to prove my vague suspicious, the police would find it.

According to Mrs. D'Angelo, Kevin Monahan remained at liberty in Rochester. Also according to Mrs. D'Angelo, some of the teachers at the school where Paula had taught had been questioned about "an incident" in the staff lunchroom earlier in the fall. Said incident turned out to be a teacher accidentally spilling hot coffee on Paula and Paula getting angry about it. The incident had been resolved when the teacher paid for the dry cleaning of Paula's jacket, although everyone who'd been there said it had been Paula's fault, as she wasn't watching where she was putting her big feet and collided with the other teacher. Paula had not been popular, my landlady informed me, with either her fellow staff members or the students and their parents. However, she grudgingly admitted, not being popular was rarely grounds for murder. Young Eddie, Mrs. D'Angelo's network reported, was in therapy to help him deal with the sudden death of his mother.

That, I thought, was a good thing.

Wednesday, we awoke to sunny skies and a good foot of fresh snow. Perfect for the beginning of Christmas week. As it was now only eleven days to Christmas Eve, Rudolphites had more important things on their minds than a murder and police investigation. Tonight was a full dress rehearsal of *A Christmas Carol*, and Friday would see the sold-out premiere presentation of the play. Sue-Anne had organized an after-party, and all the movers and shakers in this part of the state, and many from beyond, had been invited to attend. (Actually Wendy had organized the party and the guest list, but Sue-Anne took the credit.) The Saturday performance was also sold out. The production would take a break on Sunday for the annual children's party at which many of the town's residents would be involved. My dad, AKA Santa Claus, and Alan, AKA head toymaker, would be the stars of the afternoon, and most of the senior class at Rudolph High would have supporting roles as elves. I'd been roped into putting in an appearance as Mrs. Claus, and Victoria's Bake Shoppe would be responsible for the catering of kid-friendly foods and mountains of Christmas cookies. My mom's children's vocal classes were scheduled to sing Christmas carols at the party.

Next week, in the run-up to Christmas the following Monday, Mom and some of the adults she taught, dressed in full

Victorian-era costumes, would stroll up and down Jingle Bell Lane singing carols for the entertainment of shoppers. It was a heck of a lot for Mom to do as well as appearing in the play and directing the musical components. She complained bitterly about the pressure. Dad sympathized with her, brought her tea and toast in bed in the mornings, and reminded me that Mom never hesitated to say no to anything she didn't want to do.

Dad popped into the store that afternoon as I was ringing up a collection of tree ornaments and a stuffed reindeer. The woman I was serving turned at the sound of the chimes over the door. She audibly gasped and swung back to me. "Oh, my goodness. Is that Santa himself in civilian clothes?"

The little girl with her, the one who'd carefully selected the reindeer as a gift for her brother, stared, open-mouthed and wide-eyed.

"It might be." I touched my index finger to my lips. "Please, don't tell anyone. He likes to be incognito when he's checking to see who's been naughty and who's been nice."

"It will be our secret, right Madison?" said the woman.

Madison said nothing, so awe-struck was she. My dad was dressed in jeans and one of his beloved ugly Christmas sweaters, this one a hand-knitted thing showing Rudolph's smiling face with a giant red battery-operated light for a nose. A red woolen toque with a white pom-pom bouncing on the tip was perched on his head. No matter how he dressed, Dad always looked like Santa Claus, with his bushy gray beard and eyebrows to match, red cheeks, sparkling blue eyes, and big round belly.

"Ho ho ho. And a merry Christmas to you!" he bellowed at Madison and her mother.

"Merry Christmas, Santa," the woman said. Madison said nothing.

When they'd left he gave me a smile that was just my dad. "Things are hopping in town, honeybunch. Lots of excitement about the opening of *A Christmas Carol*. Grace tells me a state senator has reservations at the Yuletide Inn for the weekend. Ralph and I had lunch at the Touch of Holly earlier, and they say they're fully booked for tonight through the weekend. Such is the same with most of the hotels and restaurants."

"Always good to hear."

"Ralph and I had to admit that perhaps Sue-Anne's excessive expenditure on this party of hers isn't entirely out of line. It's bringing extra publicity to Rudolph."

The store was busy, but Chrystal and Jackie seemed to be handling everything so I could relax for a moment and have a chat with Dad, while keeping an eye out. "How's Mom? Pre-performance nerves started yet?"

"Thankfully not yet, but I'm expecting them. She's dismissing the entire production as of no consequence, but Friday night will be her first time in front of a paying audience in a theater for several years." Dad glanced around the store and spotted the new display tucked into a back corner. "Those children's books are new."

"I'm trying them out, see how well they do."

"You need to place them more prominently. So people can see them."

"I'm not competing with the bookstore, Dad."

"The bookstore sells Christmas decorations and ornaments. Even some dolls."

"But not primarily. People come in here looking for gifts, so we want to provide them with one-stop shopping, that's all."

My father headed to the small book rack. He selected a copy of each volume and carried them to the front window. He put them on a side table and climbed into the big picture window, where he began rearranging my lovely display. I hurried over. "Dad, what are you doing? I have everything exactly the way I want it."

"A few minor adjustments, honeybunch." He waved at a family passing by, who laughed and waved back. "If you have items in stock, you want people to know about it."

"But, but . . . this is a décor store. If I have books in the window, people will come in looking for books other than those, and I'll have to send them to the bookstore."

Books prominently arranged to his satisfaction, Dad returned my Christmas morning display to some sort of order and clambered out of the window. "I'll be off. I'm going to your mother's dress rehearsal tonight. Would you like to come?"

"Are they allowing an audience?"

"Of select invitees. Aline has invited me. And I am inviting you. Having us in the audience will calm her nerves."

"Sure." I had nothing better to do. Alan was furiously finishing his last minute orders as come Sunday he'd be busy with his head toymaker role, and Vicky and her staff were working all hours to bake enough cookies to feed a stable of reindeer.

Only about five minutes after Dad left, a woman ran into the store. "Oh, thank heavens. You're a lifesaver."

"I am? How so?"

She pointed to the display window. "All my daughter wants for the new baby for Christmas is a copy of *The Polar Express*. I've searched bookstores all over, but it's out of stock everywhere. And then, what do you know, I was walking past and saw a copy in your window. I never would have thought to come in here otherwise. It's a genuine Christmas miracle!"

So gobsmacked was I, I could think of nothing to say. I lifted my right arm and pointed to the small shelf of books, tucked into a dark corner. Realizing I probably looked much like the Ghost of Christmas Yet to Come, I dropped my arm.

"There it is!" She clapped her hands. "How wonderful. Oh, and you have a copy of the children's illustrated version of *A Christmas Carol* too. Perfect. We're taking the older grandchildren to the Saturday show. Look at those lovely dolls. A Santa doll will make a nice addition to the book as a gift."

I know my dad isn't Santa Claus.

But sometimes, I wonder.

Chapter Fifteen

The penultimate dress rehearsal for *A Christmas Carol* was due to start at six-thirty, and my dad always likes to be early. For everything. As instructed, by five to six, I was standing on the sidewalk outside Mrs. Claus's Treasures waiting for Dad. Jackie had left a short while ago. She'd been nothing but a bundle of nerves as the day progressed. Chrystal would wait a few minutes more for those last-minute shoppers and then lock up the store for the night.

"What's this?" Margie Thatcher called from her own doorway. "Leaving early, Merry. You have a highly slapdash approach to the running of your business."

I ignored her as Dad pulled up. I hopped into the car. "I'm surprised they didn't ask Margie to play Scrooge."

Dad gave Margie a cheerful wave, and she scowled in return. He chuckled as he pulled into traffic. "That would indeed be typecasting. But remember, honeybunch, Scrooge has a conversion at the end, and he becomes kind to everyone. I'm afraid Margie, like her sister before her, is past that."

Dad, I knew, had tried over the years to befriend the Thatcher sisters, to draw them into the full life of the Rudolph community. He had not succeeded, but he still made an attempt to be friendly.

"Do you remember Al Thorne?" Dad asked me.

"No. Who's he?"

"I suppose you wouldn't. One of the old gang from our high school days. He moved to Texas not long after we graduated, to be with a woman he met at college. The woman, far as I remember, didn't last, but Texas did. Anyway, he's in the area for a short visit, staying with his parents in Rochester. I'm going down tomorrow for an impromptu reunion. Not good timing with Christmas week about to begin, but I'd like to see him. I've been invited to stay overnight, as one or two beers might be involved."

"Have fun," I said.

*   *   *

Jackie wasn't the only one suffering from nerves. Desmond Kerslake paced up and down in front of the stage. Catherine Renshaw sat in the center of the front row, her foot swinging wildly in the air and the fingers of her right hand tapping a rapid rhythm on the armrest. Irene Dowling was a few seats down from her, chewing on the end of a tape measure.

The theater was mostly empty, but a handful of family members and guests had come, and they whispered excitedly to each other. "I wonder who invited them?" Dad waved to Randy Baumgartner and John Benedict.

"Dave French is trying to close a deal to buy an old motel in Muddle Harbor," I said. "It was likely him, trying to make friendly."

"I hope the deal goes through. Lloyd French had grand dreams of having a chain of budget motels when he first took over the Carolers', far bigger dreams than business sense. About all he could ever manage was to keep that one place running. If his son can do what he couldn't, maybe he'll give Dave some credit for once. Their relationship's always been a difficult one, and folks say Dave only agreed to come back and help out because his mother begged him."

"Nice he was able to get involved in the theater then," I said. "Give him an escape from parental disapproval."

"What would you know about parental disapproval, honey-bunch?" my father asked with a chuckle.

"Nothing whatsoever. Although I do remember when I was in tenth grade and I started going out with Mike McIver . . ."

"The less said of Mike, and all the McIvers, the better," Dad said as he led the way down the center aisle to the third row.

The stage curtains were open, revealing George Mann on his knees, hammering at what was supposed to be the front door of Scrooge and Marley, judging by the hand-painted sign over his head. Several people in costume watched.

"Looks like there might be a problem. Take a seat, Merry, and I'll see what's happening." Dad slipped up the stairs at one side of the stage, and reappeared onstage seconds later. "Something the matter here, George?"

George mumbled around the nails in his mouth.

"Will you hurry up with that?" Desmond yelled. "I need to get this thing started. We're ready to go."

"You need a collapsing set less." Dad rummaged in George's toolbox and came up with another hammer.

Desmond buried his head in his hands.

"Perhaps you can tell Ian to jump over the stairs, rather than walk down them," Irene suggested.

"That would work fine if we had Dave in the role," Catherine snapped. "Ian's more likely to stumble and break a leg."

"Will you shut up about Dave once and for all!" Desmond said.

"Careful, old man." Dave clattered the chains draped around him. Although made of paper-mache, they didn't so much clatter as rustle. As well as the chains he wore a threadbare suit. With his broad shoulders, mop of thick dark hair, and general good looks, he looked nothing at all like the ghostly presence of a bitter old man.

"Where's your beard and wig?" Irene asked him.

"They itch. I'll put them on before I come out. To bring the house down with my one song and one scene."

"Leave those stairs for now," Desmond said. "We can move around it tonight, and you can fix it tomorrow before final rehearsal."

"Better not," Dad said. "I have to go out of town tomorrow, and I don't get back until shortly before the curtain rises on Friday. George is more than capable, but if anything else needs fixing, two of us is better than one."

A woman walked out of the wings, probably a member of the chorus, dressed in a long brown dress under a fringed shawl and a white bonnet. "It doesn't fit!" she shouted. "Irene, do something."

Irene jumped out of her chair. "What do you mean it doesn't fit? I adjusted Eddie's costume to fit your sons only yesterday."

"Aaron, get out here," the woman said.

A boy about eight years old edged onto the stage, his cheeks and the tips of his ears pink with embarrassment. He wore a brown checked shirt under a brown jacket showing about three inches of wrist and lower arm, short pants that weren't intended to be short, straining to fasten around his middle, and thoroughly modern sneakers. Presumably this was the new Tiny Tim. He looked even less suited for the role than Eddie Monahan had. "That was Anthony who was here yesterday for the fitting," the woman said. "I told you the twins would alternate the role."

"By twins," Irene said, "I thought they'd be the same size so they could wear the same costume."

"I never said they were identical twins. Aaron's had a growth spurt."

"Then get Anthony down here!" Desmond yelled.

"He has Boy Scouts tonight. Then a birthday party tomorrow."

Jackie came on stage. Her costume had been, as she'd asked, adjusted to best show off her assets. Mrs. Cratchit was supposed to be a working class woman, scarcely able to afford an adequate sized goose for her family's Christmas dinner. Jackie's dress was made of a dark green fabric that shimmered and swooshed as she walked. The elbow-length sleeves and the low-cut bodice had been trimmed with white lace. A pair of her own earrings, streams of silver that almost touched her shoulders, were in her ears and her long hair pinned up under a feathered fascinator. "I can't work with a ringer," she declared. "That's not the boy I rehearsed our scenes with yesterday."

"Well, you'll have to," the boy's mother said. "Aaron's here now."

"I can't have cast members changing willy-nilly!" Desmond yelled.

"Oh, do sit down," Irene said. "This is amateur theater, not even off-off-Broadway. You work with what you have. Although you'll have to find some suitable footwear for the boy, whichever boy puts in an appearance, Andrea."

Desmond turned on the wardrobe mistress. His eyes almost popped out of his face. "You might not care, Irene, but let me remind you we have theater professionals coming opening night to see our show, and I expect it to be the very best it can be. No, I expect it to be better than it should be."

"So you keep endlessly reminding us." My mother emerged from the wings. "Which, let me assure you, is doing nothing to calm people's nerves."

"That ought to do it," George said as Dad helped him struggle to his feet.

"Better get Ian out here to give it a try," Dad said. "Is he the only one who'll be on the steps?"

"No," Mom said. "As Scrooge approaches front and center to deliver his opening lines, several members of the chorus climb the steps so as to be seen as they sing behind him." Mom's Ghost of Christmas Past costume was fabulous, I thought—a high-necked, floor-sweeping, unadorned white gown, with wide sleeves that flowed past her fingers, topped by a large-brimmed white hat decorated with white flowers with a hint of gold sparkles sprinkled through them. Her face was powdered stark white, her eyes thickly outlined in black, her lips a slash of red. The costume had been designed to fit over a dress so she could instantly slip out of it when she took center stage as Belle, Ebenezer's lost love, for her grand solo. And then, back into the ghost getup for the next step of the journey through the old man's memories.

"Better get them all climbing up and down, then," Dad said. "To test it out."

"This is a nightmare," Desmond moaned.

"You think this is bad," Mom said. "You should have been backstage at La Scala for the opening of *Tosca*. None other than the prime minister of Italy, a representative from the Vatican, and the American ambassador were in the audience, and—"

"Perhaps a story for another time, Aline." Dad gave her a fond smile.

"Chorus!" Desmond yelled. "Take your places on those steps. I know it's not time yet, but I want them tested out."

Various cast members had gathered in the wings, waiting for rehearsal to start. They trooped forward now. They looked great in a variety of long dresses and aprons, capes, black trousers and frock coats, tall hats or bonnets, Some hurried forward, beaming from ear to ear, excited to play their role. Others hedged nervously, overcome by anxiety.

Ian eyed the steps. "Are you sure these are safe?"

"That's what you're going to find out," George said. "Get on with it. I haven't got all day here."

Tentatively Ian climbed the steps to stand at the doorway of Scrooge and Marley, constructed to look as though the building was falling down through neglect and a failure to pay to have it maintained. There were only two stairs. If the set did crumble beneath him, I doubted it would do him much harm, but it would be embarrassing in front of a full theater. When nothing gave way, Ian confidently stamped on the top step.

"Now the rest of you," Desmond said.

Members of the chorus leapt into place. Some tapped nervously at the boards, some jumped up and down as though trying to make it collapse. It held.

Dad slapped George on the back, and the older man beamed. "I'll be off. Call me, Noel, if you need anything." He threw a look at Catherine and Desmond. "Seein' as to how my home-made wine isn't good enough for your fancy party."

Dave laughed. "Imagine serving that plonk to the audience we're expecting. I can see the reviews now: 'French's stellar performance as Jacob Marley, the sole highlight of the night, spoiled by alcohol poisoning.'"

My mom turned on him, her face such a mask of fury her makeup threatened to crack. "I've had about enough of you. You and Desmond both. This is an amateur theatrical production, and all these people are volunteers. They've joined this group to have fun and to promote our town. Not to be your props in a ridiculous attempt to impress some supposed Broadway big shot. Friday night is not your night, either of you. It's for all of us. All of them." She lifted her arms to indicate the cast, every one of them watching her. White fabric flowed around her like fog or smoke. "It is not going to be anyone's big break. And you, Catherine, need to get off your high horse as well."

Ian let out a bark of laughter and clapped enthusiastically. "That's telling 'em, Aline."

Catherine's eyes narrowed and her lips tightened. She threw Ian a poisoned look before turning on my mother. "Well, pardon me for wanting to get the best performance we can."

"And you will get the best performance these people can deliver. With all of their heart and soul. But they can only deliver what is possible, given the circumstances. You, Catherine, need to decide if you want to be the artistic director of a company that doesn't need one, but does appreciate your financial largesse, or to go back to New York, where you seem to think you belong, and try to get your foot in the door there."

"Now see here, this has gone far enough." Bruce Renshaw had taken a seat halfway back. He stood up.

"Shut up," Catherine said. "I can fight my own battles."

Bruce dropped back down, a somewhat sheepish expression on his face.

"Battle?" Mom said. "This is no battle. I am expressing my opinion. You may disagree, or not." She stepped backward and went to stand next to Dad. He put his arm around her shoulders.

Her in full makeup and ghost costume. Him in ugly Christmas sweater, still holding his hammer. My parents really were a study in contrasts.

All was quiet for a long time.

"I don't wanna be in this dumb play anyway," Aaron whined. "This stupid costume is stupid."

"Be quiet," his mother snapped.

Desmond stepped forward. He puffed out his chest. "Let us begin. Everyone, full rehearsal will commence in five minutes. Please take your places. Noel, can you lower the curtain, please."

"Got it," Dad said.

"I want one full run-through, start to finish. The way—" he coughed, "it's done on professional stages."

Ian held up one hand. "Before we do that. You've forgotten someone, Desmond."

The director looked around. "Who?"

"Paula, of course. Paula was an important member of this troupe for many years. She loved to act, she loved Rudolph. She was hoping her young son, Eddie, would follow her example."

Irene swallowed a retort.

"I think a moment to remember Paula would not be amiss," Ian said.

"An excellent idea, Ian," Mom said. "You're quite right."

"Very well," Desmond replied impatiently. "A moment."

The scattering of people in the theater seats got to their feet, the Muddites among them. On stage, people bowed their heads or folded their hands. A couple of women in the chorus put their arms around each other. Aaron shifted his feet and tugged at his mother's dress. She swatted his hand away.

The silence lasted about ten seconds before Desmond cleared his throat. "Now that that's done, it reminds me. Who's the understudy for Mrs. Cratchit?"

"I am," Jackie said. "I mean I was. After Paula's tragic demise, I stepped into the role. I'm fully prepared and excited about making my—"

"I mean the new understudy." The cast all exchanged glances and shrugged. "Don't we have one?"

"Looks like we don't," Ian said. "Does it matter?"

"Of course it matters. Unlike what some people might think—" A poisonous look at my mom, which she returned with sweet smile. "We need to have actors available if needed. Particularly for Mrs. Cratchit."

"Why particularly for her?" someone asked.

"In case our current Mrs. C. is arrested for murder, of course." Desmond turned to Jackie. "You are the prime suspect, isn't that correct?"

Someone gasped. Dad said, "that's unnecessarily blunt, Desmond."

Jackie blinked rapidly. Tears filled her eyes. The woman next to her, carrying a mop and pail, gave her a sideways glance and edged slightly way.

Jackie burst into tears and ran off stage, tripping over her long skirts as she fled.

Chapter Sixteen

"Surprisingly, the rehearsal went well after all that," I said.

"Maybe next year they should put on *Black Christmas*. Get the mood right," said Vicky. Do you remember when we were fourteen and a bunch of us from school snuck out of town to catch it in Muddle Harbor, because it was banned in Rudolph?"

"I remember. It was absolutely dreadful. Not worth incurring our parents' wrath."

"Kept me awake for weeks."

"The worst was Dad sadly shaking his head in disappointment and telling me that movie was contrary to the Christmas spirit we know and love in Rudolph. All of which is beside the point."

"Before you get to the point, pass me that cutter, will you? The big one."

I handed Vicky the largest of her metal gingerbread figures. It was midafternoon on Thursday, and I'd escaped from the store to grab a quick lunch at Victoria's Bake Shoppe. Traffic coming into town and on Jingle Bell Lane was clogged, the sidewalks were packed, and Mrs. Claus's had been hopping all day. We'd had more snow last night, and the snowplows and homeowners with their shovels and snowblowers had been out early. As had been Mrs. D'Angelo, armed with her own shovel, when I left for work. She'd known (of course she had) that I'd been at rehearsal last night and wanted to hear every salacious detail. I escaped on the grounds of a busy day ahead.

Which hadn't been a lie.

Even at three in the afternoon, the lineup at the bakery had been so long, I'd snuck in the back way to get my order. I found Vicky elbow deep in gingerbread dough and briefly told her about last night's rehearsal. The scent of warm pastry wafting out of the oven, of sugar, cinnamon, and nutmeg rising from Vicky's dough, and curried butternut soup simmering on the stove filled the room.

I breathed it all in. The smells of Christmas. Is anything better? "I suppose it's natural enough," I said. "Nerves are stretched to a breaking point. Everyone's on edge. After last year's flop, they need this year's production to be a success. Different people have different reasons for being involved in the show and thus differing expectations of what they want to get out of it. Such as young Aaron who doesn't want to be in the play at all, yet he managed to give an adequate performance as Tiny Tim. Mom gave Desmond and Dave a stern talking to. And, not incidentally, Catherine as well."

"I wish I'd been there to see it. Was Jackie okay? That was a mean thing for Desmond to say in front of everyone." Vicky worked steadily as she chatted. She rolled out the dough to a thick rectangle and began cutting out the human-like shapes. Vicky didn't believe in overly decorated cookies: after they were baked she'd add a touch of icing to represent eyes and mouths and just a hint of clothing.

"I'm beginning to not like Desmond all that much," I said. "He's as self-centered as the rest of them. I know he's under pressure, but really, that was uncalled for. As for Jackie, she recovered after a few minutes of me consoling her. More of those stretched nerves. She was more upset thinking Desmond wanted to kick her out of the part than the suggestion that she might be arrested for murder any minute. She did an okay job. I might think her acting a bit over the top, but at least she remembered all her lines, and as Mom went to great pains to remind them, it is amateur theater. I'll admit I didn't stay until the end. I left after the Ghost of Christmas Past had done her bit."

Vicky scooped pink icing into a bag. One of her assistants lifted a sheet of fragrant individual-sized turkey pies out of the large oven.

"You're busy here, I'm busy there," I said. "I'll be off. Thanks for this." I picked up the hefty bags of food I'd called ahead to have prepared for me. Along with a sandwich for my lunch and cookies as treats for my hardworking staff, I had soup and a bacon and spinach quiche to take to Alan's for a late dinner tonight. The store wouldn't close until nine thirty, but Alan said he'd be working late himself.

* * *

My phone rang at midnight. Alan and I were curled up on the couch watching an old James Bond movie with Pierce Brosnan as 007. Mattie snoozed on the rug in front of the fire, and Ranger napped with one eye open. Before dinner we'd had a long walk in the nighttime winter woods, to shake off the stresses of the working day, as fresh snow fell on our heads and shoulders and covered the naked branches of the trees and the rushing waters of the creek.

"Who on earth would be calling at this time of night?" I put down my mug of hot chocolate and struggled, reluctantly, out of Alan's arms to check the phone. My heart gave a jolt, and I was immediately pulled out of my comfortable languor when I saw the name on the display. "Mom. What's wrong?"

"Merry." Her voice trembled in a way I'd never heard before. "Someone's . . . I think . . . someone is in the house."

I swung my legs off the couch and sat upright. "Now? You mean they're there now?"

Alan took one look at my face and leapt to his feet. In the background, James drove far too fast through crowded city streets as pedestrians ran for cover and vegetable carts were upturned. Alan grabbed the remote and froze the screen, leaving 007's expensive sports car suspended in midair.

"Have you called the police?" I asked.

"No. I'm . . . not entirely sure."

"Do that. Now. Never mind, I'll call them. You get out of the house." I jumped off the couch and ran for my coat, boots, and car keys. "I'm on my way."

"I think they've gone. I don't hear anything more."

"You can't be sure of that, Mom. If it's not safe to leave your bedroom, go into the bathroom and lock yourself in."

Alan beat me to the door, snatching his keys off the hook as he passed. "I'll drive."

We were out of the house before Mattie and Ranger knew what was happening. Their questioning barks followed us to Alan's truck.

"I'm hanging up now and calling 911," I said. "Alan and I are on our way."

Alan didn't have to be asked to step on it. Snow had continued to fall when we were in the house, but his truck was used to the conditions. Fortunately plows had been at work on the highway leading to town, and he could push past the speed limit. "If a cop tries to stop me, they can follow us," he said as we tore down the dark, empty road.

I called 911 and told the operator what Mom had told me. I gave her the address and she said, "I'll have a patrol car there as soon as possible."

We arrived before the cops. The street was quiet, most of the houses wrapped in darkness, holiday decorations switched off for the night. Streetlamps shone on swirling flakes of snow. Alan pulled into the driveway, and I was out of the truck before he'd come to a complete halt.

I ran around the back, heedless of his cries of, "Merry, wait!"

The lamp over the kitchen door was off. I fumbled on my chain to locate the right key and fumbled more to get it in the lock. Then I had it and the door flew open. "Mom! We're here!"

Alan grabbed my arm, "Merry. You have to wait for the police. The intruder could still be in the house."

"But my mom. I have to see to my mom."

His blue eyes stared into mine for a few seconds. I hesitated. I was still gripping my phone in my hand. It buzzed, and I was so startled I almost dropped it. Instead, I stabbed at the button to answer. Mom's voice was so soft I could barely hear. "I hear voices downstairs. Is that you, Merry?"

"Yes, we're here. Alan's with me. The police are on their way."

"I'm in the bedroom. I think . . . I'm pretty sure he . . . they . . . whatever . . . are gone."

"I'm coming up," I said.

I shook Alan's arm off and ran through the kitchen, heading for the hallway and the stairs leading to the second floor.

The hallway was unexpectedly chilly; a strong, icy draft blew against my face. I ignored it and took the stairs two at a time. I heard Alan's footsteps behind me as he spoke into his own phone, telling the police we were in the house.

I charged down the hallway and into my parents' room, yelling, "Mom!"

The closet door slowly opened and my mother stepped out. "Merry, Alan, good evening," she said. "I'm sorry to have disturbed you."

In the distance, sirens broke the silence of the neighborhood.

"I'll go down and meet them," Alan said. "Your mom might like a cup of tea, Merry."

"What an excellent idea," Mom said. She was dressed in a peach floor-length satin nightgown with a lacy décolletage. Her feet were bare, the toes painted a cheerful bright pink. She looked down at herself. "Hand me that robe, will you, dear. If I'm to receive visitors in my nightwear I should try to look as presentable as possible."

I studied her face. "Are you okay, Mom?"

"I'm fine dear. Now." She gave me what she thought was an encouraging smile as she put her hand to her heart. I couldn't help but notice the hand was shaking. Not as calm and collected as she wanted me to think. "I had a fright, that's all."

"Can you tell me what happened?"

From downstairs came the sound of boots hitting the floor and several people talking at once.

"Let's join the others, shall we," I suggested. I took her arm, and she let me lead the way.

We found Candy Campbell and Officer Williams at the bottom of the steps with Alan. "We're going to search the house, Mrs. Wilkinson," Candy said. "Is that okay with you?"

"Please do. Although I'm confident whoever was here has gone."

"You shouldn't have come in by yourselves," Candy said to me. "You should have waited for us."

"My mother needed me," I said. "I didn't know how long you'd be."

She didn't look as though she completely agreed with me, but she let it go.

"Wait outside until we give you the all clear," Williams said. "It's cold, but maybe you can wait in a car."

"My truck," Alan said.

"There's a strong draft in the hallway," I said. "As though a window's open. That's not normal, not at this time of year. Alan, take Mom outside, please, and I'll show the police what I mean."

I ran down the hallway without waiting for anyone to agree. Or not. Mom's music room is an extension specifically built onto the back of the house for that purpose. She used to rehearse there when she was performing, and it now serves as her classroom and studio. In order that her students can come and go without tramping through the house, French doors open onto a flagstone path that curls around the house to join up with the front walkway. The door to the music room was open and a strong cold wind blew through. "Mom would never leave a window open in these temperatures," I said to Candy and her partner.

They exchanged glances and nodded. Williams jerked his head at me, telling me to stand aside. I did so. My heart pounded in my chest.

Candy shoved the door open with a shout and her partner ran in. No one screamed, shots did not ring out, so I gathered my courage around me and ventured in after them. The piano stood silently in its corner, dust cover in place; an oil painting of

Mom as Carmen hung above it. The laptop and speakers were untouched, and the rows of books and bound sheet music on the shelves lining the walls did not appear to have been disturbed. Framed posters from Mom's performances in her glory days covered the walls, and a bust of Mozart stared at us from the top of a bookcase.

One of the French doors stood partially open. Shards of glass covered the carpet beneath it, slowly being covered by a light dusting of fresh snow. The pages of a book open on the center table fluttered in the breeze. I was in my winter coat, but a chill ran down my spine.

My mother, for all her elaborate clothes, diva airs, and stories about her glory days, was anything but a fanciful woman. If she said someone had been in her bedroom while she slept, then someone had been in her bedroom while she slept. I knew that, but still, I'd hoped she'd been dreaming.

"Looks like your mother did have an intruder after all, Merry," Candy said.

"Did you doubt it?" I asked.

"People imagine lots of things in the night," Williams said. "I'll check upstairs."

I spotted something out of place on the carpet and stepped forward. Candy shouted, "leave it," but I ignored her and bent over to have a closer look. It was, of all things, a white bed sheet, one corner caught in a door hinge, crumpled and cast aside as one might throw off a coat without caring where it landed.

Chapter Seventeen

I bundled my Mom into her coat and boots, and Alan and I took her to my place while the police finished searching the house and called for someone to come and take fingerprints. Mom told me not to worry my father, but I ignored her as I'd ignored Candy Campbell earlier and gave him a call. I explained what had happened, as calmly and succinctly as was possible. He said he'd had a couple of beers with his friends earlier so didn't want to drive but would try to find a cab. Mom grabbed my phone and insisted she'd be all right until the morning. Alan and I went into the kitchen to give her some privacy while they talked. When we emerged with tea and toast, I was relieved to see some of the tension had left her face. "Your father will be here first thing in the morning," she informed us. "Earlier, if I know him."

We settled in the living room. It felt strange to be in my own place without Mattie's bulk filling every corner. No doubt he thought it strange to be at Alan's without me. I hoped he and Ranger wouldn't get up to too much trouble while we were gone.

Mom had told the police briefly what happened, but once we were settled on my couch, Mom with a heavy throw gathered around her shoulders, Alan asked if she remembered anything more.

She shook her head. My mom rarely faces the world, or even her own family, without hair done and full makeup applied. Tonight she looked so pale; her cheeks shrunken and the shadows beneath her eyes deep. "Nothing new. I don't normally go to bed before midnight, but with the opening of the play tomorrow, which I suppose is now today, it's going to be a very long day so I decided to turn in early. I read for a while and then drifted off. I thought I heard a noise downstairs, but you know what old houses are like when the wind gets up. It's always creaking and moaning."

I knew. This house was much the same. I'd almost expected Mrs. D'Angelo to be standing on her front porch when we drove up. But the lights remained off and the property quiet in the falling snow. I guess even Mrs. D'Angelo has to sleep sometimes.

"I tried to get back to sleep," Mom continued. "Unlike when I was touring, your father and I rarely spend nights apart these days, so I told myself I was being nervous in his absence, jumping at nothing."

"You likely heard the glass on the music room door breaking," I said.

She shuddered and took a sip of her tea. "I might have fallen asleep again, because the next thing I knew, I was not alone. Someone, something, was standing by my bed, looking down at me. I thought I was dreaming at first. It was . . . white, the arms not visible, the shape shifting. Remarkably similar to the Ghost of Christmas Past. I remember thinking how odd that was. In all my years I've never dreamt I was living one of my own roles."

"Is that your part in the play?" Alan asked.

"One of them."

"Did you see the face?" I asked.

"No. It was white, that's all I noticed. I mean excessively white. As in applied with theatrical or clown makeup, as though an exaggerated version of my own costume. The face might also have been partially covered by a hood or a sheet. Everything happened so very fast, I didn't notice a lot of details. I told Candice that."

"It, whatever it was, said nothing?" Alan asked.

"Not a word. The cloth moved, and a finger pointed at me. Directly at my face. It was then I knew this was no dream. I must have screamed and attempted to climb out of the far side of the bed. It was all so . . . confusing. Confusing and terrifying. By the time I got out of bed and turned to face it . . . it was gone. I heard footsteps rapidly descending the stairs. I immediately called you, Merry, and hid in the closet until you arrived. However, now that I come to think of it, the closet was not a particularly adequate hiding place. The door does not lock."

Alan and I said nothing. Mom took another sip of her tea.

"It sounds to me," Alan said at last. "As though this person, whoever it was, intended to do nothing more than frighten you, Aline."

"That was more than enough, thank you," she said.

"Agreed. If they'd wanted to do more . . ." My voice trailed off. I shook the image away.

"This person must have known Noel was away," Alan said. "It can't be a coincidence. As you said, Aline, he doesn't usually go out of town overnight, particularly not at the start of Christmas week. Who knew he'd be away tonight?"

"It was no secret," Mom said. "I don't know who he might have mentioned it to."

"He told everyone who'd been at the dress rehearsal Wednesday night," I said. "He said, in full view of the entire company, he wouldn't be able to work on the set the following day, if something went wrong, because he was going away."

* * *

I insisted on settling Mom into my bed for what remained of the night. I took the couch, and Alan offered to sleep on the floor, but I reminded him we'd left the dogs at his house. They hadn't even been let out one last time.

"You sure you're going to be okay?" he asked me.

"I'm sure. The intruder isn't going to come here, and Dad'll be here in a couple of hours."

I walked Alan downstairs to the outer door. "You'll call me if you or your mom need anything?" he said. "If anything . . . out of the ordinary happens, don't hesitate."

"I won't."

"I'll bring Mattie to the store in the morning. Let me know if your plans change and you don't go in."

"I will." I kissed him and he pulled me close. We stood together for a long time, simply holding each other.

"If I'm going to go, I'd better," Alan said at last. "The play opens tomorrow. Tonight now. Do you think your mom's up to performing?"

I chuckled into his chest. "Are you kidding? According to her she sang Waltraute in *Gotterdammerung* at Covent Garden with a fever of a hundred and two and a full body rash. And that was nothing compared to the time—"

He kissed me again and then let me go and stepped away. "Point taken. I'll drop Mattie in the morning, and pick you up shortly after six tonight as arranged."

"I've just remembered. My car's at your place."

"Do you need it today?"

"I shouldn't."

"Then we can pick it up on the weekend. Before that, I guess you're expecting me to dust off my suit."

*   *   *

I doubt if Mom got any more sleep than I did. Dad made it from Rochester to Rudolph in record time and he was hammering on my door at six AM. I gave my parents a few moments of privacy and went into the kitchen to prepare another round of tea and toast.

Mom sipped the tea, ignored the toast, and said, "I'd like to go home now, Noel."

"No hurry, sweetheart. I called Diane Simmonds as I got near town. She'll meet us at the house at seven thirty."

"That will give me time to dress and prepare for visitors," Mom said. She was still in the nightgown she'd had on last night. Candy asked us not to go back upstairs at the house until the bedroom had been thoroughly checked. "Then, I'll need to get some rest and put all this fuss and bother behind me. I have a performance to give this evening."

"I haven't forgotten," Dad said. He didn't bother to ask her if she was up to it after the fright of last night.

"Do remember to get your suit from the cleaners, Noel. I'd prefer you not wear casual clothes this evening."

He gave her a fond smile and me a wink. "I'll be on my best behavior."

"We're expected to attend Sue-Anne's after-party. Someone told me a senator or two is coming. I do hope the town rises to the occasion. George Mann might not agree, but that does not mean serving his homemade wine."

My parents left and I got ready for work. I expected a busy day before Mrs. Claus's, like many of the shops on Jingle Bell

Lane, would close early so people could attend (or appear in) the opening night's performance of *A Christmas Carol*.

My apartment seemed so empty without Mattie. I hoped he'd had a good night and hadn't worried too much about where I'd gone in such a rush.

The store wouldn't open for a few hours yet, but I decided to go in early. Not only was I too restless to go back to bed, but plenty of tasks always need to be seen to when the store's closed. I munched on Mom's uneaten toast while I showered and dressed for work. That done, I put on my outdoor clothes, and then tiptoed down the stairs, holding my breath and trying not to make a sound on the old floorboards. I opened the door slowly and carefully, shut it silently behind me, and darted across the snow-covered lawn as the weak winter sun slowly rose in a clear sky. I'd discovered a loose board in the back fence one summer and hadn't reported it to the landlady to be fixed. It made a convenient exit route if I needed to sneak away unseen. Police cars had clogged the street in front of my parents' house last night, lights flashing and sirens blaring, officers running in and out, shouting to each other. Mom had been bundled out of the house with a coat thrown over her nightgown and driven away in Alan's truck. Attracted by the commotion, lights had come in on nearby houses, curtains moved, and people stepped onto their front porches to see what was going on. I'd long suspected some members of Mrs. D'Angelo's network were neighbors of my parents.

My instincts were spot on. As the loose board flopped into place behind me, I heard Mrs. D'Angelo's voice approaching. I peeked through the crack in the fence. She wore an unbuttoned coat, and her feet were stuffed into rubber boots decorated with images of colorful umbrellas. She was talking on her phone as she came around the corner. "Joan, I'm on my way to check now. Before Merry goes to work, I want to pop in and make sure Noel and Aline are all right. Quite the kerfuffle at their house last night, I heard." My landlady let herself in the back door with her key and her voice faded away.

I congratulated myself on having the foresight to kick up snow behind me as I'd crossed the yard in an attempt to hide evidence of my passing.

* * *

The first person through the doors of Mrs. Claus's Treasures on Friday morning was none other than Detective Diane Simmonds. I doubted she'd come to get her Christmas shopping done. "Do you have a moment to talk, Merry?" she asked.

I considered saying no, as the second through fifth person came close behind her and they had that sharply focused, determined gift-hunting look on their faces I love so much. Fortunately Jackie arrived promptly on time this morning. She'd be leaving at three to get ready for the play, and Chrystal was coming in at noon to work until early closing at four-thirty.

"You've been to my parents' house?" I asked the detective.

"Yes. I left them a short while ago. I'd like to talk to you about what you observed last night. Your office?"

Jackie tore her attention away from greeting the customers. "What happened last night? What about Merry's parents? Does this have anything to do with the play? It'll be a disaster if Aline drops out. People are coming just to see her."

"Merry?" the detective said.

"Mom's fine," I assured Jackie. "She'll be there, right on time."

As Simmonds and I walked into the back I heard a customer say, "The play? You mean *A Christmas Carol?* We have tickets for tomorrow. We wanted to go to the opening night performance but it was sold out."

"You'll love it," Jackie said. "It's going to be absolutely fabulous. I myself have a small but vitally important solo part. I'm playing Mrs. Cratchit as well as being a prominent voice in the chorus."

"Did you hear that, Marlene?" the woman said. "We're actually talking to one of the stars of the play."

There'd be no living with Jackie now.

Simmonds and I went into my office, and I shut the door. "Have a seat," I said. I dropped into the chair behind my desk.

She looked around the room. "Where's Matterhorn? This place seems empty without him."

"As a bonus, the carpet's dry. He's at Alan's. We left in such a rush last night after Mom's call, we didn't even stop to bring the dogs."

She took the offered chair. "Which is why I'm here. I was notified this morning of an apparent intruder at your parents' house last night. The call was flagged for my attention because of your mother's association with the Paula Monahan killing."

"I wouldn't say 'association' is the right word. Neither is 'apparent.' There was an intruder, no doubt about it."

"You and Alan Anderson were at the house when officers arrived in response to the 911 call. Can you tell me what caused you to go there and what happened then?"

I did so.

"You didn't see any evidence of this intruder, other than the broken door and the sheet on the floor?"

"No. Whoever it was had gone by the time we arrived. It normally takes about fifteen minutes to get from Alan's to Mom's.

We probably did it in ten. Maybe less. The roads were . . . uh . . . not busy at that time of night."

"Understood."

"Mom said he . . . or she . . . whoever . . . didn't stay after she'd woken up. Mom jumped out of bed and the person fled. I don't recall seeing a car parked on their street, though I suppose they wouldn't have been dumb enough to drive their own car and park it right outside."

"You never know. If criminals weren't morons, we wouldn't catch half of them. I showed a photograph of the bedsheet to your mother. Plain white, mass produced, cheap, clean. She claims she doesn't own one like it, but she did check the linen closet and the contents appear to be undisturbed."

"Which means they brought it with them. And, as most people don't call on friends in the middle of the night bearing bedsheets, I can only assume wearing it to frighten Mom was their intent."

Simmonds nodded. "We've fingerprinted the music room and your parents' bedroom as well as the staircase. It was a cold night, so it's more than possible our intruder was wearing gloves, but we can hope. The sheet's been sent for DNA analysis. If we get lucky, a hair or eyelash or something similar rubbed off on it."

"Doesn't everyone these days know about DNA? Why would they leave the sheet behind?"

"It was snagged on the door, caught on a hinge. I suspect that happened as the intruder left, and they were in too much of a panicked hurry to take the time to free it."

"That's good then."

"If I don't have a DNA sample to compare it against, anything we find isn't worth much. I have to ask you Merry, if you can think of any reason someone might have broken into your parents' house to attack your mother."

"Is attack the right word? She wasn't harmed."

"She was badly frightened, although she's attempting to pretend she wasn't. I consider that an attack, but I won't know if this person had further intentions until I determine the reason behind the intrusion."

"If they meant to harm her, they would have, surely."

"We don't know that. Did the attacker hear something that caused them to believe someone else was in the house? Your mother says she immediately rolled off the other side of the bed. Did the attacker fear she was going for a gun or a knife? Or that your mother has a black belt in karate and was getting into position to attack?"

"This has to be related to the killing of Paula Monahan."

"Why do you say that?"

"First, you yourself made the connection. Second, my mom doesn't have enemies. She might tell you that some Estonian or Swedish mezzo-soprano has it in for her because she got the better role, but really . . . Even if that ever happened, which I doubt, Mom hasn't sung professionally for several years now. It has to have something to do with *A Christmas Carol*. Although," my voice trailed off, "I can't think what."

"I asked your mother if she'd remembered anything about Paula Monahan's death since we last spoke, and she says no. I also asked her who the understudy for her part is."

I sincerely hoped it wasn't Jackie.

"A woman by the name of Iris Kincaid. Do you know her?"

"I don't think so."

"Your mother told me Iris has been in the company for many years and has always been content to be an extra. She's the understudy for your mother because, in Aline's words, she's the one with the best voice. But she is, again according to your mother, nothing but terrified at the idea of stepping in."

"My mom's a hard act to follow."

"Nevertheless, I had an officer pay a call on Ms. Kincaid this morning."

"And?"

"Her husband and visiting daughter and son-in-law tell us everyone in the house was awake at midnight because Ms. Kincaid was either pacing up and down or locked in the bathroom being sick."

I gasped. "You think she was poisoned? Maybe someone's out to get the entire theater company."

"She had pre-performance jitters. Her husband says it happens every time, the night before opening." Simmonds shook her head. "I can't understand why people are so passionate about doing something they apparently hate so much it makes them physically ill."

"You know my dad wasn't home last night?"

"I do. I can't help but think that was more than a coincidence. Who knew he'd be away?"

"It was no secret. He might have told friends, or the staff at town hall. He mentioned it Wednesday at the dress rehearsal."

"He didn't tell me that. Who heard him?"

"Everyone. Not only the usual suspects, meaning the cast and crew, but a handful of people were watching. Randy Baumgartner and John Benedict from Muddle Harbor among them. Bruce Renshaw also."

"Why do you specially mention them?"

"No reason." My phone tinged to tell me I had a text and I glanced at it.

Alan: *Mattie and I are pulling into the alley now. Can you
    unlock the door?*
Me: *Be right there*

"It's Alan, bringing Mattie," I said to Simmonds. "He needs
me to let them in."

She stood up. "I'm finished for now. You'll call me if you
think of anything?"

"You know I will."

She gave me a half-smile. "Not always. Oh, what's the dress
code for tonight?"

"You mean at the play? Pretty fancy, according to Mom.
Special guests have been invited and the town's putting on an
after-party. Are you coming?"

"I am. I called the mayor on my way here and told her to get
me a ticket." Simmonds grinned. "She said none are available,
the performance is completely sold out, and the party is by invitation only. I told her in that case, I'd take her seat for the show,
and I am inviting myself to the party. I suspect she'll manage to
find an extra ticket somewhere."

Chapter Eighteen

I'd spent a lot of time thinking about what to wear to the gala performance. What passes for the glitterati of Rudolph and environs were going to be in attendance along with several special guests. Chief among the glitterati was my own mother. You can be sure she'd have something mighty snazzy to put on when she took off her costume, and she'd have more than a few words to say if she didn't think I was suitably presentable.

When I lived in Manhattan and truly did move among the most influential people in the American design world, I had some suitable outfits. I'd been nothing but a lowly paid worker, but when I went to parties and events for the magazine, I needed to look as though I belonged. I gave those clothes to charity shops when I left that life behind me. Not a lot of opportunity in Rudolph to dress as though I was going to a megastar's Christmas party or to the opening of an art gallery show.

I'd finally decided to make a statement by being low key and understated, and bought a floor-length navy-blue skirt and matching jacket to wear over a white satin shirt. I'd accent the outfit with the ruby earrings I'd inherited from my late

232

grandmother, and shoes with heels so high I never wore them because they pinched.

Alan arrived at my house not long after six, looking so handsome in a gray suit with thin blue threads and a blue tie that was a perfect match to his eyes that I almost suggested we not worry about making the first act.

But we'd arranged to go with Vicky and Mark Grosse, so that would never do.

"You look," Alan said, "absolutely fantastic." He gave me an exaggerated wink. "Do you think anyone would notice if we arrive late?"

"Great minds think alike," I said. "In answer to your question, you can be sure my mother would."

Vicky texted me to say they were on their way. I told Mattie to guard the apartment and we left.

Alan and I rounded the corner of the house in time to see Mrs. D'Angelo and her date descending the stairs from the porch. Her hair was sprayed into a stiff helmet, and imitation diamonds glittered from her ears and around her neck. A peek of pink satin showed from underneath the hem of her tattered winter coat. Her date was none other than George Mann, farmer and the show's lead set constructor. His thin hair was slicked down with a copious quantity of oil, and even across the yard I could detect the faint scent of the mothballs that had been protecting his suit since he wore it last.

We exchanged greetings. "I've a couple bottles of my good wine in the truck." George gave Alan an exaggerated wink. "Spread the word to those who want a real drink after the play, none of that fancy ten-dollar-a-bottle stuff Sue-Anne's bringing in."

"I don't think serving out of the back of your truck is legal, George," Alan said.

"Arrest me then," he replied as he led Mrs. D'Angelo to the rust- and mud-covered vehicle parked behind Alan. She took a strong grip on her coat and dress, and George shoved her up into the cab with a grunt.

Alan wiggled his eyebrows at me, and I laughed. "It's been a while," Alan said, "since you could purchase a Sue-Anne-approved bottle of wine for ten dollars."

At that moment Mark's car pulled up and we set off for the theater.

*　*　*

The parking lot of the Rudolph Community Center was packed. I smiled to myself as I watched the streams of people entering and leaving the building. In true small-town fashion, theatergoers dressed in their elaborate finery mingled with parents taking kids to ball or gymnastics practice, people with yoga mats tucked under their arms, and others lugging laden sports bags.

We turned right after passing through the doors and headed toward the auditorium, surrounded by the excited buzz of conversation. As we divested ourselves of our coats at racks provided for that purpose, I said to Vicky, "Nice outfit, must be new."

"Like it?"

"I sure do."

She wore a sleek black pantsuit—slim-fitting, ankle-length trousers, cashmere jacket with shiny satin lapels, stiffly ironed red shirt, red ballet flats. It suited her perfectly, with her height and slender frame and dramatic hairstyle. She'd even dyed the single long lock of hair red to match her blouse. Mark, dressed in an immaculate gray suit, smiled fondly at her. "Never one to blend in with the crowd, our Vicky."

The doors of the auditorium hadn't opened yet, and the crowd was building in the hallway outside. The line in front of the cash bar was long.

"Can I get you something?" Alan asked me.

"No thanks. I'll save it for the party later."

"Wouldn't mind a beer myself," Mark said. "I wonder how long before they open the doors? Stuff any more people in here and the fire department will have something to say about it. Vicky, want anything?"

"No thanks."

The men headed for the back of the line. "I see Aunt Gertrude," Vicky said to me. "I haven't spoken to her for far too long. Catch you later."

I studied the crowd. Many faces I recognized, a lot I didn't. Diane Simmonds was by herself, watching everyone. Her red curls were arranged into a softer style than normal and more makeup applied than I'd ever seen her wear. She'd dressed for the occasion in a multicolored dress with a wide flaring skirt and put small diamond earrings in her ears. But the purse thrown over her shoulder was big and clunky and no doubt contained a lot more than tissues, a lipstick, and a few spare dollars. That, along with the expression on her face and the way her eyes never stopped moving, marked her out as what she was: a cop, working. The chief of police had come, resplendent in his dress uniform, and at the moment he was chatting to the fire chief, also in uniform. Mrs. D'Angelo spotted the police chief and headed straight for him. His eyes widened in terror the moment he saw her, but he didn't react quickly enough, and she reached him before he could flee.

I saw my dad across the crowded room and made my way toward him. He also wore a nice, although slightly out-of-date, suit and a tie, which made him look like Santa Claus dressed up for a fancy night out. "How's Mom?" I asked.

"She slept most of the day, which did her good. She says she's recovered from the incident, and I hope that's true. Fortunately, tonight's performance gave her something else to think about. As for the performance . . ." His voice dropped. "I think she's extremely nervous. She hasn't sung in front of a paying audience for a long time, and never before to her hometown crowd other than a few Christmas carols or accompanied by her students."

"That's probably good. It never serves to get too sure of yourself."

He ruffled my hair. "How did you become so wise, honeybunch?"

I smiled at him. "I had a good teacher."

"Evening all. It's looking to be a big night." Russ Durham joined us, followed by Kyle Lambert, big black Nikon around his neck next to a homemade card hanging from a lanyard, announcing that he was "PRESS."

"I trust you know not to take pictures while the performance is in progress," Dad said sternly.

"Yeah. Right. Got it. Russ told me like about a hundred times." Kyle lifted his camera. Dad put an arm around me and we smiled as Kyle took the shot.

"Catherine and Bruce are arriving now," Russ said. "Why don't you get a couple of pictures of them. She looks amazing."

And she did. Diamonds were in her ears and around her neck and wrist. Her dress was a crimson taffeta, the sleeveless top low cut and tight fitting, the skirt flaring out and sweeping the floor behind her as she strolled through the crowded space, exchanging greetings, hugs, and air kisses as she passed. Bruce, dressed in a suit that showed signs of too much wear, followed in her wake, appearing content to take a back seat on her occasion.

Russ pointed across the room. "All the town dignitaries have come, present company included. That's the senator over there. Big guy with silver hair and pink tie talking to Sue-Anne. Sue-Anne's seen Kyle and the camera. She's telling her husband to get Kyle over there and fast. There he goes, as commanded. If Sue-Anne's smile gets any broader she's going to crack her face."

"Don't be mean," Dad said. "Sue-Anne's a good mayor, and we're lucky to have her. Let her enjoy her moment in the sun."

"Speaking of moments in the sun," I said. "Here comes Randy Baumgartner. That must be his wife with him. Too bad about that outfit. He's trying to muscle Sue-Anne aside and get next to the senator for the photo. Sue-Anne's having none of it. She's holding her ground, but look, Mrs. Baumgartner's distracting her with a compliment on her dress. Randy slips in and shakes the senator's hand. Kyle takes the shot. A win for Randy!"

"This is more exciting than the play," Russ said. "And we have front row seats."

"Do you know which one's the big Broadway hot shot I've been hearing so much about?" I asked.

"Yeah, I do. I met him earlier. He was talking to Desmond a couple of minutes ago. Desmond seems to have disappeared. Some crisis backstage maybe. He's the short, round, bald guy. Looks like a movie version of a mobster. I estimate that suit cost about three thousand bucks, maybe more, and his watch is right up there too."

"Where's the party going to be held?" I asked. "Not here, surely. It wouldn't be nice for those not invited to have to pass through on their way out."

"We're using the main gym," Dad said. "The center's closing early tonight so the caterers can set up. Sue-Anne isn't at all happy about having her centerpiece gala party in a smelly old gym, immediately following the over-fifty men's basketball game, but the banquet hall was already booked for a wedding reception. She wanted to have it at the Yuletide Inn, but Ralph put a stop to that idea on the grounds of the expense."

"If the after-party gets boring and you're looking for extra-legal excitement," I said, "George has a truck full of his home-made wine."

Dad and Russ laughed.

"Now there's someone I didn't expect to see," Dad said as none other than Margie Thatcher stepped hesitantly into the hallway, her eyes as round and frightened as a deer who'd accidently wandered into a hunting lodge. Her hair was formed into a mass of tight curls, and her dress was a rather gaudy pink with lime green trim, and it looked to be about thirty years out of date. She clutched her purse to her chest. "I'm glad she came," Dad said. "I'll catch you later, honeybunch. Russ."

Dad headed in Margie's direction as the doors to the auditorium swung open and the ushers took their places.

"Let the show begin," Russ said. "Where are you sitting, Merry?"

I checked my ticket. "Row B."

"Lucky you. I'm in what passes for the nosebleed seats in an auditorium this size. I didn't realize I'd need my opera glasses."

I joined the surging crowd as we made our way to our seats and settled in. Alan soon joined me, and Dad took the chair on the other side of me. The auditorium buzzed with excitement as the audience filed in. The stage curtains were open showing a London street scene. Painted storefronts, roofs lined with chimney pots. Fluffy white stuff representing snow piled in corners and tucked against window frames. A six-foot-tall, potted Douglas fir draped with decorations stood at both edges of the stage. The Scrooge and Marley sign, tilting at about a forty-five-degree angle, hung prominently above the center of the stage.

Alan leaned across me to speak to Dad. "Nice job on the set."

"Mostly George. Be sure and mention it to him."

Sue-Anne bustled her guests in and invited them to take their places in the front row. Unfortunately, the senator sat in front of me. I'd have to crane my neck to see around him. His wife was next to him and the Broadway producer on his other side. Sue-Anne sat beside the senator's wife, and Catherine and Bruce Renshaw were farther down the row. The police and fire chiefs, and the women with them, were also in the front row. Randy Baumgartner and his party, I assumed, had been banished to the cheap seats. The seat next to the producer remained empty until everyone else was settled, and then Desmond Kerslake scurried in and sat down, muttering apologies.

The lights dimmed, the audience hushed, the music swelled. Men, women, and children dressed in an assortment of nineteenth-century garb spilled onto the stage, laughing and chatting, exchanging the compliments of the season. And the play began.

It wasn't Broadway, but no one in the audience expected it to be, and the actors did a fine job. Jackie hammed it up in the chorus, but at least she didn't shove anyone aside to get to the front. Ian might have overplayed the nastiness when Scrooge declared that the "surplus population" needed to be reduced, but he didn't overplay it too badly. The first scene ended, the lights were lowered, and George, in his mothballed suit, and the teenage kids hired to be stagehands rushed on stage to rearrange the set to create Ebenezer's cold, dark, miserly lodgings. One of the kids performed a deep bow before leaving, and the audience laughed. Sue-Anne peeked at the senator's wife, and seeing that she was chuckling, she laughed also.

Ian McIntosh hunched over a fire made of red paper propped against birch logs and pretended to eat his gruel. Dave clanked his paper-mache chains, and warned Scrooge against continuing down the dangerous path he was on. The wig and beard helped him look a lot more like the timeworn ghost he was supposed to be than when I'd seen him at dress rehearsal. He was, I thought, quite good, better than I'd expected. When he finished his song, he received a round of polite clapping. He then ominously declared that the first visitor would arrive at the stroke of one and disappeared into the darkness of the wings.

The first visitor was, as expected, my mother , as the Ghost of Christmas Past. When she stepped on stage, her flowing white gown shimmering around her, summoning Ebenezer to his reckoning, the audience burst into enthusiastic applause. She might have tried not to react, but she couldn't help the small smile that crept across her painted face. I glanced at my dad. He was almost glowing with adoration.

Alan took my hand and squeezed it, but I scarcely noticed. Seeing Mom in that costume pulled me sharply out of the play. The person who'd invaded her house Thursday night had put on a bedsheet and painted their face white. That couldn't be a coincidence. It had to be either a deliberate attempt to mock her costume or been inspired by it. Meaning, whoever had been in my parents' house last night had to know what Mom would be wearing tonight. For the play's publicity shots, she wore the dress concealed under the ghost costume, to be revealed when she'd step out of the shadows to play Belle.

The intruder had to either be a member of the cast and crew, or to have been at a dress rehearsal. It was possible Irene told someone the details of her design, but following the death of Paula I considered it unlikely to the point of impossible that the killer was not, in some way, associated with the play.

While my mother led Ian across the rooftops of London, I thought. I'd seriously considered that Paula might have been killed in mistake for Catherine. I could now dismiss that idea once and for all. The intrusion at my parents' house and the scare inflicted on my mother were clearly intended for my mother and no one else.

Why kill Paula but merely frighten Mom? If the intent of Paula's killing, as I'd also speculated, had been to disrupt the performance so much it was canceled, no one could assume a mere fright in the night would cause a hardened professional like Aline Steiner to totally withdraw her involvement. Only my mother's death or injury would accomplish that.

Therefore, putting a stop to the production had not been the intent of last night's intrusion. The killing of Paula Monahan and the attack on Mom had to be personal. Which meant I could remove Randy Baumgartner and John Benedict and any other Muddites from my mental list of suspects. Maybe I wouldn't remove them entirely, not until I knew more about the motive, but I'd demote them to the bottom.

As much as I didn't want to think about what might have happened to my mother when an intruder broke into the house, I forced myself to. Why had that person not finished the attack? Why give her a fright and then flee? Nothing had been stolen; Mom was unharmed, although slightly shaken up. Was

Simmonds right in thinking the intruder feared Mom was going for a weapon? I didn't see it. Who would break into a house and deliberately wake a sleeping person without considering how they might react?

The attack on Paula had been quick and determined and effective. It was not a so-called prank or an attempt to put a fright into her that went wrong.

Paula had been murdered. My mother had not.

What was the difference between Paula and Mom?

My line of thought was interrupted when, on one side of me, Dad shifted in his seat and leaned forward, and on the other, Alan tensed. I blinked and focused on what was happening in front of me.

The merry crowd had gathered for the Fezziwigs' annual Christmas party. The stage was adorned with a heavily decorated, and quickly movable, fake Christmas tree. Extras sipped at empty glasses or nibbled on nonexistent food and laughed heartily. Ian stood alone on the far side of the stage, dressed in Scrooge's long tattered nightgown and cap, wrapped in the shadows, watching. Something shifted in the darkness at the back of the stage, the audience held their breath. My dad sighed.

My mother stepped forward. She'd cast off the white gown and was dressed in blue. She stood alone, not moving, drawing the audience to her. And then, she began to sing.

My mother's far too old to be playing a young man's lost love, but when it comes to opera, no one much cares about such details. Belle, as Mom told me, is not only supposed to be in her late teens, but sung by a soprano. Mom's a mezzo-soprano, but tonight that mattered as little as did her age. She'd modified the song slightly to suit her deeper voice, and it worked brilliantly, giving the character a touch of wisdom and maturity, perhaps even a foreshadowing of what was to come. Her rich, powerful voice captivated the small auditorium and everyone in it. I've only seen Mom perform a handful of times, in my childhood when she was appearing at the Met and Dad would bring the kids to the city for a weekend visit. I knew she was good, but as a child I didn't truly appreciate how good.

I swear tonight the mice under the stage stopped whatever they were doing to listen. No one coughed, no one shifted in their seat.

Mom stood slightly stage right, in a circle of light and shimmering blue fabric. The other actors melted into the sidelines where, wrapped in near-total darkness, they partied on, not making a sound. Belle sang about her dreams for love. "Someone . . ." The lights were on her face, and she wouldn't have been able to see where we were sitting, but as she sang, "When that loved one is mine . . ." the years fell away and she dipped her head, ever so slightly, toward my father.

I felt, as much as heard, him suck in a breath.

The song ended. My mother blinked several times. The rest of the stage lights gradually turned up and the other actors danced across the stage. The man playing the youthful Ebenezer stepped hesitantly toward Belle, ready for their fateful meeting.

"Brava! Brava!" A man seated farther down my row leapt to his feet. The audience was shocked out of their silence, and other people began clapping and standing up. Applause and more cries of "Brava!" rang through the auditorium. Poor young Ebenezer hesitated, not sure of what to do.

My mother dipped her head, ever so slightly, in acknowledgment of the praise. I glanced at Dad. He was beaming and clapping wildly. Mom let the applause last a full minute and then she turned toward young Ebenezer, raised her right arm, dipped her hand, and graciously indicated he could begin. He hesitated and threw a terrified glance at the audience. Seeing the applause was slowly dying and people resuming their seats, "Ebenezer" took a deep, shuddering breath, and croaked, "Miss Belle . . ."

And the play continued.

My mom had been outstanding, the praise lavish, and I knew she'd be pleased.

What, I'd thought before the song began, had been the difference between Mom and Paula Monahan, that Paula died and Mom did not?

There were plenty of differences but, regarding the play, I could see only one, and that one was crystal clear.

Paula was easily replaceable, proved by how smoothly Jackie slipped into her role as Mrs. Cratchit. Paula's son, Eddie, was equally replaceable as Tiny Tim.

My mother was not replaceable. Not at all. She was, as I had just witnessed, irreplaceable. Mom might have a minor role, but she was still the star. As Jackie pointed out earlier, people had come to Rudolph specifically to see my mother, the great Aline Steiner, come out of retirement. In addition to her onstage parts, she was vitally needed to direct the singers, and even after opening night, she'd be required to keep rehearsing them and correcting any mistakes they might have made.

My mother couldn't be removed from the play without endangering it entirely.

"Drink, Merry?"

I pulled myself out of my thoughts. All around me people were talking and getting to their feet. The auditorium lights were on. "What? I mean, is it over already?"

"Of course it's not over," Dad said. "Scrooge hasn't had his great redemption yet. Are you okay, honeybunch?"

"I'm fine. I just . . . got distracted.

Alan and my dad both gave me curious looks. "If you're going to the bar," I said quickly. "I'll have a soft drink, please. Anything."

I followed Alan into the lobby, and Dad followed me. That is, Dad started to follow. He didn't get far as people kept slapping him on the back and telling him what a great job Aline was doing.

"Does your mom come onstage again?" Alan asked me.

"Yes, but not to sing a solo. She's part of the dinner party at Fred's house when Scrooge arrives hoping he can join them."

"Fred? Oh, right, Scrooge's nephew. I've never particularly wanted to go to an opera, but after hearing your mom, I might reconsider. That's a heck of a line at the bar. I might not have time, but I'll try." Alan hurried off.

I glanced around the crowded hallway. People were laughing and chatting, and everyone seemed to be enjoying themselves. I overheard more than one person telling their friends the production was better than they'd expected. I supposed that was good.

"Your mom's great." Vicky slid up to me. "I'm sorry I never got to see her perform on a professional stage."

We watched Sue-Anne proudly introducing her special guests to everyone she could corral while Randy Baumgartner tried to muscle in. Diane Simmonds stood alone in a far corner, her sharp eyes roving over the room. The police chief walked up to her, and they exchanged a few words.

Bells tinkled to tell us it was time to return to our seats. Vicky went in search of Mark, and I waited for Alan. He returned empty-handed. "Sorry, Merry. Line was too long."

I linked my arm through his. "Doesn't matter. I'm sure the drinks will be flowing at the after-party."

"If not there's always George's truck," he chuckled. We took our seats, the lights were dimmed, the curtains swooshed open, and the play resumed.

Once again, I tried to focus on the show, but once again, my mind wandered. I found myself studying the row of heads in front of me. Plenty of people wanted to see this play succeed, particularly after last year's flop. Sue-Anne cared about the reputation of the town. As did Dad and all the councilors. The store and hotel and restaurant owners. Independent businesspeople such as Alan. No doubt the chief of police and the fire chief did as well. For Rudolph to survive it had to continue to be known as a "Year-Round Christmas" destination. Particularly at Christmastime.

Someone had been angry at my mother. They'd also been angry with Paula. They'd killed Paula, but didn't dare do the same to Mom.

If my mom wasn't part of it, the play might still go ahead, but its popularity and success were not guaranteed.

I could think of only two people who'd clashed with both Paula and Mom, who also cared about the play and had their personal pride riding on its success: Catherine Renshaw and Desmond Kerslake.

At that moment, the senator leaned across the Broadway producer and whispered something to Desmond. The director nodded, but he didn't take his eyes off the stage. Ian and the large man pretending to be the Ghost of Christmas Present, who'd earlier been Fezziwig at the company party, were watching the Cratchit family preparing for their Christmas feast. Jackie stepped forward. She hesitated. Her bodice heaved. The audience held its breath. I held my breath. "Now children!" Jackie bellowed. Everyone let out a sigh of relief.

I tried to focus on what was happening on the stage, but my mind wouldn't stop returning to the puzzle. The music room was situated at the back of my parents' house, not visible from the street. Had the intruder been prowling the property under cover of darkness, searching for the best way to enter, or had they previously known its location and that the French doors opened directly into the garden? Footprints would have been left in the snow. I made a mental note to ask Diane Simmonds what a search of the property had found. Had someone been sneaking about searching for possible ingress, or had they gone directly to the music room knowing it was there?

If the latter, they must have previously been in Mom's music room. That didn't narrow the suspect list down much—Mom had coached most of the singers in the production at the house. On the other hand, a small sign by the driveway indicated the direction to the music studio. Easy for anyone to assume that meant there would be a side door even if they'd never seen it.

*　*　*

I slowly became aware that all around me people were getting to their feet. I blinked and refocused. The curtain had come down, the audience was applauding enthusiastically. "Merry?" Alan looked down at me. "You okay?"

"Absolutely. Great job. Loved every minute of it." I also leapt up.

The curtain rose. The chorus stepped out, giggling and bowing, clearly delighted at the enthusiasm of the audience response. Those with minor speaking or singing parts came next, including a beaming Jackie, who dropped into a curtsy so deep she must have rehearsed it for hours.

There'd be no living with her now.

247

Dave came out alone. The applause increased. In front of me the guy from Broadway said something to the senator as he lifted his hands in a salute. Dave noticed, his eyes flicked, and he smiled.

Then came Mom and Ian, to a burst of thunderous applause. My mother swooped into a deep curtsy, which after years of experience she hadn't needed to rehearse. Ian lifted her hand and pressed it to his lips. Someone in the audience threw a bouquet of flowers. Aaron, the boy who'd played Tiny Tim, rushed forward to scoop them up and present them to Mom.

Everyone stepped back and beckoned to the wings. George Mann and Irene Dowling edged onto the stage, both beet red with embarrassment. Mom took one step forward and gestured to the front row of seats. Neither Desmond nor Catherine needed any prompting to get up and turn to face the auditorium. More applause. They smiled graciously at each other.

Finally, everyone trooped off the stage, and the lights were turned fully up.

"I didn't think it was that good," Alan said to my dad. "To deserve that amount of applause, I mean. Other than Aline, who blew the roof off with her song."

"Hometown crowd," Dad replied. "Most everyone here tonight has a relative in the cast or crew. I have to admit, they exceeded expectations. Except for Merry's mother, of course. I wouldn't have expected anything less than a stellar performance."

We slowly filed out of the auditorium, heading for the after-party.

"Desmond did a good job," I heard the Broadway guy say to Sue-Anne. "With what he had to work with." He laughed. "For a minute there, I expected Mrs. Cratchit to faint dead away, and the kid who played Tiny Tim doesn't exactly look as though he's lingering at death's door. What some of the singers might lack in vocal range, or even talent, they made up for in sheer enthusiasm. Which is precisely what I want to see in amateur theater."

Waitstaff were ready for us when we entered the gym, armed with trays bearing flutes of Champagne. The bar had been set up in here and a line of non-Champagne drinkers immediately formed in front of it. Other young people serving as waiters circulated, offering canapes. I recognized many of the kids as those who'd put on their elf costumes on Sunday for the children's party.

"Drink, Santa?" a pretty girl said as she held out her tray.

"Don't mind if I do." Dad accepted a glass.

Alan drew me to one side with a soft hand on my arm. "Several times when I looked at you, you seemed lost, Merry. Didn't you like the play?"

"What I noticed of it was fine. I had things on my mind."

"That's what I was afraid of. You need to let the police sort it out, Merry."

I smiled at him. He didn't even have to ask what precisely had been on my mind. "I should. But I can't stop myself thinking about it."

"I know." He gave me a smile so warm it had my toes tingling. He gestured to the crowd and said, "Diane's here. Obviously she's not working undercover." He was right about that. The detective stood alone against a wall, a glass of water in one hand, watching everyone and everything. "Unlikely the guilty party's going to be so intimidated by her presence they'll walk up to her and confess all."

"She knows that," I said. "She's just taking it all in."

Excited whispers started at the doorway to the gym and spread through the room. Conversation died as people turned to look at what was happening, and applause broke out as the cast made their entrance. Mom and Ian came first, the rest of the players following. Irene, George, and the crew brought up the rear of the procession.

Catherine hurried forward and wrapped my mom in an embrace. Notably, she did not do the same to Ian. I'd seen Rachel McIntosh before the play began, laughing and chatting with friends. She slipped up to Ian now, and put a hand on his arm, establishing them as a married couple. Catherine greeted her with icy coolness, and the look Rachel returned was anything but friendly. The affair between Ian and Catherine might be over, but Rachel would not be forgetting anytime soon. Ian took his wife's hand and they walked away. Catherine gave a barely noticeable shrug and turned to lavish praise on Irene for the costuming.

Mom had scrubbed off the stage makeup and reapplied a touch of blush, lipstick, and mascara. She looked every inch the diva in a quilted green, red, and black jacket worn over wide-legged black linen pants and a black silk V-neck shirt.

Sue-Anne grabbed Mom's arm and almost dragged her across the crowded room to meet the senator and other honored guests. Russ and Kyle, and Kyle's camera, joined them.

The Broadway producer gave Desmond a hearty slap on the back. Alan and I headed in the direction of Vicky and Mark, but Jackie stepped in front of us. "So, what did you think, Merry?" She held a glass of Champagne, and her eyes were bright with excitement and pleasure.

"You were great," I said honestly. Maybe not Broadway great but perfectly fine for a small-town amateur production.

"I was so nervous. I hope you didn't notice."

"No one did," I said, not so honestly.

"See that guy talking to Desmond? He's a big shot on Broadway. I'd love to meet him. Come on, you can introduce me."

"Me? I don't know him. I don't even know his name."

"That doesn't matter. Tell him you're Aline's daughter. That'll be good enough." She gave me a good strong shove in the men's direction.

"If I must," I said.

"I'll catch you later, Merry," Alan said. "Congratulations, Jackie."

I didn't need to interrupt anyone. Desmond saw me coming and said, "Frank, here's someone you'll want to meet. Get over here, Merry. Merry, have you met Frank Kendale? He's visiting us from the great city of New York. Frank, this is Merry Wilkinson, Aline's daughter."

Frank's gaze didn't pass over me, searching for someone more interesting to talk to. Instead he looked genuinely interested. "Pleased to meet you, Merry. Are you as talented as your mother?"

I laughed. "Totally and completely tone deaf, but Mom doesn't mind. Not too much anyway. My three siblings are all in show business."

"Might I have met them? I do some work on the periphery of Broadway on occasion."

"My brother Chris is as musically talented as me, but he loves the theater anyway. He's a set designer."

"Don't recall the name, but if I run into him, I'll say hi."

I could almost feel the rays of impatient energy behind me as Jackie bounced on her toes wanting to get into the circle. Frank turned his attention to her. "You were Mrs. Cratchit, right?"

"Yes! You noticed me!"

"Not an easy role to play," he said. "A young woman such as yourself portraying a life-worn working-class mother."

He hadn't praised her performance, but Jackie took it that way. "Thank you. Thank you so much. I watched plenty of productions on YouTube to get an idea of exactly how I wanted the part to work. Not that I copied anyone, of course. I want to give the character of Mrs. Cratchit my own individual spin. I—"

"I always knew my old pal Desmond had a keen eye for talent," Frank said, neatly cutting Jackie off. I decided I liked Frank Kendale very much. He'd changed the subject while letting Jackie still think she was involved in the conversation. "He and I go way back. I always figured he could have gone far in show business, but he had other ideas."

"I love the theater," Desmond said. "But the cutthroat world of putting on major productions simply wasn't for me. My wife, Lorraine, hated Manhattan with a passion. When she got ill, that made up my mind once and for all. We came back to Rudolph for her to spend her last years in the town she loved."

Frank's smile disappeared, and he dipped his head. "Great woman, Lorraine." He slapped Desmond on the back again. "Far too good for the likes of you, but I never could convince her of that. Try as I might."

Desmond smiled at his old friend.

I'd been wrong when I considered the possibility that Desmond might have killed Paula in a desperate attempt to improve the play, to impress the producer in a last-ditch attempt to salvage his reputation and get himself back to Broadway. Frank Kendale had come here to support his friend, under the full understanding of what amateur theater was.

"Congratulations, Desmond." Dave joined us. "Great job. You pulled it off." He carried a glass of beer.

"Thanks. Dave French, meet Frank Kendale."

They shook hands. "You've got a powerful voice, Dave," Frank said. "I enjoyed Marley's solo."

"Thanks." Dave peeked at me out of the corner of his eyes. "I had some coaching from Aline Steiner herself."

"She brought the house down with that number, all right."

"Did your parents not come tonight, Dave?" Jackie asked. "You couldn't keep my mom away." She smiled at Frank. "That's her over there, trying to get close to Aline. She's so excited at being a stage mother."

Dave's face tightened ever so slightly. "My mom wanted to come but . . . my dad doesn't believe in spending money on what he calls frivolities." He gave us all a forced smile.

"Sorry to hear that," Frank said. "Obviously it's my line of work, but I firmly believe the arts are vitally important to the health of society in general."

"So true," Jackie gushed. A waiter presented a tray of canapes. Nice spicy little pastry things. We helped ourselves and he moved on to the next group.

Only Dave didn't take one. He shifted his feet. "Don't know if you had a chance to read your program yet, Frank, but my bio points out that I have Broadway and Hollywood experience. I was on the way up, things looking good, but I wanted to take some time off to help my folks when my dad took sick. I'm intending to get back at it soon and pick my career up where I left off."

"Good luck with it," Frank said. "Des, I haven't met Aline Steiner yet. Why don't you introduce me? Who's that guy she's with? The one who looks like Santa Claus enjoying a rare night away from the North Pole."

I laughed. "That's my dad."

He looked genuinely embarrassed. "Oh. Sorry. Didn't realize."

"Don't apologize. My dad is Rudolph's Santa Claus. If you're staying in town for a few days, you can see him in full gear and action Sunday afternoon at the town's children's party."

Dave interrupted, not interested in Santa Claus or a children's party and not ready to let Frank go yet. "I heard you've produced some Broadway shows, Frank."

"A few."

"More than a few," Desmond said. "Frank's a big player behind the scenes."

"Maybe you could give me a few tips. How to break back in, I mean." Dave's laugh came out more like a strangled cry. "I knew when I took time off it'd be hard to go back. Things move on, right? A couple of introductions here and there would help." He gave Frank a weak smile.

"Yeah," Frank said. "It's a tough business, all right. I'm not working tonight. Call my office sometime." He started to turn away. Notably he did not offer Dave his card or give the actor his personal number.

"Congratulations, Dave!" Randy Baumgartner was next to join our little group.

"Thanks," Dave said. "I couldn't have done it without this guy." He indicated Desmond. "And Aline of course."

"What'd they have –? Oh, I get it. Yeah, your bit was okay, although your part was small. I kept expecting you to come back. Small but important, right? No, I mean congratulations on the deal."

Dave flushed with embarrassment.

"Deal?" Desmond asked politely.

"The motel deal. Dave here pulled off a deal to buy an old motel in Muddle Harbor." Randy pulled business cards out of his suit pocket and shoved them at Desmond and Frank. "Randy Baumgartner, mayor of the aforementioned town. If you're ever thinking of putting on another play, we can find you the space in Muddle Harbor. Particularly now the motel's going to be renovated and spruced up. That's your plan, right Dave? He drove a hard bargain, let me tell you. I never figured Ted would go that low, but good old Dave here managed."

"We all have our talents," Frank said.

Dave's expression was one of pure fury. "I told you, Randy. I was acting for my father. He'll be back on his feet any day soon and then I'll be leaving town and picking up my acting career."

Randy's face crinkled in confusion. "You did? I don't remember that. You assured me you're in it for the long haul. Interested in building a few more budget motels if that new highway comes closer to town." He lowered his voice and gave Dave a broad wink. "I had a quick chat with the senator earlier. He'll see what he can do."

"Des," Frank said. "You were going to introduce me to Aline Steiner. I can't take the chance on her leaving early."

"Don't worry," I said. "My mom never leaves a party early." Not a party at which she's the center of attention.

"Why don't I do that?" Jackie leapt into the conversation. "Aline gave me special individual instruction and plenty of tips on how to look the best on stage. I'm the manager at one of Merry's stores, and Aline and I are like really close."

Jackie had given herself, unknown to me, a promotion. And me, at least one new store.

They walked off, leaving me alone with Dave and Randy.

Dave's eyes were narrow as he watched Jackie, chattering nervously all the while, lead the two men in the direction of my mom, basking in the adulation of people offering their congratulations.

Dave.

Dave, whom Paula had called "totally and completely" unsuitable to play Scrooge. Dave, who desperately wanted a bigger part in the play, but had been refused.

I'd remembered that my mother had gotten angry at Dave and Catherine in front of the entire ensemble, accusing them of letting their egos take over and forgetting this was amateur theater. I'd forgotten, until now, she'd included Dave in that insult.

Dave.

I looked into his face. Dark, angry eyes, as cold as chips of ice, stared back at me.

Oblivious to the currents swirling around, Randy chattered on. "That highway'll be good for you, Dave. Good for Muddle Harbor. You folks in Rudolph better watch out, Miss Wilkinson. Muddle Harbor's on the verge of greatness and we'll be giving you a run for your money."

"That's nice," I said.

"I better grab that senator again before he leaves. Maybe he can pay a visit to Muddle Harbor on his way outta town. Yeah, I'll suggest that."

Dave and I were left alone. Alone in a room packed with people.

"Are you that ambitious, Dave?" I asked.

"I don't know what you're talking about."

"What did my mother ever do to you? Why pull that stupid prank? Or was it a prank? Were you stopped before . . . you could do whatever you'd intended?"

His eyes flicked as he looked across the room. Catherine, radiant in her triumph. Desmond proudly introducing his old friend to my mother, the diva. Mom, thoroughly in her element. Jackie and the rest of the bit players, giddy with excitement. Sue-Anne and Ralph Dickerson being interviewed by Russ for the paper. Kyle, trying to get Ian and Mom together for yet another photo.

I hadn't noticed Kyle taking any pictures of Dave. Dave, almost certainly, had also noticed that.

"Maybe your mother needs to be reminded she's not the big opera star anymore," Dave said in a voice so low and so cold I shivered. "She's a bit player in a low-rent production staffed by a small-town bunch of wannabes. That costume Irene made up for her might as well be a bedsheet."

"No one in this company's a wannabe," I said. "Except, maybe, for Jackie. And you. They're in it for the fun of it."

"Fun," he spat. He walked away.

"Crostini, Merry?"

"What?"

"Would you like a crostini?" The smiling young waiter held up his tray of offerings.

"Oh. You startled me. I'm sorry I snapped. No. I mean, no thanks."

"Okay."

I looked around the room. Everyone seemed to be having a great time. Except for the possible exception of the senator, who'd been cornered by Randy Baumgartner and whose expression indicated he was hearing far more about Muddle Harbor's plans for expansion than he ever wanted to know. Alan was chatting to Vicky and Mark. Mom was with Desmond and Frank while Jackie hovered at the edges of the group. Ian and some other members of the cast were posing for pictures for fans. Rachel stood just out of the picture frame, watching her husband. I hoped they'd be able to get over their problems.

Dave joined Catherine while Bruce lined up at the bar.

Everyone was here. Except the two people I most wanted to see: my dad and Detective Diane Simmonds.

I've gotten in trouble before, thinking I was in control of a situation and not immediately telling Simmonds what I suspected. I was not going to do that again.

I made my way across the crowded room, searching for her. She might have gone out for a breath of air or even decided to call it a night and head for home. I'd give her a call and hope she answered.

The sounds of the party fell away behind me as I stepped into the hallway. I took my phone out of my small evening bag. The lights were dim behind the reception desk, and no one else was around. I started to place the call.

Someone grabbed my arm. The phone was plucked out of my hand.

"Calling someone, Merry?" Dave French asked.

Chapter Nineteen

"I'm . . . uh . . . checking in with Alan. It's time we were on our way. Work tomorrow, you know."

"Funny you'd come into the hallway to phone him when you walked right past him just now." Dave shoved my phone into his pocket. "I'll hold onto this for you, why don't I? Let's go for a walk."

"I don't want to go for a walk."

"But I do." His grip tightened on my arm. He leaned toward me and stared into my eyes, and I did not like what I saw there. "You're a nosy little thing, aren't you? Always poking around where you have no business being."

I tried to pull away and dig my heels in. But he had a firm grip on me, and those heels were so high I was thrown off balance. "I'm not going anywhere with you."

"I just want a nice chat, Merry. I know what you're thinking and you're wrong. Why don't you let me explain the error of your ways to you?" He pulled me along with him, heading away from the party and the front entrance, going in the direction of the auditorium. All the lights in that wing of the community center were off; the dark hallway loomed in front of us. "You're so interested, I bet you'd like to see behind the scenes of a theater. As miserable a little theater as this one is."

"Killing me's not going to get you a role on Broadway," I said.

"Killing you? Why would I kill you, Merry? Then again, I now know you're tight with that detective. It might have been a mistake, jumping Paula in your place. But I saw my chance and I took it. Fortune favors the brave, isn't that what they say? You need to keep a better eye on your store. Anyone could walk in and rob you blind."

"What did poor Paula ever do you to?"

"Do to me? She laughed at me; she insulted me. I'm stuck performing in an *amateur* play with a two-week run, directed by a guy who hasn't had a new idea in twenty years, and didn't have the chops to stick it out on Broadway, playing second fiddle to a washed-up opera diva who doesn't know she's washed up, and an old man without the sense to know when it's time to give it up. All I get is put-downs from my father and sneers from those who, like Paula, think they're my equal. I've had enough of it. I saw that miserable Paula go into your store, and I followed her. I intended to give her a fright, put her in her place. But when I saw how easy it was to catch her off-guard, no one around . . . I did what I should have done earlier."

As he talked, he continued pulling me down the dark hallway. I breathed. *Stay calm, Merry. Just stay calm.* Dave was a big guy, and he had a firm hold on my arm. But we were not in the middle of nowhere. This was a public building; we were only a few feet away from a crowded party. Unfortunately, everyone was having such a good time at the party, they weren't listening for sounds of someone needing assistance.

"As for your mother . . . yeah, I considered getting rid of her too, but I figured it was too close to opening night. Might risk the whole production, or the big shots might not bother to come."

I took another breath. I braced myself. Then I let out a scream and pulled backward as hard as I could. Dave whirled around and his mad eyes stared into mine. He jerked me toward him with so much force my feet slipped on the polished floor. He put one arm around my chest and slapped the hand of the other over my mouth. A couple more struggling steps and he was using his body to push open the door to the auditorium. I struggled, both to get away and to breathe. "Will you shut up," he said. "I don't want to have to hurt you."

That, I did not believe.

If he did kill me, I wanted to leave as much evidence behind as I could. I scratched at the hand over my mouth and tried to reach his face. He grabbed my hair and wrenched my head back. Together, wrapped in a deadly embrace, we stumbled into the auditorium.

"Hey, man, what's going on?"

The dim light that came in with us showed two of the younger members of the chorus as they leapt apart, guilt written all over their faces. The boy stepped forward. "Find your own place, why don't you."

"Hey!" the girl said. "What are you doing? Merry, is that you?"

Dave shoved me toward them with a growl. I stumbled on my awkward heels but managed to keep myself upright as Dave turned and bolted out of the auditorium.

"Are you okay, Merry?" the girl said. "That didn't look nice, but we'll leave if you want us to."

"No, we won't," her boyfriend said.

"Call the police!" I shouted as I sprinted out the door and gave chase.

Dave was running back down the hallway, heading toward the lights. He reached the reception desk and hesitated, wondering which way to go. An elderly couple came out of the gym, a duet of canes tapping the floor in front of them. Dave whirled around. He saw me, coming his way. "I wasn't going to hurt you, Merry. I only wanted to talk. I have to make you understand this production might be my last chance to get my career back on the track it deserves, and naturally it's important to me nothing interferes with that. Not a pack of talentless hacks or a blasted budget motel deal. You need to calm down."

"I am calm. You are not. We need the police here," I said to the couple. "Call them, please. I've lost my phone."

They stared at us.

Dave made up his mind and shoved open the doors leading to the outside. He wouldn't get far. The wisest thing for me to do would be to wait for the police to arrive and then, calmly and concisely, tell Detective Simmonds what I'd surmised and what Dave himself had confirmed.

But, despite what my dad said only a few hours ago, I am not wise. I followed Dave. My lungs gasped against the sudden attack of icy cold air as I stepped out of the building. While we'd been enjoying the play and then the after-party, it had started to snow, and heavily this time. The strong lights over the parking area shone on swirling flakes; the cars were covered in several inches of the stuff. A snowplow lumbered down the street, yellow lights flashing. A car pulled slowly out of the as-yet-unplowed parking lot, taking care in the fresh deep powder.

Dave sprinted across the lot, presumably heading toward his own car. I ran after him, my high heels slipping in the snow, the cold penetrating my thin stockings. As Dave passed George Mann's battered, rusty old truck, George stepped out from behind it, directly into the path of the fleeing man. Strong yellow light from the top of the pole above them shone down. "Hey, Dave. Welcome. The more the merrier. I've brought some of my own homemade stuff. That's good enough for the rest of us, right?"

Startled, Dave slipped. George reached out a hand and grabbed him to keep him from falling. Another figure stepped into the light, and then another. Mrs. D'Angelo and Margie Thatcher clutched plastic glasses full (or not so full) of red liquid. They were in coats, gloves, and scarves, and had a decided glow to their cheeks that I suspected was caused by more than the invigoration of the performance and the cold of the night.

"Get out of my way, you old fool!" Dave gave George a hearty shove, and the older man fell back with a startled cry. He struck the hood of his truck but managed to remain upright.

"What the—?" George stared at Dave in shock.

"That wasn't very nice," Mrs. D'Angelo said. "Who do you think you are?"

I'd told the young lovers and then the older couple to call the police. I strained my ears for the sound of sirens but could hear nothing. Had they made the call, or assumed I wasn't serious? I should have run into the party, shouting for help. The chief of police himself was still there.

Too late now. "Someone call the police!" I yelled. "He killed Paula. He attacked my mother. He was going to kill me."

"What on earth are you taking about?" Margie turned to Mrs. D'Angelo. "Never mind her, Merry always did have a wild imagination."

"I'm not—"

"That's right," Dave said. "Pay her no attention. She's nuts."

George had recovered from the surprise of the unexpected attack, straightened, and took a step forward. "I've never known Merry to make things up. Make the call, Mabel, and we'll let them sort it out. In the meantime, Dave, come and have a drink while we wait." He stretched his hand out to take Dave by the arm.

Dave punched George full in the face. This time George crumpled to the ground without another sound. Mrs. D'Angelo and Margie were momentarily frozen in shock. I ran toward them, but my useless shoes couldn't find purchase on the fresh snow. I grabbed at a car to keep from falling. The cold of the metal stung my bare hand.

Mrs. D'Angelo let out a cry and fell to her knees next to George. She cradled his head in her lap and cried, "George, speak to me. George."

Dave pulled car keys out of his pocket and sprinted across the lot. Later, in the calm light of day, I realized he had nowhere to go. No chance of getting away. But at the time I wasn't thinking. I was acting on pure instinct.

I glanced at Mrs. D'Angelo and George. His eyes flicked open and he let out a low groan. Mrs. D'Angelo burst into tears. Behind me, I could hear people shouting, asking what was going on. Margie Thatcher jumped up and down, yelling, and waving her glass in the air with such vigor wine splashed over the rim. "Get help! We need help out here."

The lights of George's truck were on. I let go of the car I was clinging to and grabbed for the driver's door of the truck. I wrenched it open and swung myself in. As I'd hoped, the keys were in the ignition. I looked at the control panel. It resembled nothing I'd ever seen before. A long metal pole, which I took to be the gearshift, was attached to the back of the steering wheel, not rising up from the floor next to the driver's seat. I'd heard of standard transmission. I had no idea how to drive one though.

Margie Thatcher clambered in the passenger door. "Do you know how to drive this, Merry?"

"No."

"Not much good then, are you?"

"I guess not."

My door was wrenched open. Detective Diane Simmonds said, "What on earth is going on here?" Behind her I could see people streaming out of the community center in their finery, heedless of the cold and the falling snow. Many were shouting into their phones or taking pictures of the scene.

"Dave," I gasped. "It's Dave French. He killed Paula. He's making a run for it."

"He won't get far," she said. "You better get out of there. You're going to freeze."

I swung my legs out the door and jumped down. "Someone has to go after him. Who knows what he might do thinking he has nothing left to lose?"

Simmonds grinned at me. "Taken care of."

She pointed and I followed the direction of her finger. Dave had been driving too fast through the unplowed parking lot. His car had come to a sudden halt, the hood buried in a snowbank, wheels spinning, snow flying. As I watched, he stumbled out of the car, into the waiting arms of several police officers.

Chapter Twenty

Hot tea was pressed into my hands. I gripped the cup and took a sip, letting the welcome warmth fill me. Gradually, I stopped shivering.

"Believe it or not," I said to the circle of people watching me. "I decided not to intervene, but to tell Detective Simmonds what I believed had happened. Dave realized what I was thinking and he followed me out of the gym intending to stop me calling her. Oh, by the way, he put my phone in his pocket. Can I have it back?"

"'Fraid not," the detective said. "It'll be taken into evidence."

I groaned.

We were back in the gym of the Rudolph Community Center. I'd been guided to a chair, someone had draped a coat over my shoulders, and someone else had brought me a mug of hot, sweet tea.

The party ended abruptly and everyone unceremoniously sent out into the night. Only my mom, Alan, Vicky and Mark, and Jackie had been allowed to stay. In the background, the waitstaff watched us while quickly closing up bottles and whisking away uneaten food.

By the time I'd clambered down from the truck and watched Dave being arrested, an ambulance had arrived and medics were struggling to get George to lie still so they could check him over. He was trying to sit up and insisting he was fine, but they wanted to take him to the hospital to be examined anyway. My dad, who arrived on the scene at the same time as Diane Simmonds, told George not to be a fool. He wasn't a young man, and he'd had a blow to the head when he hit the ground, never mind a punch to the jaw.

George eventually gave in, and Dad and Mrs. D'Angelo were allowed to ride in the ambulance with him to the hospital.

The elderly couple I'd earlier seen in the hallway had hurried (as fast as they could) into the gym and shouted for help. The police had been called, and many of the partygoers hurried out to see what was going on. Russ and Kyle were among the first out the doors, Kyle ready to take the Pulitzer Prize–winning shot. The chief of police was now outside, supervising the scene himself while Diane asked me for my statement. A few moments ago, I'd heard Russ trying to talk his way back into the gym, and Candy Campbell, guarding the door, telling him to get lost.

"I did try to find help," I said. "So no one can be angry at me this time, right?"

"I can," Alan said. "Sometimes, Merry . . ." His voice drifted off and he simply shook his head.

"The things you get up to," Mom said.

"I'm sorry about that, Merry," Simmonds said. "Looks like I dropped the ball. I was about to leave, thinking coming here tonight had been a waste of time. Other than enjoying a good show, that is. On my way out, your dad and I got chatting. My daughter's having trouble making friends at school, and knowing how involved your parents are in the community I wanted some suggestions as to activities she can participate in. I confess I suggested we step outside so I could indulge in my one-a-day smoking habit, and we went out the back way. I am sorry."

"All's well that ends well," Mom said. "I trust Noel didn't join you in partaking in this smoke? One a day or not."

"No, Mrs. Wilkinson, he did not."

"Glad to hear it."

"All of which is beside the point," Simmonds said. "Take me through what happened, Merry."

"Can't that wait?" Mom said. "My daughter needs to rest. She's had a considerable shock and a traumatic experience."

"I'm fine," I said.

"You are not," Mom, Alan, and Vicky said simultaneously.

"I need to go down to the station and talk to Dave anyway," the detective said. "I'll get a full statement from you tomorrow. Before I do that, though, I need to know one thing. Did Dave French confess to killing Paula Monahan?"

I thought for a long time. Everyone watched me. "As good as," I said at last.

"As good as is rarely good enough."

"He said he made a mistake following her into my store. But only because it was my store and he didn't realize how much I'm . . . in his words . . . tight with the police. He said he saw his chance and took it, although I suppose he never exactly said, in so many words, what that chance was."

"It's a place to start," she said.

"Why?" Mom said. "What sort of threat would Paula have been to Dave?"

"Oh, my gosh." Jackie clutched her face in her hands, her eyes wide. "Was he out to get the Mrs. Cratchits? The Christmas Cratchit Killer? I might have been next. I need to sit down."

"Don't be ridiculous," Mom snapped.

I said, "You're perfectly safe, Jackie. Paula was no threat to Dave, but she'd mocked him and he didn't care for that." I reached out one hand and my mother folded it into hers. "Same as you, Mom. He knew he couldn't kill you without endangering the run of the play—tonight's grand opening in particular—so he decided to put a fright into you."

"Diane," Mom said. "You might want to look into the possibility of there having been incidents in other productions Dave's been involved in. This sort of behavior rarely comes out of nowhere. So many people want to be stars and there are so few real opportunities and so much ego is on the line." For once, she didn't launch into a story about a conflict she'd been involved in or observed—she merely gripped my hand all the tighter.

"I'll make some calls to that effect," Simmonds said. "As for now, looks like I have a long night ahead of me. I'm going down to the station. See what Dave has to say for himself."

"He'll try to weasel out of it," Vicky said. "He'll say Merry misunderstood or overreacted or something."

Simmonds gave us all a knowing grin. "Dave French was observed by a substantial number of respectable citizens punching an elderly man in a totally unprovoked assault. I'll be laying that charge immediately, and then we'll see what comes up. Something always does. They never can stop trying to explain themselves."

Chapter
Twenty-One

Dad had called from the hospital to say they were keeping George in overnight, but only as a precaution because of his age. He was sitting up, telling the nurses if Dave hadn't taken him by surprise, Dave would be the one needing their care.

I'd been bundled off home, and Alan tucked me into bed. I slept surprisingly well, considering the fright I'd had that night, and awoke to sunlight streaming through my windows and the scent of coffee and bacon drifting out of the kitchen. I grabbed for my phone, needing to check the time, before remembering it had been taken as police evidence. Heaven knew when, if ever, I'd get it back.

Alan's tousled blond head popped into the bedroom. "Thought I heard you moving around."

"What time is it? I have to get to the store."

"Coffee's on and breakfast will be ready soon. Diane called a few minutes ago to say she's on her way to take your statement about last night and to let us know what's been happening."

"But . . . but . . . the time? The store?"

"It's ten thirty."

"Ten thirty!" I threw off the covers. "On the second last Saturday before Christmas!"

Alan sat on the edge of the bed and pushed me back down with a gentle touch. "Relax. I called Chrystal and asked her if she could come in early today, and Jackie's already there. They can manage for a few hours."

"I suppose. Did you speak to Jackie? She's got to be wired about last night."

"I didn't, but Chrystal said she'll call me if Jackie seems distracted." He gave me a kiss on the forehead. I reached for him, but he pulled away with a laugh. "You have just enough time for a shower and to get dressed before Diane gets here."

By the time I walked into the kitchen, showered, dressed, and feeling at least partially back to normal, Diane Simmonds was sitting at the table drinking coffee and digging into a plate piled high with bacon, eggs, and toast. She'd changed out of her evening wear into jeans, T-shirt, and leather jacket, scrubbed most of the makeup off, and run her fingers through her hair, but the circles under her eyes told me she'd not been to bed. Mattie sat at her feet, tongue lolling, drooling on everything, staring at her through enormous brown eyes overflowing with adoration. He didn't even bother begging for scraps of bacon.

She put down her fork, picked up her coffee cup, and gave me a grin when I came in. "Good morning, Merry."

Alan put a steaming mug in front of the spare chair at the table. I sat down. "You seem pleased with yourself, Detective," I said.

"Early days yet, but we're making progress. I need you to come down to the station later today and make a proper statement. Alan tells me you don't have to be into work until later this afternoon."

"Actually I should—"

"One o'clock should do it. In the meantime, I can fill you in on some of what's been happening. Last night, Dave French insisted that you'd gone totally, and I quote . . . nuts on him, ranting and raving and making wild accusations. He'd been trying to calm you down. He says you ran out into the snowstorm and he followed, afraid you'd hurt yourself."

When I finished sputtering with indignation, and Alan had stopped growling, Simmonds continued. "Not much he could say, when I told him I have several pieces of cell phone footage showing him punching George Mann, a man almost twice his age, hard enough to knock him to the ground, and then attempting to flee. Without, apparently, concerning himself with your welfare, which he'd been so concerned about a few short minutes ago. The attack on George was sufficient for me to arrest him for assault and to hold him overnight. He got on the phone to a lawyer, and said lawyer arrived first thing this morning. I interviewed Dave, in the presence of his lawyer, about the accusations against him."

"What did he say to that?" Alan asked.

"He said he'll plead guilty to the assault on George, although he was confused and not acting like himself. When I asked him about Paula and your mother he began, as they usually do, justifying himself. Somehow, people like Dave French always seem to think that if they explain themselves to me carefully enough, I'll totally see their point of view and let them go with a pat on the head and a request to please not do it again. His lawyer knew better, but once Dave started, he couldn't stop talking. He pranked, in his words, your mother, because she needed to be taught not to be so full of herself."

"Bit late for that," I said. "Oops. Did I say that out loud?"

Alan, who was standing behind me, his strong woodworker's hands resting on my shoulders, chuckled.

"From there," Simmonds continued, "Dave managed to segue, again despite his lawyer's warnings, into telling me Paula was so startled when he came into the shop on the afternoon in question she lost her footing. He grabbed her scarf in an attempt to keep her from falling. And . . . ."

"And?" Alan and I chorused.

"At that point his lawyer finally got him to shut up. But he'd said enough. He's confessed to being at the scene, and he quite obviously didn't try to help her. Not that there was anything accidental about it, and I'm confident of being able to prove such in a court of law." She grinned at me and put down her empty coffee mug. "We've got him for all that. I intend to add the attempted murder of you to the charges and for that I need your statement. See you at one, my office. Thanks for the breakfast, Alan. I've had a long day already."

* * *

"Dave French truly was typecast as Marley then," my mother said.

"Looks like it. Except for the coming to see the error of his ways part." Despite a heaping helping of Alan's eggs and bacon after Detective Simmonds left, I'd agreed to meet my parents at Victoria's Bake Shoppe later in the afternoon. Alan had taken me to the police station at one before going home. He needed to see to Ranger, and then he expected to put in a couple of all-nighters to get stock made to replenish the local shops for the last-minute Christmas rush.

At Mrs. Claus's, I found Chrystal overwhelmed while Jackie held court telling everyone who was interested, and many who were not, about her spectacular triumph as Mrs. Cratchit as well as the takedown of the "*Christmas Carol* Killer," which she herself had, if not personally participated in, been witness to.

I dragged Jackie off stage (i.e. my store floor) and into my office, where I delivered a strongly worded lecture on not only the value of a day's work for a day's pay but the inadvisability of spreading gossip about any killer in town, never mind associating his name with Christmas in America's Christmas Town.

"Whatever," she said. "You haven't forgotten I'm leaving at five, I hope? I have a performance to give tonight, remember."

I sighed. "I remember."

"I hope Frank comes back to see the show again. I talked it over with Kyle last night and he thinks I delivered my opening line a bit too softly. Tonight I'm going to speak up more." She'd walked out of my office, saying, "Now children. Now! Children! *Now* children."

"Oh, by the way. I have a new student. Someone you know," Mom said as she nibbled on the edge of a piece of gingerbread.

"Who?" I asked.

"Candice Campbell. Last light, when you and Alan left, your father was still at the hospital with George so I called a cab to take me home. Candy was outside the community center, doing what I believe they call guarding the scene. She told me she wants to take lessons from me."

"Can she sing?" Dad asked.

Mom shrugged. "I've no idea. I told her to make an appointment in the new year and we will start from there. She's hoping, she told me, to join the theater players."

I groaned. "I hope you're not having anything more to do with them, Mom. Dave French might be gone, but I don't see

Catherine and Desmond getting on any better from now on. Never mind Jackie's convinced her chance of stardom is at hand. As for Candy . . ."

Mom sipped her tea. "Desmond called me this morning. He wanted to check in, make sure I wasn't too disturbed by the events of last night."

"Meaning your daughter being chased through a snowstorm by a deranged killer?"

"And her chasing him in return," Dad said. "No. He was concerned that Aline would have been upset by the abrupt ending of the party."

"You theater people really are a single-minded lot," I said.

"He mentioned he's considering proposing the company put the play on again for Christmas in July."

"Might be a good idea," Dad said.

"It's a terrible idea. I trust you said no, Mom." I knew I was wasting my breath. She had that look behind her eyes. The one that meant she was already working out vocal arrangements and stage movements.

* * *

Mom headed for home to prepare herself for tonight's repeat performance, and Dad and I strolled together down Jingle Bell Lane, back to Mrs. Claus's Treasures.

A substantial amount of snow had fallen last night, and the temperatures had risen to just below freezing. People were bundled up in coats and scarves, carrying bulging bags of gifts, edible treats, and cheerful wrapping paper. Decorations filled the store windows, lights twinkled from wreathes on the light standards, and cries of "Merry Christmas" and "Happy Holidays" rang out as friends greeted each other.

When we reached Mrs. Claus's Treasures, Dad said. "I'm hoping you can give me some idea as to what I can get your mother for Christmas, honeybunch."

"Not a clue. I'm afraid you're on your own this year, Dad. Next year, I bet if you ask Chrystal to make her something truly personal and individual, she will. But this year—you've left it too late." *As usual*, I thought, but didn't say. I gave my father a spontaneous hug.

He smiled and said, "what brought that on?"

"Nothing in particular. Thinking about Dave and Lloyd French maybe."

Dad frowned and shook his head and said nothing.

I wasn't looking to excuse, or even explain, what Dave had done. He couldn't excuse the callous way he killed Paula because she'd offered him some mild insult and he took his chance for revenge, or the way he'd frightened my mother. But from the little he told me, I believed Dave's relationship with his father might have had a lot to do with his . . . issues. The elder Mr. French openly scorned his acting ambitions, and Dave's ego was so wrapped up in wanting to be a star it was all-consuming. He came home to help his parents after his father's stroke, because his mother asked him to. And then, as thanks, his dad mocked his interest in show business and refused to even attend the play that was so vitally important to his son. It was all so very sad.

"Have I ever thanked you for being a good father?" I asked my own dad.

"Not that I can recall. But, as perhaps you'll find out yourself one day, honeybunch, thanks are never needed, not between a parent and child."

The door to Rudolph Gift Nook opened and Margie Thatcher stepped out. She headed toward us. I braced myself.

No doubt a complaint was coming about me not watching my store closely enough, or blaming me for George Mann getting a punch in the face.

"Margie," Dad said, as cheerfully as ever. "Good afternoon."

"Noel. Merry. I . . . I . . . I brought you something. She thrust a gaily wrapped package in my hands. "If I don't get a chance to chat to you again, I wanted to say Merry Christmas." And she smiled. She actually smiled.

"Merry Christmas to you, Margie," Dad said.

"Thank you," I said. "This is . . . very . . . thoughtful."

"No need to get me anything in return. I wanted you to have a small gift, that's all. I enjoyed Mrs. Wilkinson's play last night, Noel. I wasn't familiar with that story, although everyone else seems to know it, and I found it very . . . thought provoking. Please tell her that for me." She turned to go back to her own store.

"Margie," Dad said. "If you've no plans for Christmas dinner, why don't you come to our house this year? We always have a good-sized group. We enjoy a big meal, maybe play a few games, sing a few carols. Come to think of it, it's all very Dickensian."

I stared at my dad.

Margie blinked. "You . . . No, I mean, no, I have no plans. Thank you. I'd like that, Noel. Thank you. Merry Christmas." She slipped away.

When she was gone I looked at Dad. He gave me a wink.

"A true Christmas miracle," I said.

I know my dad isn't Santa Claus. But sometimes I wonder.

"Bless us, every one," he said.

Acknowledgments

F irst of all I'd like to thank all the cozy readers who begged
and petitioned for this series to return. Little warms an
author's heart more than knowing that readers truly enjoy the
world you've created. A Merry Christmas and Happy Holidays
to you all, no matter the time of year.

Thanks to Kim Lionetti, agent extraordinaire, and Matt
Martz and the rest of the team at Crooked Lane for listening
to readers (and to me!). And, as always, a big thanks to Sandy
Harding who takes what I've written and makes it as good as it
can be.